SHELTER FROM THE STORM

CALLE J. BROOKES

LOST RIVER LIT PUBLISHING, LLC
SPRINGS VALLEY INDIANA
EST. 2011

Other books by

Calle J.
Brookes

ROMANTIC SUSPENSE

PAVAD: FBI ROMANTIC SUSPENSE

Beginning (Prequel 1)
Waiting (Prequel 2)

Watching
Wanting
Second Chances
Hunting
Running
Redeeming
Revealing
Stalking
Ghosting
Burning
Gathering
Falling
Hiding
Seeking

FINLEY CREEK SERIES

TRILOGY ONE (TEXAS STATE POLICE)

Her Best Friend's Keeper
Shelter from the Storm
The Price of Silence

TRILOGY TWO (FINLEY CREEK GENERAL)

If the Dark Wins
Wounds That Won't Heal
Hope for Finley Creek (bonus novella)
As the Night Ends

TRILOGY THREE (FINLEY CREEK DISASTER)

Before the Rain Breaks
Lost in the Wind

MASTERSON COUNTY NOVELLA SERIES

Seeking the Sheriff
Discovering the Doctor
Ruining the Rancher

Denying the Devil

SMALL-TOWN SHERIFFS

Holding the Truth

SUSPENSE/THRILLER

PAVAD: FBI CASE FILES

PAVAD: FBI Case Files #0001
"Knocked Out"
PAVAD: FBI Case Files #0002
"Knocked Down"
PAVAD: FBI Case Files #0003
"Knocked Around"
PAVAD: FBI Case Files #0004
"White Out"

Calle has several free reads available at
www.CalleJBrookesReads.com

For my grandfather, the best man I have ever known.
You will be missed.
Oct. 2015

For my grandmother, who gave me the courage to try. Without you and your love of romance, I never would have made it this far.
Feb. 2016

For my papaw, whose children loved him deeply, and will always miss him.
Oct. 2017

Calle J. Brookes is first and foremost a fiction writer. She enjoys crafting paranormal romance and romantic suspense. She reads almost every genre except horror. She spends most of her time juggling family life and writing while reminding herself that she can't spend all of her time in the worlds found within books. CJ loves to be contacted by her readers via email and at **www.CalleJBrookes.com**. When not at home writing stories of adventure and wrangling with two border collies and a beagle puppy, CJ is off in her RV somewhere exploring the beautiful world we live in, along with her husband of she can't remember how many years and their child.

FCA22019

SHELTER FROM THE STORM
Copyright © 2016 by Calle J. Brookes

All rights reserved. Printed in the United States of America. No part of this book may be used or reproduced in any manner whatsoever without written permission except in the case of brief quotations embodied in critical articles or reviews.

This book is a work of fiction. Names, characters, businesses, organizations, places, events and incidents either are the product of the author's imagination or are used fictitiously. Any resemblance to actual persons, living or dead, events, or locales is entirely coincidental.

For information contact:
www.callejbrookes.com

Book and Cover design by CALLE J. BROOKES

First Edition: OCT2016

10 9 8 7 6 5 4 3 2 1

What I am looking
for is not
out there,
It is in me.

-Helen Keller

SHELTER FROM THE STORM

FINLEY CREEK: TSP
BOOK 2

Chapter 1

THERE WAS A STRANGE WOMAN sitting in his car, demanding he take her home with him. Any other night and he might just have considered it.

But not tonight. Not when his brother Elliot was counting on him to keep the woman Elliot loved safe.

"Get out of my car." Chance Marshall leaned over the redhead who had installed herself in the passenger seat of his rented SUV. She didn't back away.

There was no way in hell he was taking this woman back to Texas with him tonight. He didn't even know who she was. Not really.

Just a vague family connection that she had claimed. If he *did* know her, it had been well over ten years since he'd seen her, hadn't it? Why had she climbed into his car and refused to get out? What was he supposed to do with her?

"No. And don't curse at me. I don't like it." She leaned her carrot-red head back against the seat. "Get in the car, Chance. Or don't you care that I found something that may help you? May help your brother?"

Chance had never laid his hand on a woman before in his life—with a few notable exceptions while on the job with the Texas State Police and the Texas Rangers back in the early days of his career—but this woman left him no choice.

He grabbed her arm with one hand, then slipped his other hand under her long, skinny legs and gripped. He pulled.

She got caught in the seatbelt. She hooked her arm around the headrest. He cursed again. Then again when she laughed. "I do not need this right now. Get *out*."

She smiled, then pushed the sunglasses up to rest on the top of her head, revealing pretty light-brown eyes. "Tough.

Gabby's my best friend. One of my only friends, to be honest. If she's in trouble, I'm going to be there."

Gabby was the woman his brother had feelings for, the woman his brother was going all ape-shit overprotective over. The woman some asshole had terrified. Threatened. The fact that this girl mentioned Gabby and the trouble the other woman was in told him that she probably was a genuine family connection. And a very loyal one, apparently. He admired the sentiment, but the stupidity—it was beyond foolish. "Don't be a damned idiot. What are you going to do to protect her?"

Light-brown eyes bore right through him. "Whatever I have to. Gabby's my best friend, Chance. And I love her."

For the life of him, he thought the girl meant it. And she was a girl in a lot of ways. At first glance, he'd thought she was younger than she actually was, but she was still a good decade younger than him. And innocent. Very naive.

What the hell was she thinking, getting in a strange man's car this way? Didn't she have any more self-preservation than this? "What's your name? Why did you track me down?"

"You don't remember me. That's ok. I'm Brynna. I was just a little girl when we knew each other. My father and mother were good friends with your parents. But you were a teenager when I was there the most. And then…after you moved out, I was there quite a bit. We didn't see you very much. Which was ok, because I know you never liked me. I never really liked you, either."

He vaguely recalled a bunch of redheaded girls in his parents' home. Had she been one of them? "Why are you really here?"

She stared at him for a moment out of those disconcerting eyes. This girl-woman had eyes that could twist a man's gut into real knots, didn't she? "I've found something, I think. And Gabby said you were nearby."

"So why are you in St. Louis?" How the hell had this creature found him? He'd always paid cash for everything, and there wasn't anyone other than his brother that he'd told where he'd be. And even that was just an occasional occurrence. He wasn't exactly the type that was easily tethered.

"My sister is here, with PAVAD. Have you heard of it? I tracked your cell phone to find you, after Gabby told me you were up here when we were chatting online earlier today."

Of course, he had heard of the FBI's PAVAD division. He had contacts in every federal agency in the country—contacts he'd deliberately cultivated in his work—and he'd heard quite a bit about the relatively new FBI unit that was supposedly unstoppable.

He'd used this trip to speak to a St. Louis field agent who'd worked the murder of Chance's family ten years earlier. Chance had been called to St. Louis speak to a grand jury about a previous kidnapping case he'd worked as a private investigator.

Ten years ago, he'd been assigned to the same team as Art Kendall. Chance had wanted to get the guy's impressions about that day.

He wasn't so sure he trusted the reports the Texas State Police had given him.

And Chance would be following every lead, no matter how long it took. "Aren't I just the lucky one?"

He'd met with the field agent after the man's shift had ended, which was why Chance was in the FBI parking garage at nearly eight at night. The parking garage shared with PAVAD. Had the girl been waiting for him all this time? In a dark garage, alone? With little defenses?

Damn it, the girl-woman needed a keeper.

She blinked up at him; in the dim light of the interior lamp, her skin glowed, and her eyes were remarkable. What was it with those eyes of hers? They were gorgeous, but made him feel like a damned slug. "I don't really understand sarcasm. At least, that's what I've been told. Why are you lucky?"

Was she for real?

"Never mind. Other than Gabby's friend, who are you exactly? What do you know about my brother?"

"I have something that is extremely pertinent to the murder investigation that I know you are still working. But I need to speak with my bosses before I can share it. But I didn't want to wait to talk to Benny. I wanted to talk to the chief of my TSP post. Your brother. Elliot. What I found is going to be hard on Gabby. I was chatting with her to check on her and she said you were up here, too. I don't drive. You are going back there. It was logical that we ride together. So I found you myself."

She grinned at him, revealing dimples and a beautiful smile complete with a tiny gap between her front teeth.

"So you came up this way to show me?"

"No. Not exactly. I was here anyway. I was visiting my sister and brother-in-law, who both work with PAVAD. I need to get back to Texas tonight. And I need to check on her. On Gabby. She tends to freak out over scary stuff like this. Since it's about your family, it made the most sense that I find you and you drive me home. See. Logical. Logical."

"Let me get this straight. Gabby's with my brother. I know that part. But you aren't capable of finding your own way home? How exactly is that working out for you?"

"I *have* found my way home: you. I don't drive. I never learned. We have a common purpose. You want to catch the bastards who killed your family. So do I."

Why did the word *bastard* coming from her lips sound so wrong? Because of the sweet doll-like appearance? The obvious innocence on her face? Chance pushed those thoughts away. This girl was bound to give a decent man fits. An honorable one. He wasn't the least bit decent, and he was for damned sure not honorable. He didn't have the time to screw around with this girl. Woman. Girl-woman, that's what he would call her—it suited her better.

But he doubted he was getting her out of his car any time soon.

"Of course I want to find the killers."

"So do I. So does Gabby. And your brother, too. Shouldn't we work together on that? I'm very good at what I do, you know? Some of my work is now being used by the FBI. By the FBI. It's cutting edge, or so they say. You drive me home; I'll work in the car. I share what I have, you do the same. An *I-show-you mine, you-show-me-yours* kind of thing. Except with clothes on."

Seriously? This girl-woman was just asking for trouble someday, wasn't she?

"Who controls you? You have a family out there? One of your sisters? Parents? Handlers?" Someone had to. There was no way this creature had been released on the unsuspecting world completely on her own, right?

She stared at him for a moment. "I don't think I understand you. I live with my father, if that's what you're asking. My mother died five years ago. Five. He's home now. He and your dad were partners twenty years ago, you know?"

"*Beck*. You are one of Kevin Beck's daughters." That made things perfectly clear. He'd met Kevin Beck on many occasions and had liked and respected the man. Beck had been a little younger than his dad, and had four or five kids, all a little younger than Sara and Slade. And all girls, he thought. All red-haired pretty girls who gave everyone who knew them fits. *This* was one of them, then. He tried to recall if any had had hair quite that carroty. There had been one. And he hadn't liked her when he'd been a teenager, had he? Something about her had annoyed the hell out of him back then. "Your dad should have whipped your ass *years* ago. You *don't* get into strange men's cars. I'm surprised you didn't know that."

She looked at him like he was the idiot. "You're not strange. Well, not unknown strange, I mean. You may do weird things that I don't know about, though. I guess you could be strange that way. I've known your family my entire life. Known you. Known you. You poured pancake batter on my head when I was six. Which was really mean. And your brother is with my best friend right now. See? I do know you."

"Still. You don't know me now. I could kill you, beat you, rob you, rape you, assault you right now, and then dump you along a dark road somewhere. Or bury you. Where you'll never be found. Have you thought about that?" He leaned down in the open passenger door. Because the girl was for damned sure not getting out. And now that he knew *who* she was, he couldn't just kick her to the curb and let whatever happened to her happen, could he?

Kevin Beck had been his sister's godfather. His parents had reciprocated with the Beck brat closest in age to his sister, the one with the carroty red hair. *This* girl. Damn it.

That meant something to Chance. It had to.

Like it or not, he was stuck with her for a while, wasn't he? At least until he delivered her to her father, along with a clear lecture to her and a reprimand for the older man for letting her out of his sight long enough for her to get into trouble.

He got close enough that he could see the faint flecks of gold in those peculiar brown eyes of hers. She didn't so much as flinch away, though he knew having him in her personal space like that had to bother her. Hell, it would bother him. But this one was an extremely cool little customer. "What do you say about that?"

"I'd say I've already texted my sister Mel and told her where I was and who I was with." She smiled at him like she'd won something. "And Jarrod. I texted him, too. He gets a little freaked out if he doesn't know where I'm at or what I am doing. Especially this late at night."

"Who's Jarrod?" Boyfriend, possibly? She was a damned beautiful—if irritating—girl-woman. There had to be a guy involved somewhere.

"Jarrod's with the TSP. Detective Foster." Chance remembered him; he'd met Foster hanging around Gabby. For some reason, he couldn't see this girl-woman with Foster, though. The other guy was too hard, too cynical, to be with a girl-woman like this. "In your brother's post. He's a detective. And a friend. But shouldn't you get in and start driving? We have a long night ahead of us. And I think it's going to storm some more."

"It's not going to storm."

"Oh, I think it will."

—

IT stormed. Chance should have known it would. It didn't seem to bother his companion, who'd slipped earbuds in delicate little ears.

Something about Brynna Beck bothered the hell out of him. Made him a bit snarly. And, if she was the Beck he was remembering, always had. Whenever she'd been around, she'd grate on his nerves to the point he'd want to scream.

It was the way she looked at him, the way she talked. She used to repeat everything anyone ever said in a monotone, like a voice recorder. She didn't seem to do that now. It had driven him nuts. As had the way everything normal had seemed to bother her as a kid. He tried to recall the last time he'd seen her—had she been at the funerals? He didn't remember. No surprise—he'd buried four members of his immediate family that day.

He looked at her—she had to be around twenty-three or

twenty-four. A little younger than his sister, Sara, would have been. Kevin Beck had brought his family to Chance's college graduation, hadn't he? That was the last time he remembered seeing the Beck family, when he'd been twenty-two.

So this girl would have been about twelve then. He vaguely recalled a thin little girl hiding behind sunglasses and headphones. She'd told him congratulations, then followed her older sister to the duck pond nearby. He hadn't given her another thought since then.

This was that girl.

He looked at the sunglasses on her head. The headphones in her ears. Some things hadn't changed, had they?

She shifted, and he was just able to make out the full-grown female curves in the dim glow from her laptop.

Well, some things *had* changed over the last ten years, hadn't they?

She thrummed. Practically vibrated in the passenger seat of the rental. Her bag was at her feet, and her fingers typed at the speed of a freight train. She'd occasionally hum, little sounds of concentration that seriously pissed him off. Made him wonder when else she would hum. *What* else would please her enough to have her making that sound.

Did that damned Foster make her do that?

She's promised to show him hers. He was manfully keeping his thoughts on the professional rather than the other areas of his body that idea, that image, flooded. Trying to, anyway.

This was his parents' goddaughter. That they'd been dead ten years mattered little to his body.

Kevin Beck's annoying little daughter. Hell. He'd never had a thing for younger women before. He wasn't about to start now.

He shifted a bit in the driver's seat.

Beautiful, intelligent, loyal—and apparently as mad as the hatter ever was.

So why was he having so much trouble keeping his eyes on the road and off of her?

She finally pulled the earbuds from her ears and sighed, about two a.m. He'd decided it would just work best if they drove straight through the night. He'd expected his companion to fall asleep, but she hadn't. "Yes, Gabby has to have what else

I need. Damn it. I didn't want to have to show her what I found. It will upset her too much. Gabby gets upset a lot."

"And what is it that you found?"

"You know about the emails Gabby's been getting, right? I've been looking for three years to find some sort of connection between the IP address and the Finley Creek Texas State Police branch. I've found nothing, and I haven't told Gabby. I don't want her getting scared again. It's almost like someone knows exactly what I am doing as I'm doing it. Even though I'm not *supposed* to be working on the Marshall case and I've told no one. Not even my sister, Mel. But I've checked every computer I use. Mine, Gabby's, my personal ones. If they're using spyware, I can't find it. And that means they are very, very good."

"That confident in your skills?"

She blinked at him again. Did he have *moron* written on his forehead or something? "Well. *Yes*. I've designed some seriously kick-ass software for law enforcement—as has my older sister, Carrie. We know what we are doing. I gave her a cloned hard drive from both mine and Gabby's laptops. She hasn't been able to find anything, either. But I know something has to be there. But I can't find what. Can't find what."

"And that's why you have that sticker over the webcam?"

"Yes. And after what Gabby told me happened to your sister…how the killers saw Gabby, too. Well…I'm not stupid. Not stupid at all. I don't want someone spying on me. But this is Gabby's laptop. Benny has mine today; he's upgrading it. I borrowed Gabby's. We built them together. Together."

Chance looked away from her for a moment. His sister, Sara, had been killed while on a live webcam feed to her best friend, Gabby, ten years ago. Gabby had hit record as she'd called 911. But it had been too late for Chance's family.

All he had left was his brother Elliot.

"You've been friends for a while?"

"Four years. We met once or twice with Sara when we were kids. At your mom's house. But Mel was more Sara's and Slade's friend than I was. I was too young. But Gabby and Sara…they were older than me."

"Yes." Gabby had been his sister's constant companion from about the age of ten or eleven, he thought.

"I'm younger than Gabby. Mel's older—she and Slade were

the same age. Whenever we'd visit your house, I'd stay in the kitchen with your mom while they played. Mel and Sara and Slade. They'd play with Jillian and Sydney. My other sisters."

"But not you?"

"Too loud for me." She said it so matter-of-factly. "I'd rather make cookies with your mom. She didn't talk to me like I was weird. And she wouldn't let them be loud in her kitchen. She was my friend, too. I loved her, a lot. I still miss her."

"Me, too." There was something in her tone that told him far too many people probably had looked at *her* differently. "Why weird?"

"I wasn't quite as good at communicating back then as I am now. You know that. You used to laugh at me for it. I remember."

He winced. He couldn't remember it, but he probably had when she'd annoy him too much. Most of the time, he'd just tried to stay away from all of the little kids running around his parents' house. Now he wished he hadn't. He wished he'd spent as much time with his younger brother and sister as he possibly could have back then.

It was easy to miss what you'd lost, wasn't it? Rather than appreciate who you had. Chance had learned that the hard way.

The last words he'd ever shared with someone in his family had been harsh. An argument with his youngest brother, Slade, over something so stupid he barely remembered it.

What he remembered most about that kid was signing the hospital paperwork to cut off life-support and letting Slade die three days after their parents and younger sister.

"It's ok. I've forgiven you for it. You weren't the first. Nor the last. I'm weirder than most women. And I know it."

She was very direct. No artifice. He had to admit that was a bit of an oddity. "I see."

"I don't think you do. Ever heard of Asperger's. You know, kind of like autism? Although they are lumping it in with autism now."

Who hadn't? "Yes."

"I'm on it, you know. The spectrum. For years I thought I was the only one in the family. The only one. Then two years ago we found my missing sister. I'm not. Carrie's just like me.

Only she has pervasive developmental disorder—not otherwise specified. PDD-NOS. I am high functioning. So is she. We don't know who is higher functioning, though. Probably her. She's lived on her own before. Before she got married. I haven't. I've always lived with my father. But Carrie was lost for so many years. She didn't have our family like I did."

Chance was having some trouble keeping up. But Asperger's explained a lot, didn't it? The slightly repetitive, halting speech pattern, the lack of a filter—possibly. He didn't know much about it, but he remembered a little girl who hadn't talked so well back then. Who'd twitch and rock when upset. *He'd* somehow always seemed to upset her back then. Until he just made a point of staying away. "Ok, missing sister? How was she lost?"

"Carrie was kidnapped by a murderer when she was nine. He took her to Oklahoma, and she went into foster care there. Then she ran away when she was fifteen and lived on the streets. I saw her in a computer forensic trade journal and recognized her. I mean…she looks like me and everything. So I did some digging"—which Chance took to mean *hacking*—"in her files. She's a year and a half older than Mel."

"I'm sorry for what your family went through." He'd never heard anything about Beck having a missing child out there. Had his father and mother known?

"We didn't know about Carrie. I mean, my dad and mom did. They did. But not the rest of us. But we've found her now. We saved her life when that murderer tried to kill her again a few years ago. We got there just in time to help save her and some other people. She jumped off a roof and landed at Mel's feet. I was down on the street, by all the sirens. Jarrod made me stay down there with the Missouri police. I could just see the fire. It was terrifying. My dad was up there, too. He almost got shot. Now she's married with a baby. My niece Madeline."

"I'm glad it worked out for you." Family sagas and drama just pissed him off. He wanted no part of them. Not that he resented people who had those kinds of connections—but he didn't want to hear about them. To be reminded. "So what did you find on that laptop?"

"Oh. I have to show you mine first, huh?"

He wished the interior light was on, that he could see her face. Did she realize what kind of sexual innuendo she kept using? Chance knew himself as exactly what he was—he was a damned caveman at times. Especially when it came to females and sex. She'd gotten him thinking of one thing with her *I-show-you mine* earlier.

Damn it. This woman—she still grated on his nerves but in an entirely different way than she had as a child. Did she realize that?

Somehow he doubted she did.

A keeper. The girl-woman needed a keeper.

He would not be lusting after Kevin Beck's innocent little daughter.

"Do you realize how that sounds?" He pulled the car to a stop at the intersection. He hadn't taken the direct route. He'd chosen to go due west from St. Louis and take the highway that went south into Finley Creek. There were faster ways, but they were the obvious. Chance never took the direct route—it was safer to go an alternative than what people would have expected. He knew that. But they also needed to stop.

They needed food and a break. A restroom. Caffeine. Then they'd keep going.

She turned toward him, just as headlights flooded her window. Headlights that weren't stopping. "What—"

Chance grabbed for her, knowing as he did that it wouldn't matter in the least.

He was too damned late to get her out of the way.

Something crashed into the passenger side.

Into Brynna.

Her scream was a sound he would never forget.

Chapter 2

BRYNNA FOUGHT THE HARD hands that dragged her from the broken window. She knew they weren't there to help her or Chance. "Let me go! Chance! Help!"

Brynna screamed as loud as she could.

But she knew the truth—it was the middle of the night in a small town that probably had less than eight hundred people total. And most of those were probably sound asleep. She'd be lucky if a coyote heard her cries out here.

"Do you have her?" one of the men asked.

"I got her. What about her computer? There will be one. Or more."

Her laptop had been on her lap. Her tablet and phone were both in the bag at her feet.

What about Chance?

Was he dead? Why wasn't he trying to help her? Brynna kicked at the man holding her. She couldn't see him; it was too rainy. Not even the moon illuminated the road.

Where was Chance? Was he dead? Where was he?

She fought panic. Mel said not to panic when something bad happened. Her sister said that was how people made mistakes and got themselves killed. She would not panic.

"Let me go."

"Shut it, little bitch," the one holding her said. His hands tightened.

"Don't kill me."

"Don't tempt me."

The other man stepped closer. He was tall. Just as tall as her brother-in-law Sebastian. Sebastian was well over six feet, like six four or six five. But this guy seemed old. Older, at least, like her father. The one holding her was shorter, chunkier, and his hands were way too tight.

"She's just a girl," the tall one said. "Young. How old are

you now, Brynna?"

"Twenty-four. Almost twenty-five."

"Yes, that's about right. You're just a baby. I don't know what he was thinking. She's got nothing to do with any of this. Never should have been brought into this."

Brynna was the worst at interpreting peoples' tones, and she knew it. But she thought she heard actual disgust. Why?

"Where's your laptop, little one?" the tall one asked.

"In…in the car."

"Keep her here. I'll get it and check on Marshall. Don't hurt her."

"Put a bullet in him. That will end part of our problem," the one holding her said. He tightened his arms around her, right under her bra. Brynna fought to breathe, and blood was dripping into her right eye. She thought her head had slammed into the window before the window had shattered. Before they had knocked the glass in with something.

They'd been after her, definitely. Hadn't they?

Because of what she'd found on her laptop?

"And bring every damned law enforcement agency down on our heads? We're not in Texas, after all. He does not have any TSP on his payroll in Oklahoma, you idiot. An interstate crime will bring too much attention."

The one holding her snorted. "But it would end that problem, at least. He's worse than his old man. Both sons are. Kill them and be done with it. Like we should have ten years ago. Then we'll have a bit of fun with Red here."

"Do *not* mention ten years ago to me. You know better."

Old man? Chance.

They were talking about Chance's father, weren't they?

About killing Chance to end the problem. Brynna tried not to hyperventilate. Ten years. The killers. Sara's killers. And they had *her*.

What was she supposed to do now?

She'd never felt more alone in her entire life.

Chapter 3

CHANCE WOKE JUST AS they were pulling the girl from the car. It took him a moment to remember what had happened. To remember the blinding headlights and the sound of a large vehicle accelerating. Straight toward them. Toward Brynna.

He heard Brynna screaming, yelling his name.

The terror he heard was something else he would never forget.

He grabbed for the gun he always wore. It was gone, and he didn't have time to search for it. He'd just have to improvise. He slipped from the driver's side quietly.

In the dark, with his black clothing and his dark hair, they'd have one hell of a time seeing him. He didn't know who, he didn't know how many, and he barely knew where—but he was going to use every advantage he had.

They were not going to hurt that girl any more than they already had. His parents had loved that girl; he owed it to them to keep her safe.

No matter what he had to do, he was keeping her safe until he could return her to her father where she belonged. He cataloged his impressions of the area right before the crash had happened. Small town, one all-night gas station—he could barely make out the chain's sign in the distance. No houses that he could remember passing. Remote, wooded. Isolated.

They'd followed them, hadn't they? How else would they have known Chance was turning off in this particular spit in the road?

—

THEY were moving quickly. Chance thought about jumping

the tall one when he returned to the rental SUV. But he didn't. Not until he found Brynna.

Chance skulked through the rough grass on the embankment. She called out again, frightened and frantic. And then she cried out from pain.

He hurried toward the sound of her cries—and toward the sound of an idling engine.

Not the truck that had hit them, then. They had another vehicle waiting. Why? And why had they pulled Brynna from the SUV instead of him? A kidnapping attempt, then.

Had she been the target? It made sense.

No one should have been able to find *him*. He had always made a point of keeping any connections to his whereabouts extremely tenuous. He rarely ever told Elliot where he was, and for good reason.

Some of the things he'd done over the last ten years were more than just dangerous. They were deadly.

But a young computer tech? She wouldn't have even thought of half the precautions he used just walking to the bakery two blocks from his apartment.

If someone wanted *her*, they would have found a way to get her.

And they had. It was just his shitty luck that he'd been there with her when it happened.

Maybe it was *their* shitty luck. He wasn't letting them get away with that girl. If they got her to that waiting vehicle, Chance wouldn't have a snowball in hell's odds, and he knew it.

He had to get to her.

Keep crying out, baby; I'm coming for you.

Chapter 4

BRYNNA KNEW HER TEARS were ticking off the guy holding her, but she couldn't stop them. She'd never been so scared in her life—except when her mother had died and when her sister Mel had been shot. She didn't know what to do.

"Shut up."

"I can't." And she wouldn't. Why would she make it easy for them to abduct her or kill her? Shouldn't she fight like crazy? Wasn't that what Mel would do?

Carrie certainly had. Her eldest sister had jumped off of a multistory building to escape a kidnapper and murderer.

But this guy was so much bigger than Brynna was. Stronger.

She sniffed.

So she'd have to be *smarter,* that was all. How was she supposed to bring a man so much bigger than her down?

A *man.*

Of course. Her father had been very specific when he'd first taught her and her sisters about men and some of the things they'd try to do. And how to defend themselves.

Aim true and aim hard.

And when they least expected it. How could she make him think she was a big wimp? "I'm sorry. I'm sorry. You can take my laptop, and I'll not stop you. I promise. Just don't hurt me. Don't cut me. Please. Just take it and go."

He snorted and ran the pocketknife over her left breast. "Real fighter, aren't you?"

Brynna shook her head. "No, no, no. I don't fight. My sisters do. I just want to go home. Go home to my dad."

His grip tightened, and he pulled her off her feet. "So what will you give me if I promise to let you go?"

His hand dropped to her backside, and he squeezed suggestively.

Terror immediately threatened to erase her plan from her head. She recoiled.

No. She wouldn't give him sex. She wouldn't.

But she could play along for a moment, couldn't she? "I d-don't know what you mean."

"Sure, you do. You're a beautiful girl, a very beautiful girl. I'm sure you've done it before."

She shook her head. "Not that. I…" She'd never traded sex for anything in her life.

He softened around her, turned more suggestive than threatening. "Oh, you *are* going to be a lot of fun. Let me get rid of my partner, and you and I will get to know each other. And then you can go right on home to your family in the morning."

She'd vomit first. But Brynna nodded. She needed him off guard. "O-ok."

He shifted his weight and faced her more fully. His hand on her neck pulled away. He tangled his fingers in her hair.

Her assailant shifted again, widening the distance between his legs just enough.

Brynna rammed her knee into his groin as hard as she could and screamed.

And then *he* was there. A dark shadow, cursing and angry. And tangling with the monster who had held her. "Run, Brynna, run! Don't stop. Go!"

Chance. He wasn't dead, after all.

Brynna ran.

Chapter 5

CHANCE AIMED FOR EVERY dirty point he could with the son-of-a-bitch who'd had his hands on Brynna. He'd give it to the girl: she'd surprised him with the giving-in ruse she'd pulled on the big bastard.

He doubted the fucker had expected the knee to the dick any more than Chance had expected her to do it.

Smart girl. And determined. Her father had obviously taught her one little trick every girl-woman should know.

He punched the guy in the face a few times for good measure, then heard the guy's partner yell something.

Run up behind him.

Chance stood and drove his fist into the taller guy's solar plexus.

The guy was older and in less decent shape. That was probably the only advantage Chance was going to get, and he knew it.

In the meantime, Brynna had disappeared into the sparse woods, somewhere.

Chance would only have a few seconds to find her, before they were separated for good out there. Or she fell down a magic rabbit hole or got eaten by a pack of coyotes or something. Or these sons-of-bitches caught up with her.

"Stay the fuck away from her." If he had his gun, he'd blow a hole right through both of them. But he didn't. He had nothing but his fists. So he would use them.

From somewhere nearby, he heard her cry out. Had she fallen? Hurt herself even more?

The sun was rising. They'd be able to spot her in that red shirt of hers, even through the rain that was picking up again. If he got to her first, they might have a chance of getting enough distance between them.

And he doubted the sons-of-bitches wanted their vehicles

close enough to the totaled SUV to be identified. No. If they stayed too much longer, they ran the risk of traffic stopping to see what had happened.

Chance took a gamble that they wouldn't shoot him in the back or follow, and ran toward her call. The two men ran the opposite direction. Toward their vehicles.

He found her on a service road about an eighth of a mile north of the intersection. It was nothing but gravel and mud, but she kept going.

"Brynna! Brynna, you can stop now."

Chance caught up to her easily. It was clear she was tiring.

He reached out and stopped her. She fought, just like he'd expected. "It's ok, Brynna. It's ok. They left. We're alone now."

"Chance?" She stilled, then wrapped small feminine hands around his shirt. The way she clung to him told its own story. "I thought they'd killed you. They talked about the night your family died. It was *them*. They killed your family. And they had me. I thought they'd killed you too. Killed you. Killed you."

"I'm tougher than that." He touched her hair, soaked with rain. Fought the urge to go after them again—for his family. And for *her*. "We're not giving up."

"They have my laptop."

"Yes."

"I cloned it. I gave a copy of the hard drive to my sister Carrie. I don't want them to go after her."

"Who did you tell you cloned it?"

"Carrie. Gabby."

"Just those two?"

"Yes. In private."

"Then I think it'll be ok."

"We need to get to one of those hard drives." She buried her face in his chest. "But I don't want them to go to Carrie. Not if I don't have to. She has a baby, and I don't want Maddie hurt."

She had a family, didn't she? This skinny redhead with the magic eyes and the odd way of talking had people that she loved, who loved her.

Damn it, those fucking bastards had no right to pull her into the middle of this. He stepped back from her but wrapped one hand around her fingers. "We need to get out of here. We don't know if they'll come back or not."

"Our car?" Her voice broke as she looked around. "We're in the middle of nowhere."

"It's totaled. We can't drive it. We'll go back. You'll hide while I search for my gun. Then we'll decide what to do." He pulled his cell free. No signal. "Your phone?"

"In my bag. I think they took it."

Chance stilled. "They have your cell. Your wallet? Address?"

"I think they knew all that anyway. But I have my wallet and my money."

"You're probably right about that. Did you text anyone?" How much information did the assholes now have access to? She'd said it was like someone was watching her. Maybe someone was.

"I told Gabby that I was going to find you. That was it."

"So they know Gabby knows. Decision made. We head back to Finley Creek." Better keep to the people who were already involved than getting some other innocent member of this girl's family messed up in it.

It took him less than five minutes to return to the rental and find his gun under the seat. He had an extra magazine in his pocket—one reason he favored cargo pants—and having it and the weapon made him feel a little bit more secure.

A little, not much.

Brynna was huddled right where he'd left her next to a culvert.

Poor kid looked like a drowned red rat. Pitiful.

Sweet and vulnerable and nowhere near equipped to deal with the kind of world they were in. Was this how his brother had felt the first time he realized Gabby was still a part of this?

He wasn't going to follow the same path his brother had. No matter what this girl-woman touched in him. "Get up. We need to get moving."

Chapter 6

HER SIDE BURNED. HER feet burned. But Brynna kept going. Chance had her arm in his hand as he dragged her through the brush and into the woods surrounding the narrow highway they'd taken. He'd said the roads were too dangerous now. And they were too far from a house to go for help. Not with the storm approaching. How much more of this could she take?

Until she got home. She would do anything to make sure she made it back to her father and her sisters. Baby Maddie. She'd just held her only niece two days ago, and she'd been so happy, so beautiful.

Brynna loved that baby so deeply. The thought of dying before she could see Maddie and Carrie and Mel and Jillian and Syd and their father again made her want to vomit.

She needed to tell them she loved them again. At least one more time.

No matter how miserable she felt being dragged through the Oklahoma woods by a madman—and she wasn't certain Chance Marshall was entirely sane—she would keep going until she made it back to her family.

"Keep up." He stopped for a second, just long enough to glare down at her from those weird green eyes.

"I'm doing the best I can."

"Do better. Unless you want to do dead. Either the storm is going to get us or those bastards will. Unless we find shelter."

"I'm *trying,* ok? Some of us aren't GI Joe, you know?" She pressed her hand against her side again.

She was still bleeding, wasn't she? But bleeding was better than dead, wasn't it?

She pulled in a sharp breath. "Let's keep going. I'll be ok."

He pulled her closer, until less than eighteen inches

separated them. "How badly did he hurt you?"

"I'm ok. Ok. He only cut me twice, twice. Let's keep going." She'd think of her family one by one, if she had to, to focus. "I want to go home. I want my family."

"Why the hell did you have to wear a red shirt? Redheads shouldn't wear red." He grabbed the band of her shirt and pulled.

"It's pink. Redheads aren't supposed to wear *pink*. And I think that's a stupid rule. I like pink. And red. I don't like yellow, though."

"Can you shut up for a minute, please? Why the fuck didn't you tell me he cut you this badly? Are you wanting to bleed out? How deep?"

"It was car glass, I think. When they knocked out my door window. It cut me in a few places when they pulled me out the window. And he had that knife. What would you have done if I had said it? Stopped running for our lives to put a bandage on? I don't think so." She tried to pull her hand free but he wasn't going to let her go until he was ready to, was he? "Let's keep going. Before this guy goes after Gabby and your brother. Gabby's already lost one best friend, I'd really prefer she not lose another."

His face tightened, and Brynna got it—the best friend Gabby had lost had been his baby sister. "I'm sorry I said that. About your sister. I remember her. She was older than me but was always nice. I'm sorry."

"Don't mention it." He reached into his bag and pulled out a white undershirt and a knife. He cut the cotton quickly. "Hold up your shirt."

She obeyed. He wrapped the makeshift bandage around her and then pulled a roll of duct tape from the bag. With a few strips of tape, he had the cotton in place. "Let's go. We'll fix you up later. As soon as we find shelter."

"It's going to storm some more."

"You always state the obvious?"

"Yes. It's easier that way."

"Then let's get going."

But his hands were far gentler this time when he led her over the rocky embankment.

Chapter 7

SHE WASN'T A COMPLAINER; he would give her that. He'd seen far stronger people crumble under horrible circumstances. But this girl-woman kept going.

He needed to find them some shelter; the rain wasn't stopping, and the wind was picking up. The storm she'd predicted was coming.

Maybe more. He'd lived in Texas his whole life. He knew how tornados were. And it was prime season for it.

"Brynna, baby, we need to find some shelter."

"Where?" She looked around the Oklahoma woods. From what Chance could figure they were still somewhere north of the Texas border.

She was shivering, and shock was taking hold. She'd been up all night, in a collision, and almost abducted. And now he was dragging her through the woods on foot—in a thunderstorm.

No.

They needed to rest. Then they could find help.

Not that he trusted any damned one else.

"Come on, Bryn. We'll find a spot to rest."

"I'm trying." She was gasping for breath, wasn't she? She wasn't just tired.

Something was wrong. Chance scooped her up. She didn't weigh much at all. "Wrap your arms around my neck. I'll get you there."

"I'm sorry. I know you can go faster than I can."

"Shut up. I'm not going any faster than you can make it. You know what Elliot would do if I showed up in Finley Creek without you? Not to mention Gabby. She scares me."

"Gabby? I don't think she could scare anyone. She's more likely to *be* scared of everyone."

So literal, wasn't she? Chance smiled. "My brother loves

her. And she loves him."

"Already? I know she *likes* him. But you can't fall in love with someone that fast. It doesn't work that way. Love takes time and interests and trust. How can you trust someone after only a week? That doesn't make much sense."

"Love isn't logical. They might not have admitted it to each other or to themselves. But the emotion is there. I could see it." He remembered his parents. The two of them shouldn't have clicked, but they had. His mother had been like Gabby was—light, happy, seeing the world as a beautiful place. His father had been more like Chance—untrusting and world-hardened.

But they'd been married for thirty years before they'd been murdered.

Thirty years wasn't exactly nothing.

"It should be," she said. "People find mates who... well...*match* them. Shared interests and goals. That kind of thing. It's not like it is in books or movies. People don't meet and fall in love like that. Well, almost. I know a couple that were on the run last year. They were nuts about each other, I guess. They came to our house for help."

"Running from the cops?" He kept walking, just letting her talk. "And they came to you?"

"To our house. And they were running from a corrupt FBI agent. He tried to kill them. He shot my friend. But she survived. He is my sister's husband's brother. They fell in love."

"See, it can work that way." Not that it would for men like him. But those that were looking for that—well, more power to them.

"I think that's crazy, though."

And this girl-woman was an expert on love? "You've been in love?"

"I thought so. A few times. But those relationships didn't work out."

"Why?" Normally he wouldn't bother asking such questions. But the idea of Brynna involved with someone irked him on some level. And made him wonder. What kind of men had she been drawn to? He could hazard a guess—brainy, computer types. Pale and weak.

Still, how could a guy not take one look at her and have those kinds of thoughts?

"Tell me."

"Why? Are you going to tell me about all the women in your past?"

Then again, the way she challenged a man in such a brutally honest way—some guys *would* find that off-putting, wouldn't they? "Just curious. Does this Jarrod guy treat you well?"

"Jarrod? Yes. He picks me up and drives me to work almost every day. He drives Gabby, too. I used to ride with my sister Mel before she got shot. She was Jarrod's partner for a few years. She got me my job with the department after I got my degree in computer sciences. And I'm good at it. Benny says I'm one of the best."

"Bennett Russell?" The guy would know. He'd been one of the pioneers of computer forensics. Everyone associated with the Finley Creek TSP post was aware of that.

"He's the best boss. He lets Gabby and me pretty much do what we want as long as we find what we're looking for. And he makes it so that we don't have to deal with too many of the officers and detectives. They can get really pushy sometimes."

"How so?"

"Sometimes they like to get in our space. Lean over our shoulders to look at our screens. I caught this guy playing with my hair once and *sniffing* me. Benny chased him out of our office and spoke with the guy's commander. Then there was the guy who was convinced Gabby was in love with him and needed him to marry her and let her be a stay-at-home mom to his four kids. Yeah. Jarrod took care of that guy, but I don't know what he said to him. Gabby was actually speechless. Mel was laughing like a lunatic after that one. I don't like people in my personal space. I think it's just rude."

She wrapped her arms around his neck. Chance didn't miss the irony. There were only a few ways *they* could get more into each other's personal space. Didn't she realize that?

"I think I can walk again. I mean, my side hurts. And so does my head, a little. And my arm, but I don't think it's broken."

She was damned lucky. If they'd been going any faster, those sons-of-bitches would have killed her on impact.

But they hadn't intended to.

They'd just wanted her dazed and easy to handle. They

hadn't meant to kill her right away, but to take her. For what? To see what she knew first, and then kill her?

If that was the case, odds were good they'd try for her again.

Chance tightened his arms around her.

They'd have to kill him before they ever laid a hand on this girl-woman again.

"Chance? You can put me down now."

Chapter 8

HE PUT HER DOWN carefully. She questioned whether that was such a good thing or not. Her legs felt like bubble gum at the knees, and her side burned. She didn't know if it was rain or blood soaking her shirt and the top of her jeans, but she suspected it was both.

That monster had cut her just because he could. What would make someone do that? Hurt someone just because?

She had never understood that. Probably never would.

Brynna had rarely hurt anyone in her life. She'd defended herself from bullies a time or two—when Mel wasn't around—but they'd always hurt her first.

Her father and older sister had made sure she knew how to fight back. She might not like the idea of violence, but she wasn't going to let herself be a victim. She was proud of how she'd kicked the monster in the groin and ran. She hadn't let him kidnap her. Or touch her. That mattered.

"Where do you think we're going?"

"I'm looking for a cabin or shed. Something to get us out of the storm for a while. Once it clears, we'll walk to where we can get cell service."

"Ok." Lightning crackled across the sky, and Brynna jumped. She wasn't as afraid of storms as she used to be, not really. She'd always known to take appropriate precautions during tornado weather. But walking through the woods during a storm was not something she ever wanted to do again.

"We'll find someplace, soon."

How did he know? "How?"

"Have faith, baby."

"I'm not a baby."

He sighed. "I know that. It's an expression."

"I figured. But why call me that? It's like…something you

call someone you like. Someone you know. Elliot calls Gabby that."

"Our father called our mother that. It is just habit. Don't read anything in it. We're not like your friend on the run."

Of course, they weren't. That was silly that he'd even think that. "I know that. I'm just curious. Trying to figure you out. Trying to forget that that guy cut me with his knife and that it hurts. Really hurts. Talk to me. Please?"

He sighed. Was he annoyed with her? "Ok. What do you want to talk about?"

"Anything but why we are out here. Are you attracted to me?"

"What?"

Brynna felt like an idiot for a second. "It was just a question. Elliot is obviously attracted to Gabby, and he uses *baby*. So I wondered—"

"Are you for real? You don't just ask a guy if he's attracted to you."

"Sorry." She couldn't deny the embarrassment. She was just glad it was still too dark for him to see her face clearly. "I just…sometimes I can't filter what I'm thinking. And it comes out. Comes out."

"I get that. And for the record, I'm not a liar."

That didn't make any sense at all to her. "Ok. I never said you were."

"I'm just saying I can't lie to you. *Yes*. I could be attracted to you. In a different time and a different place. Not when I'm busy trying to find a nest of vipers who may or may not be trying to kill the only people in this world I still care about. Including my brother and your Gabby. Hell, they are the only ones I'm concerned with besides myself."

"Not me? You'd let them kill me?"

"Of course not."

"Sorry. Sometimes I'm not very good at communication with people I don't know all that well. Or even those that I do. Gabby just tells me, 'I don't understand, Brynna. Try again.' That works out well for us."

"Gabby again."

"Yes. We got each other's backs, you know. We each have different issues, Mel calls them. Mel and Jarrod just get us, I guess."

"Jarrod again. He one of those guys you've had a relationship with?"

She laughed at that. "No. I've never slept with Jarrod. I did kiss him once, though."

—

"Seriously?"

"Yes. But while I enjoyed it—he's a really good kisser, Gabby's kissed him too, and we've talked about it, how good he is at it—Jarrod is just too grumpy sometimes. I didn't want to sleep with him. So I didn't. He probably wouldn't have objected. I think he enjoyed kissing me."

How many men had this little irritant slept with? The very idea pissed him off. "I see. You compared."

"Not like that. We didn't compare technique or anything. Just told each other when it happened. And said he was really good. Probably the best kisser yet."

"You know, guys don't want to hear about other guys' ability."

"Why would it bother you? You're not attracted, remember? Not in this lifetime. I'm not sure I believe in more than one lifetime, but it does kind of make sense."

"I'm beginning to think nothing about *you* makes much sense. Let's just keep walking."

Brynna pulled in a deep breath. "Ok. I can do this."

She took a single step. And then another. Chance started after her.

He almost stopped breathing when she slipped a small hand into his. The girl-woman *trusted* him, didn't she?

Well, hell.

All he could do was keep walking.

Chapter 9

THEY FINALLY SAW IT. A flash of gray in the woods. Chance pulled her behind him while they hiked closer. Someone had dragged an old FEMA trailer to the middle of the forest. Chance figured it was a makeshift seasonal hunting cabin. He didn't give a damn who had put it there, it was shelter.

But that didn't mean they were just going to walk up to the door and say, *Hey, pal, let us in.* If it was just him, sure. Why the hell not?

But with a beautiful woman, so damned vulnerable, there was no way he was risking her. He looked for a place to hide her while he checked the place out. There was a large tree with a small, hollowed-out trunk. "Stay right here. I'll be back for you once I take a look around."

"It said *No Trespassing.*"

"Extenuating circumstances. Stay here. Take this." He gave her his tactical knife.

She took it hesitantly. "What for?"

Seriously? "Protection, Brynna. Someone comes at you, you skin them with this. And scream really loud."

"Ok. Don't take too long. I…have to pee."

"Yes, ma'am."

The place was abandoned. It took him less than five minutes to figure that out. The lock was easily picked, and he took a look inside. Dusty, old. But it had blankets. And clothes. He took a quick look around the outside again.

There was a root cellar with canned vegetables—mostly outdated—and at least a hundred two-liter soda bottles filled with water.

Pay dirt. Food, water, and shelter. Three basic ingredients for continued survival.

Now for Brynna.

He found her huddled right where he'd left her. "It's old

and dirty. But we'll be warm. Get inside. I'm going in the root cellar to grab some food and water. Will you be ok?"

"Of course."

"Good. Get out of your wet clothes as soon as you get inside."

"What?" She looked at him like he was crazy as the wind sent the branches above them crackling.

He almost said screw the trailer and dragged her into the root cellar. Food, water, shelter, protection from the storm—who cared that the root cellar was only half the size of the trailer? At least, they wouldn't have to worry about being crushed by a falling tree.

But they needed blankets and a bed. Or two.

Lightning flashed and thunder cracked. She screamed and leaped at him.

"Fine. Then. Root cellar. We'll stay there until after the storms." He'd dump her in the cellar, then go to the trailer and grab some blankets and anything else they would need. Maybe he'd get lucky, and there would be a lamp or something.

"I don't like the dark. Or wet cellars."

"And I don't like tin cans on wheels crushed by falling trees. Just get inside and wait for me." He handed her the small tactical flashlight he always carried, and his cell phone. "Hit the button on the left. There should be enough light to hold you until I get back."

"Where are you going?" He'd be a real idiot if he missed the panic in her words at that, wouldn't he?

"To grab some blankets and anything else we might need. Get down the stairs and wait for me. Go."

—

BRYNNA went. She forced herself to think of it one way—safety from the storm. And Chance was right: the storm cellar would be much better than that old trailer. It was just…

Brynna had never liked being underground all that much. And cellars were dark and scary, and you didn't know what else was in there with you. What if there were snakes in there?

What was she supposed to do then?

She used his light and checked every corner. She didn't see anything bad. There were radios and weird-shaped lamps—but no snakes or anything else.

There weren't any blankets, though, and she was absolutely freezing. And her side wasn't just burning; it felt like razor claws had dug into her and were ripping, ripping, ripping her flesh.

Weakness hit her near the bottom of the crude wooden stairs. She sank onto the plank bench in the center of the shelter and pulled her knees up to her chest. And waited, his cell phone clutched like a lifeline in her hand. There was no signal, but it was light. Of a sort.

It seemed like forever before the shelter door opened and he hurried down the stairs. He carried a big, black trash bag. He dropped it at her feet. "I put the blankets in a trash bag so they'd stay dry. And I found this. It's a crank lamp. It'll give us enough light while we're down here."

She'd seen those types of lights before. He quickly cranked it up and, after a few long moments, had a blue-tinted light shining between them.

Brynna took a second to get a *real* look around. It was a sound little shelter, wasn't it? It wouldn't hold more than three or four people comfortably for too long, but there were canned goods along the back shelf, water, and if she wasn't mistaken, a radio.

But was there a power source? "Radio. Radio."

"I see it. I think it cranks like the light." He walked past her, his big body brushing hers in the small space. Brynna shivered.

He'd felt so warm—and she was freezing. "Can I get a blanket, please?"

"Take off your clothes."

"Huh? I can't get naked with you."

"We're both soaked. You're hurt. Take off your clothes, dry that hair with one of the towels I found. I found some boy's jeans and a sweatshirt in the trailer. They'll be too big, but they're clothes. I'll turn my back, if you're shy."

"You don't have to make fun of me."

"I'm not."

"You said you weren't attracted. I don't think you'll peek."

"Honey, in spite of what you seem to think *I am a man.* A

healthy one. I'm attracted. But I'm not asshole enough to act on it."

"Why?"

"Are you for real? Because women like you are the kind that expect hearts and flowers and forever. I will never be a forever kind of man. So while I might want to strip that shirt off of you myself and taste what's beneath it, that's something I will never do. Not unless we both agreed we knew the score. And I don't think you even fully know what game we'd be playing."

"I'm not a virgin, you know."

"I don't want to even think about that."

Chapter 10

NO. THAT WAS SOMETHING he wasn't going to let himself think about. Brynna in bed with a man, naked beneath him. Touching him. Being touched by him.

He wanted to find that man and rip his fucking balls out through his nose. Just to start. "Just get changed. I'll turn around."

"Ok."

He listened for a moment to the sound of her pulling the blanket out of the trash bag. Knew she was taking off her shirt. She gasped and keened, the sound filled with pain.

He turned around.

The white cotton shirt he'd used as a makeshift bandage hours ago was soaked completely through. Blood dripped from beneath the edge of it and down her flat stomach.

Holy hell, he hadn't realized she was bleeding that badly. And it had been going on for hours?

Fuck. "Sit!"

She sat. "I don't feel so great."

"No wonder. I'm surprised you have any blood left."

"There's about five and a half liters of blood in the average body. Adult, anyway. If I'd lost that much I'd already be dead—and we'd have noticed by now."

"Did you just make a joke?"

"I'm not humorless, you know."

"Just bloodless. Hold still, baby." He used his knife and cut the white cotton away. He moved the crank lamp closer. "It's still bleeding."

"It should be clotting by now. Unless the rain water kept the platelets washed away."

"You a doctor now?"

"No. Jillian's a registered nurse, though. Or she will be when she finishes her program."

"Who's Jillian?"

"She's my little sister. She's eleven months younger than me. She was an *oops!* that my parents weren't quite expecting. She's the nice one of us. Although she is the one who bit your hand that day you dumped pancake batter on my head. I help her study for her tests sometimes. She has reading difficulties—she's dyslexic. I read the books to her, and she answers the questions."

It sounded so normal when she said it. So normal and so young. This girl hadn't been out of college all that long, had she?

"How many of you Beck girls are there?"

"There used to be just four of us, until we found Carrie. I wish we'd had her forever. She gets me."

"And your other sisters don't?"

"Of course, they do, but sometimes they don't understand what it's like. But they love me, and I love them. Like you love Elliot, I'm sure."

His brother. Hell yes, he loved his brother. He might not show it that often, but he loved him. He'd die for him, in a heartbeat, if that's what was asked of him.

Easily.

"We're going to have to get the bleeding stopped."

"With what?"

"I don't know yet. This should have had stitches hours ago." There were two deep gashes he knew weren't from car glass. Chance pushed the rage away. No one should have ever touched this girl. Hurt her.

"He used his pocket knife."

And it was no doubt filthy. Stinking bastard was going to pay, as soon as Chance figured out who he was. "We'll need to clean it and find either some glue or some thread and a needle."

"Glue?"

"Superglue. It works well on shallower cuts. And we'll need to make sure there's no glass left."

"My shirt rode up when they pulled me out the window. I think I was dragged over what remained."

"I think you have bits and pieces still in your skin." Shallow, and painful, no doubt. And probably covered with all kinds of filth from the road.

They needed to get the wounds cleaned with some sort of antiseptic before something really nasty set in, didn't they?

He knew basic first aid, but not enough to reassure himself that she was going to be ok. "Stay here. I'm going to check the shelves to see what I can find."

She nodded and shivered. Something about the way she sat with such hopelessness stirred something in him.

"Brynna?"

She looked up at him. Chance couldn't help himself; he brushed a kiss against sopping wet red hair. "You'll be all right. This time tomorrow, you'll be at home with your family. I swear."

She looked at him and then shook her head. "Please don't make promises you might not be able to keep."

Chapter 11

HE FOUND WHAT HE NEEDED on the back of the bottom shelf. A small, discount-store-brand sewing kit. The needles were probably as weak as shit, and the thread was the cheap kind, but it would keep her from losing any more blood, wouldn't it? They needed an antiseptic or disinfectant or something.

He found nothing. Just canned food. Bottled water.

And baking soda. It wasn't the greatest antiseptic, but it could be used to flush some bacteria out, couldn't it?

Anything was better than nothing.

He wished whoever had packed this little haven had thought to include whiskey or anything containing alcohol. He looked around. Nothing. They had water and an old box of baking soda.

It would have to do.

He found small scissors no bigger than his thumb in the sewing kit. And his Swiss army knife had small pliers.

Chance opened one of the two liters of water and poured half the water into an old bucket in the corner. He cut the top off the bottle to use the bottom half as a bowl. He mixed a third of the container of baking soda in the water.

He always carried a lighter with him, and he made quick use of it, sterilizing the pliers, one of the blades in case he needed to make any incisions to bring out debris, the scissors, and one of the needles. He dipped each piece in the water to let it cool after using the lighter. He arranged each tool neatly on a hand towel he'd found in the trailer.

He just prayed the towels were as clean as they looked. He soaked another towel in the soda mixture and used it to wash the skin on her side.

She still wore a bra. A simple little piece of red satin, no doubt picked out to be less visible under her red shirt.

He forced himself not to wonder if she had on matching panties beneath the jeans. Now definitely wasn't the time to think like that, was it?

He picked up the two-liter and poured some of the water over the worst injury. Where that asshole's knife had sunk into her pretty skin. It wasn't too bad of an injury, though the top two inches of the wound looked deep. And still bled. "I'm going to have to put in stitches. Just a few. Can you handle it without passing out on me?"

"I'm not a wimp."

He thought of all she'd been through, how she'd yet to really crumble. Annoying and puzzling as hell, but he wouldn't call her a wimp.

Far from it. "I never thought you were. Dig your fingers into my legs if you need to. I'll do this as fast as I can. But it will hurt."

"I know. Just do it." She closed her eyes. Small hands clenched his knees.

Brynna had small hands, even for a woman. Why did he find that so damned alluring? "Ok, baby, here we go."

Chance worked quickly. It wasn't the first time he'd done emergency stitches; he'd sewn up a colleague or two during his time with the TSP and Texas Rangers—but it was the first time he'd sewn up a civilian woman.

She might work for the TSP, but Brynna was no cop. Not at all. She was just an innocent girl-woman who'd fallen into some seriously evil shit.

He finished with the needle and thread and tied it off. He trimmed the ends as close to the skin as possible. She would scar. That he had no doubt of. He'd put in ten small stitches. He'd cut up a third towel to use as bandages, and found more duct tape in the supplies.

"Now let's get the glass or whatever it is out of your skin."

She nodded, but didn't say a word.

She didn't say anything while he pulled out more than a dozen shards of glass. Didn't open her eyes.

But he knew it hurt her. But she never complained. Not even when he put in six more stitches across three lacerations. She just…dealt.

Wimp? There wasn't a damned thing wimpy about her.

When he was finished, he grabbed a final towel himself and

went to work on her hair. He wished he'd found her a brush.

Something so normal, so ordinary. Something that she could use to control at least one thing about this situation. But he hadn't. He'd found a high school sweatshirt and a pair of old jeans. Warm socks, too. No underclothes. She'd have to go without until her things dried.

He stroked the top of her red head. She looked up at him from pain-filled eyes, a dirty and faded blanket clutched to her chest.

Something in him cracked. Just right there, standing over her, something in him cracked. Some wall he hadn't even known he had.

He reached behind her and undid the clasp of her bra. "It's wet. You'll need to remove it and put on the sweatshirt until it dries. I'll go back out to take a look around while you pull off those jeans. Unless you need me to stay."

"I'm ok. I'm tired, though. Do you think we can sleep?"

"I plan on it. After I check for cell service."

"I already did. Nothing. I don't even think there's anything down here I could use to boost it."

"Probably not. Get changed. I'll come back in in five minutes. We'll make a bed there on the floor and get some sleep."

"I want my family."

"I know. And I want us to be safe. I'll get the radio cranked while I wait."

He gave her the five minutes, then returned. She was pulling the sweatshirt over her head and hanging her red bra and matching panties over the back shelf to dry.

He put what he'd found down on the bench. "I found these. We can use that metal table in the corner and make a type of radiant heater. We'll put the candle in the middle of them. It will put off enough heat to warm at least a part of this area."

"I remember seeing something like this before. Jarrod showed me."

Jarrod. Of course. "We can pop the top on one of those cans and see what kind of food we have down here." He turned on the radio and placed it on the shelf. "Cook it over this."

He placed a small, metal cooking rack over the top of the terra-cotta pot.

"That's really going to work?"

"It'll take time, but the candle will warm the pot. Enough to warm up the green beans. And…pork and beans. We found a feast."

"Uh-huh. I need to read the labels."

"Why?" Chance looked at her, wrapped up in a dirty old blanket, her hair starting to dry in red waves. She had such a pitiful expression on her little face.

"Food allergies. I'm allergic to lots of foods." She went on to list a dozen different things at least, until he felt a bit overwhelmed.

She took one can and read it quickly. She nodded and handed it back to him, giving it wordless approval. Chance took it, his fingers brushing hers.

He wanted to hold her. To feel her pressed against him, her arms around his neck. He wanted to kiss her, taste her. Promise her that everything would be all right. No matter what.

But that wasn't going to happen. "Have a little faith, woman. There's stuff you can eat right here. A feast."

"I really want to go home, Chance."

"I know. And you will." And then he'd go bastard hunting. "I'm proud of you, you know? You kicked his balls into his throat with that one."

"He said…he offered…it almost made me sick to think about it." She shivered. Chance got it—now that they were relatively safe, what they'd faced was starting to sink in. Next would come the nightmares, he had no doubt. How sheltered was she? She spoke of her family and Gabby and this Jarrod guy. But did they all circle around her, hovering and protecting? Shielding her from the real world and all the shit that went on in it?

He somehow suspected that they did.

And then this came along and shattered her sense of safety.

He placed the cans of beans over his makeshift stove and then settled onto the wooden bench next to her. His shoulder touched hers. "I have a good idea what he offered. And he was lying. They had no intention of letting you go, no matter what. You did well. You fought and you ran. You're safe."

"Because you're with me. If I was alone, I don't know what would have happened to me out there."

He didn't even want to think about it. "You'd have found safety, and you would be ok. I think you're stronger than you give yourself credit for."

"Am I? How? I know what people think when they see me, talk to me."

"Do you?"

"Yes. I've talked about it with Mel and Gabby before. I'm different from most people."

"So? Lots of people are different. Look at me."

"You don't look different. You look like Elliot."

"I suppose I do. But I don't follow the normal ways, Brynna. I stay to myself. I work when I have to. The rest of the time I do whatever the hell I please. I've been chasing killers for ten years. That's not *normal* in anyone's world."

"No. I suppose not. Is it wrong of me to say I'm glad you were with me? I think they were after me not you. And I'm scared. What if they come after me again? What if they hurt one of my sisters? We all look so much alike. Someone shot Mel in St. Louis because they thought she was Carrie. What if…"

He heard the rising panic. He held up a hand and put it on her lips. "Stop. Don't worry about that. The assholes know we're out here. They're not going to go after your sisters. And once we make it back to Finley Creek, we'll see they are protected."

"Sydney's only seventeen, Chance. Just a kid. I don't want her hurt. Any of them."

"Don't sit there and panic." He wrapped his hand around the back of her neck gently. "Don't. Panic doesn't accomplish anything."

"Mel says that."

He had a conflicting opinion of this Mel. He half suspected she railroaded her sister. But then again…she kept Brynna safe, didn't she?

"Sounds like she knows what she's talking about."

"She's not just my sister. She's my best friend, too. Just like Gabby. And Jillian."

"She's the younger sister?"

"Yes."

"You're really lucky, baby. Sounds like you have a great

family."

"I do. I know I do. But Elliot's pretty great, too. He really cares about Gabby. I was there when he saw her again. Did you know that?"

"No." His brother was bat shit over Gabby. That he knew for a fact.

"She was very nervous. But that's just Gabby. Her cheeks were bright red. I don't think he recognized her at first, though. Once he did, he just kept staring. People were watching them, but I don't think they cared." She sighed. "It was very romantic. Gabby is lucky."

"If you say so."

"You don't think so? Don't you like her?"

"How can anyone not like her? But a woman like her—a woman like you—demands too much from a man. Elliot's the kind of guy who can give her that, though. He's made for a family."

"That's so sweet. And what do you mean a woman like me? I don't think I would make too many demands on a man. I've never in the past."

"How many relationships have you been in? You're...not married, are you?"

She laughed. "No. I'm only twenty-four, Chance."

He knew. Still, how much longer would it be before some lucky bastard scooped her up and kept her? Kept her in his bed...

This Jarrod, perhaps, who wouldn't have minded sleeping with her, who she'd enjoyed kissing?

"No hurry."

"So...what kind of demands do women like me and Gabby make on men?"

"You're relentless, aren't you?"

"I've heard that before. But...I want to know what a woman like me *is*. From someone I'm not related to. And not sleeping with. Guys you sleep with say just about anything to get what they want."

Now *that* was eye-opening. She didn't sound bitter, but she wasn't a virgin, either.

Intriguing. Some guy somewhere had convinced her to have sex with him. That thought had Chance squirming on the narrow wooden bench.

If he thought about Brynna and sex in the same thought, he'd start thinking of Brynna and sex with *every* thought. That was one damned thing he doubted he'd ever be able to handle.

"That's not true. Not for every guy."

"Really? I guess you're right. Sebastian—my brother-in-law—he treats Carrie like she's a princess. I don't think *he'd* say anything to get her into bed. I'll have to ask her sometime."

"You'd ask your sister about her sex life?"

"Well...yes."

"You're one of a kind, aren't you?"

"I guess. So...what kind of a woman am I?"

"An absolutely maddening one."

"I don't understand you. Why won't you answer my question?"

"I'm not sure what the answer is. Some women...a guy comes up against that kind of woman, and all they think about is *her*. And he'll do just about anything to have her in his bed. And before the poor bastard knows it, he's picking out wedding bands and floral arrangements. *That's* the kind of woman Gabby is. And the kind *you* are."

"Really?"

"Don't sound so pleased about it. Unless you plan to capture a guy that way. You husband hunting?"

"No. I'm not ready to be married. I've not met the person I want to be in love with yet. I'm not sure when I'd have time, honestly. Maybe when I'm twenty-eight or twenty-nine. That's when Carrie married Sebastian."

He laughed. "You can't schedule love, Brynna. It doesn't work that way."

"How would you know? You've never been married, have you?"

"No." He'd come close once. About twelve years ago or so. But he *had* been too young back then. Arrogant. Nowhere near ready for a lifetime commitment. Since then he'd realized he probably never would be able to make the kind of commitment his father had. The cost was just far too great.

Chapter 12

"WHY NOT? I HAVE GOALS for my life. Why should I let something like a relationship and sex keep me from them?"

"What are your goals?"

"Finish my software program. Carrie and I are working on it. Gabby helps sometimes, too. Carrie's brother-in-law runs like this megacorporation. He's bought some of her programs in the past. He's already offered us access to his best programmers. I want to make the program and sell it for lots of money."

"Why?" Why would this girl, who still lived with her father, need tons of money? It didn't seem to fit her character at all.

"I want to buy my *own* house. There is one across the street from my dad's. I want it. But it's over two and a half million. I want it. I don't want to live with my dad forever. But I don't have that kind of money saved up."

"And working for the TSP, you probably never will."

"I know that. But the software is for law enforcement agencies to use. With the experience I'm getting at the TSP, I'll be better able to design the program. That will fetch a better price tag. I'm not stupid. I can't make my goal at the TSP."

His admiration of her grew. Maybe she wasn't quite as naive as he'd first thought. "Good for you."

"After that, I am going to work on some other programs I have in mind. There's this game app that I'm playing around with. Not as much money, but I think it'll be fun."

While she talked, she leaned against him. Chance toyed with the ends of her hair, unable to help himself. What would she do if he touched her in other places? Would she pull away? She'd said she didn't like to be touched, hadn't she? Yet she was close enough to touch him. Be touched by him.

The degree that he wanted that ensured he never would.

Brynna Beck was trouble. A rational man knew that the first

time she turned those golden-brown eyes on him.

"I don't want to trick a man into being my husband anyway. That's so dishonest."

"Yes, it is. And that's not what I meant. Women like that don't do it on purpose. They're just so…good and right…that certain men *want* to spend forever with them. Just to see them smile or hear them laugh. Touch their soft skin." Soft, pale, lightly freckled skin like that that covered *her*. Did she realize that?

She turned her head to look at him. "And the guys can't just say no?"

"No. Because before they realize it's happened, it's far too late. You think you could separate Elliot and Gabby now? No. My brother's a real goner."

"You act like that's a tragedy."

"No. But it's terrifying."

"Why? Why would a guy like Elliot be afraid of a woman like *Gabby*?"

Hell, why would a guy like Chance be terrified of the woman right next to him?

Oh shit. He had to do it, didn't he?

"Because of this, Brynna. Because of this."

He leaned down and pressed his lips against hers, exactly how he wanted to.

And she didn't push him away.

—

WOW. Brynna had never expected Chance Marshall to kiss her. Why did he do that?

Why did *why* matter? She opened her lips and kissed him back. It wasn't like she didn't know *how* to kiss someone.

She sure had never kissed anyone quite like this before, though. The blanket fell away, and Brynna slipped her hands free. She hooked one arm around his neck and wrapped the fingers of the other hand in his shirt.

He kissed like he knew what he was doing. Like Jarrod had. The other guys Brynna had kissed were kind of fumbling and a little drooly.

But Chance. Chance kissed her like he couldn't get enough of her.

His hands didn't wander. One was buried in her hair, like he was trying to hold her still.

The other was over her lap, gripping her hip.

She leaned closer. Chance was hard and lean, and it felt…different…pressed up against him.

Kind of tingly, actually.

Brynna decided right then that she'd like to do a whole lot more than kiss with Chance.

She hummed in her throat.

He jerked away, and she almost fell off the bench. "What? What did I do wrong?"

"Wrong? Absolutely nothing. But if you don't want me to strip that damned sweatshirt off of you and pull you to the floor and spend the rest of the day showing you just what you do to me, then we need to stop. Now."

"I don't understand." Would that be so bad?

"Fuck!"

"What?" She'd enjoyed kissing him. She wouldn't mind kissing him again. "What did I do wrong?"

"Damn it, Brynna. I said you did nothing wrong!"

The instant he yelled, she recoiled. "I'm sorry. I know I don't communicate well."

"Stop. Don't sit there and look at me like that."

"Like what?" Was he angry with her? He'd yelled. Why had he yelled?

"Damn it, baby, there are times it's probably just best to be quiet and not ask questions."

Chapter 13

WHY DID HE FEEL LIKE he'd stepped on a damned butterfly or broken a fairy or something equally ridiculous? She was looking at him like he'd betrayed her or something. Like he'd hurt her.

Which he most likely had, hadn't he? Had he scared her?

She hadn't flinched away too badly. But he'd upset her when he yelled. And why wouldn't he have? She'd done nothing to deserve it.

He doubted people ever yelled at her. "I'm sorry I yelled."

"Ok. I don't know why you did, though. We were kissing, and then you yelled. That doesn't make sense to me. Unless I did something wrong."

"You did nothing wrong. Except not pushing me away. What were you thinking? I'm not the kind of guy you can just kiss like that. I'll end up expecting something. Are you prepared to give it to me?"

"I don't know."

Fuck, she was going to get herself hurt by some asshole someday, wasn't she? "Listen, Bryn. You have to be more careful with guys like me."

Was he really warning Brynna away from him?

"Why?"

"What do you really know about me? Nothing. I could hurt you, baby. Don't you realize that?"

"Are you going to?"

"Well…no."

"Then isn't that what matters?"

"You kiss a guy, you're alone with a guy, and he's going to start thinking about sex. And there are some guys out there who would take advantage of that."

"Oh. You will? Even though you're not really attracted to me."

It wasn't a question. She honestly didn't get it, did she? She thought he wasn't attracted?

If he was in the market for a woman he could care about, this maddeningly complicated female would be the kind he was drawn to.

But he wasn't. And he never would be.

He wouldn't be doing her any favors, would he?

"Brynna, I'm *attracted*. I'm a man, and you're a beautiful, intriguing woman. I want to lay you down and do things to you that haven't even been invented yet. I can't help physiology. But just because my body is telling me one thing doesn't mean my head has to let it happen. I'm wrong for you. Even temporarily. And you're…you're not the kind of woman I can get involved with temporarily. So…eat dinner. There are some plastic forks on the shelf over there. I'm going to take the radio to the door and see if I can pick up a better signal. If the storm ends soon, I think we should hike out of here."

"Ok. I'm sorry, Chance. If I did anything wrong."

"You didn't. And you have nothing to be sorry for."

He left her.

The storm was worse, and he had no doubt from the looks of the sky that someone somewhere nearby was dealing with some serious Mother Nature hell. Hail of the icy kind mixed with torrents of rain. He could get a minimal signal if he held the radio up while standing on the top step leading into the shelter. He listened to the report and cursed.

They weren't going anywhere anytime soon. If it was just him he'd risk a hike out in a lull in the storm. But with Brynna—there was no way in hell he was dragging her out in severe thunderstorms. And he for damned sure wasn't leaving her alone for those bastards to find. He'd just have to find a way to keep them safe—while keeping his hands to himself.

Done something wrong? She'd practically scorched his soul with one simple little kiss. She probably had the power to sear herself into his brain if he let his guard down.

She was still curled up in her blanket, but she'd found some plastic plates somewhere. She ate her miserable little meal and watched him with wary eyes. He'd damaged the trust somehow, hadn't he?

He had never meant to do that.

Chapter 14

SHE LEFT HIM ALONE. BRYNNA couldn't figure him out. *He* was the one who had kissed her. So why was he so angry about it? And why did it matter to her, anyway?

She didn't have time to mess around with a guy like him, anyway. The two guys she'd been with before had been guys she'd known for a while. Dated for a while. And she'd shared *two* quick, hot kisses with Jarrod. So quick she'd barely counted them at all.

It wasn't like she'd just hopped into bed with them and got it on. She'd planned it and talked about it with them, and then they'd enjoyed each other.

The first time had been right after her mother had died when she was nineteen. She and Mikey had dated for another six months after that. It had only ended when he'd gotten into the college he'd wanted to attend since junior high. They still emailed each other about once a month. She'd loved him, but not like Carrie loved Sebastian.

The other guy she'd been with was a lot like Mikey, but he'd really just wanted a girl to sleep with. She'd figured that out after a month or so. She'd been twenty-one and more embarrassed than heartbroken.

Mel had superglued the locks on his Mustang. Her sister had always had her back.

Maybe Chance was right. Maybe kissing him, doing more with him, would be a big mistake, anyway?

After she ate, Brynna looked for the best spot and spread out the three other blankets he'd found in the trailer. She didn't know about him, but *she* needed to sleep. Her head was hurting from sleep deprivation and from the collision. Her side still burned, but not as bad.

He left his candles burning, and they put off a surprising amount of heat. It was cool in the shelter, and the heat helped.

She didn't say anything to him as she settled into the little nest she'd made.

He could do whatever he wanted. She was going to rest. She'd worry about what to do next later.

—

SHE snuggled up in the blankets on the floor like she'd slept there her entire life. The sight of her like that pissed him off. *She* shouldn't be there. She should be home with her father and those sisters of hers, and even that ass Foster, who probably didn't deserve her.

He could see her sitting next to Gabby, talking computers and nail polish or something. Something girly. Something safe and protected and sweet in every way that mattered.

Was this how his brother had felt, the first time he'd realized how vulnerable Gabby was?

Elliot was far gone over Brynna's best friend. Chance admitted to himself for the first time that he was starting to understand the appeal. Brynna twisted under the blankets, restless. He understood it.

Nightmares were a real bitch.

That *she,* that maddeningly irritating female, was plagued with them now pissed him off more than almost anything in his life ever had.

Chance found himself kneeling on the floor next to her before he even thought about it. Thought about what he was going to do.

She whimpered, but her eyes didn't open. That little cry was all it took to have him slipping his hands beneath her and pulling her closer. He lay down, cuddling her against his chest until she settled again.

He could smell the floral scent of the soap she'd probably used that morning. Her hair was soft and he ran his fingers through it absently. Her chest pressed against his side.

Brynna was skinny, but she had all the right curves. Damn, how he wanted to touch.

She hummed again and snuggled up against him. Was she cold?

He pulled the blankets up over her. He wanted her warm and dry and safe more than anything else in the world.

And as he dropped a light kiss over her forehead, he knew he'd fight for that, no matter what he had to do.

Chapter 15

BRYNNA HAD TO GET PAST the fact that when she woke up, Chance's fingers were wrapped around her breasts, playing with her nipples. He hadn't been awake. If he had, what would she have done?

She'd liked it. She wanted him to do it again.

But she knew he hadn't wanted that, so she'd carefully pulled away and then slipped to the opposite side of the cellar. There had to be something suitable for breakfast.

She'd hoped the storms would be finished this morning, but she could hear the wind, even at the back of the shelter. They weren't getting out of there today, either, were they?

Her watch was working just fine. They'd been there not quite one full day. How much longer could they stay there before those men found them?

Brynna had avoided thinking about them since Chance had found them this shelter, but she doubted he had. His gun was right there, near where he slept. She wasn't unfamiliar with weapons—her father and her sister had been police officers, after all. They'd both made certain she, Jillian, and Syd knew what they were doing if they ever had to touch one.

That didn't mean she had to like them. But the knowledge that Chance had one—maybe more, he was like a weird ninja warrior or something, according to Gabby, after all—made her feel a bit safer.

She had no doubt that he'd stand between her and anything those men tried to do. What she didn't understand was why? Was it because of Sara? Because of her connection to his past? Like Gabby had thought it was with Elliot, though Brynna and Mel both had opinions of that. Elliot sure stared at Gabby quite a bit for someone who was just helping out an old family connection.

Brynna thought he wanted Gabby romantically. Mel had

confirmed it, too.

But Chance didn't feel that way about Brynna. He'd made that very clear. Although…he wanted to do things with her that hadn't been invented yet. How did she feel about that?

If she let him, what would come of it?

He didn't want a future with a woman like her—that was more than clear, wasn't it? She didn't want a future with a man like him, either. What would a man like him be able to give to a woman anyway?

He was gone all the time—from what Gabby had told her. Nobody knew exactly what it was that he did. Or if it was even legal. He was cranky and bossy and looked a little ragged. Even before the accident.

He'd looked wild and dangerous, and there was no way he'd want the same things from life that she did. She wanted a house next to her family. She wanted a career that she enjoyed that brought her recognition in her field. She wanted the type of recognition Benny had. Everyone knew what he had accomplished in his field. She wasn't wrong to have those kinds of ambitions for herself.

And then when she was a little closer to thirty than she was now, she wanted to find a man to share that with her. A man with his own goals, who would appreciate exactly who she was, and who would want to be a part of her family. Who would want her to be a part of his.

And then, when they both decided the time was right, they'd have two kids to share that life.

Brynna knew exactly what she wanted.

Chance Marshall wasn't it.

No matter how much she wanted him to kiss her again, to touch her.

She wouldn't mind a blazing hot affair, but anything more than that was not something she could deal with right then.

—

SHE had heavy thoughts, didn't she? Chance spent most of the day watching his little companion. An hour after she finished eating a can of green beans for breakfast, she started prowling around the cellar, poking into every corner looking for *something* to do. She finally settled for taking apart an old radio and a clock and playing around with the gears and wires in both.

He didn't disturb her. He didn't know what she hoped to accomplish, but it was keeping her occupied while the storms raged around them, so he wasn't going to rock the boat.

She'd snuck behind the little curtain she'd cajoled him into hanging for her, and cleaned herself up using bottled water and baking soda. He'd waited just on the outside steps of the cellar to give her some privacy. Then he'd taken his turn, hovering over the small drain that had been cut into the concrete floor. He'd been in worse circumstances; he was grateful for the recycled soda bottle full of water for his shower.

He felt half human again when it was over, at least.

His little companion was still climbing the walls. Chance stared at her for a long while, wondering if he could get away with tying her to something. Just to keep her in one place, of course.

That thought led to at least half an hour's worth of fantasizing about how else he'd want to tie her down. Imagining what he'd do to her once he had her arranged just how he wanted her.

"Chance? You've been staring for a while. What are you thinking about?"

"Things I shouldn't be."

"What kind?"

"Oh, whether you're wearing that red bra and panties again. How I'd like to kiss you while you were wearing just the panties. How I want to take them off of you." He leaned forward until he could almost touch her. "I'm a man, Bryn. There are only so many things we think about when in a small, confined space with a woman who turns us on."

"What would happen if we had sex?"

For some reason, he hadn't expected the bold question. But maybe he should have. This was Brynna, after all. And she had no qualms asking anything, did she? No filters.

Just honest Brynna. "What do you mean?"

"What would be so bad about it? There are condoms over there, you know?"

Chance choked on the water he'd been sipping. "No. I didn't realize."

"By the bullets. I'm not sure why they are there. But they are made of rubber, not latex. But they are still condoms. So we'd be safe. So…what would be so bad about us having sex? You say you're attracted. I think I am, too. I liked your hands this morning."

"What?"

"Your hands were under my shirt on my breasts when I woke up. I liked it."

He *had* had a very detailed dream about her. He couldn't deny that. He may very well have been copping a feel in his sleep. Chance hadn't been that embarrassed in a *long* time. Especially with a woman. "I…uh…"

She sent him a level look, one filled with patronization. "You would not be the first man I've slept with, Chance Marshall. I know how guys are. If a woman doesn't want sex in the morning, she'd better be the first one out of the bed in the morning."

"I am not going to think of the other men you've been with."

"Two. There were only two. Mikey and I were together for almost a year until he went to school. He was a year ahead of me in school, but we were the same age. My parents delayed me in kindergarten so I could go with Jillian at the same time. I stayed here and went to FCU. That's where I met Alex. *He* was a jerk. We were only together two times. Then he did something stupid, and Mel glued the locks in his car. I was twenty-one then. How many women have you been with?"

"Uh…" He didn't want to have this conversation. He wanted to have her. "Bryn, we are not going to have sex."

"Why not? What else is there to do down here? I like you, respect you. And I know you'd treat me with respect, too. I can't see Elliot and Anne Marshall's son ever treating a woman badly."

"And once we are out of here? Then what?"

"What *what*? We go on with our lives. Our lives."

"No strings, then?" He'd had a few encounters like that, when he needed someone. But…this was *Brynna*. How could he ever liken *her* to something like that?

She was too…too…too *Brynna* to be taken casually. No matter what she said.

"Why not? It's been three years since I've had sex. It's not like I'm promiscuous or anything. Are you?"

"No. It's been about two years for me." They were sitting in a cellar, calmly discussing having a one-night stand. Him and the girl he'd known since she was born.

And damn it, he wanted her naked and beneath him more than he'd ever wanted anything in his damned life.

Chapter 16

BRYNNA WAITED FOR HIM to make his decision. She knew what she wanted. She wanted to have no-strings sex with a wildly dangerous, wildly sexy man like Chance Marshall. Was that so bad?

They respected each other, they had protection, and they could enjoy each other and walk away. Was that so wrong?

Her father and mother had taught her that sex was special and it should only be with people she cared about. Well, she *did* care about Chance. She did respect him.

And she didn't doubt that he had saved her life. That counted for something for her.

She was a full-grown woman and had the same needs as Mel or Gabby or any other woman out there. Shouldn't she also have the right to have those needs met by someone she did respect?

Still, why was she trying to convince herself? She knew what she wanted.

"Chance? Why couldn't we—shouldn't we—have sex, if we both agree it's just no strings? That we're free to go our separate ways when this is over?"

"You're serious. No ties?"

"No ties. I don't want ties. I have goals, remember? Are you attracted to me? Because I really want to know what those things you wanted to do to me are."

"Damn, I want to show you those things."

Brynna held a hand out to him. "Then show me."

—

ALL it took was that small, pale hand held out to him.

Chance melted in a heartbeat. Her words were almost without inflection, but her eyes...her eyes told him exactly what she wanted.

"No regrets?"

"I'm not in the habit of making decisions I'll regret." She let him pull her closer. Chance hadn't felt so awkward with a woman since his first time almost twenty years ago. But it *felt* like his first all over again.

"Bryn, baby..." He drew her closer and covered her mouth with his.

Chance waited until her lips softened beneath his before pressing for more. He didn't want to rush. That was one thing he knew for certain.

He wanted to take his time touching, learning, this woman.

Chance started on the baggy shirt first. It was the ugliest damned shirt he had ever seen, but on her, it was perfect. It emphasized how slender and feminine the flesh beneath it was. It tempted while it concealed.

He wanted it gone. So he made it gone, tossing it toward one of the corners of the cellar. The red bra was next.

The cuts on her skin, the stitches he'd put in her flesh himself, were in the early stages of healing. He'd have to be extra careful, wouldn't he?

"I'm not going to break. You can actually touch me." Her words were low, calm, but her hands were going straight for the shirt on his chest.

Chance laughed. "Patience, Bryn. We have all the time in the world."

—

BRYNNA gripped the shoulders of his shirt and pressed her lips to his. Something was different about this kiss from the way he'd kissed her before. She didn't have a clue what.

His fingers drifted carefully over her skin. He pulled back. Brynna dragged in a breath.

"Brynna, I think...this is your last chance. Tell me to stop unless you want this to end over there on those blankets."

Decision time.

"I don't want to stop."

And she didn't. He made her feel, in a way she hadn't about a man in a very long time. That had to mean something, didn't it?

Just because they had sex while there didn't mean they were going to be tied together forever.

She understood that.

And hadn't her parents always told her and her sisters to be with someone they cared about and respected? Who they trusted?

She didn't think Chance Marshall was the kind of man who'd hurt her.

Hadn't everything he'd done since they'd met proven that?

"I don't want to stop."

His hands tightened on her, though not hard enough to hurt the injuries on her side. "If I do anything, anything at all, that you don't like or that hurts you, you stop me right away."

"Ok." Her hands went to the buttons of his shirt. She'd seen him without his shirt that morning—he'd taken it off and rinsed it outside in the rain—and now she wanted to touch him.

He was definitely older than the guys she was used to, but he wasn't anywhere near as soft as her previous lovers had been.

Chance was all edges and muscles and strength. Her fingers trailed over his pecs. He shivered.

Brynna grinned. "You liked that."

She did it again.

—

SHE shot him a look filled with such wickedness, such female knowledge, that Chance just about lost it right there. Ripped her clothes off and gave them both what they wanted without the niceties a first time with a woman needed.

Without the niceties a woman like Brynna deserved.

Brynna. This was *Brynna*, and he was for damned sure not going to do anything that she wouldn't enjoy. And that meant leashing his caveman and slowing himself down. Besides, they had all night to explore each other. To learn.

"I can't make any promises of forever, baby. I won't."

"I know that. This isn't a lifetime commitment. It's sex, Chance. I'm not asking you to marry me or anything." She leaned forward and nipped at his neck.

He yelped, then laughed. When was the last time a woman had surprised him? He couldn't remember. "Like to bite, do you?"

Her eyes widened. "Um…"

"I'm going to taste you everywhere, Bryn. From here—" He brushed his fingers over her lips lightly. "To everywhere…"

"Um…I…think I'd like that very much."

She wasn't wearing a bra. Her breasts were smallish, but tipped with pretty little nipples. Chance brushed his fingers over the left. It tightened beneath his touch, and he laughed softly.

Whiskey eyes looked up at him.

"You're beautiful. I can't remember if I've ever seen anything more beautiful than you right now."

"You don't have say those kinds of things to me. I know I'm not beautiful. Gabby and Mel and Jillian—they're beautiful. I'm just ok. I know I'm not ugly."

"Not beautiful? Baby, that's the only stupid thing I have ever heard you say."

"It's true. I'm ordinary. They are not. Do we have to talk about this *now?*"

"No. I suppose not. Let me show you how *extra*ordinary you are. First, it's the eyes. That's what caught me first." He kissed her lightly, first over one eye and then the other. "The mouth has given me fits since the first moment you spoke to me. Not always good, that. But I can't argue that your mouth is very pretty. Not to mention the smile. That gap between your teeth is very distracting. Charming. Not to mention the small dimple in each cheek. Whenever you smile, I get the feeling that there's a private joke in there somewhere. One I can't wait to share."

Had he ever talked so much while making love with a woman? Chance didn't think so.

But then again, he'd never been with a woman like Brynna before, had he?

"Chance? I'm not sure what you're doing?"

"I'm enjoying you." He kissed her neck, lingered. She shivered. Her arms hooked behind his head, and she pulled him closer. Chance indulged her, kissing her long and hard. He snapped the useless button on the too-big jeans and slipped them down her hips.

Brynna wasn't wearing *any* underwear. Within seconds, she was naked on the blankets, and he was leaning over her. "Baby, no matter what anyone has ever said or whatever crazy idea you've gotten in the past, there is nothing just *ordinary* about you. You are so beautiful that a man loses what little brains he does have. And once he knows you're looking at *him* that way, there's only one thing he'll ever be able to say. And that is just how perfect you are."

He touched her, far more reverently than he ever had any other woman, and she touched him right back. Give and take, touch and kiss, it was hard for him to tell where she ended and he began.

She was far more passionate than he would have ever expected. She was far less tutored than she claimed with her whole experienced self. Chance had to smile about that.

She might not be completely innocent, but the way her eyes widened and she gasped for breath told their own story.

Chapter 17

SHE'D NEVER BEEN TOUCHED by a man in quite the same way before. It defied every logical thought she'd ever had about sex. Brynna had always likened sex to something that a body needed, and it was best to engage in it with men that she trusted and respected.

Chance was definitely that; but nothing could explain just *how* his hands made her feel. The way his kisses had her burning, had her stomach tightening and her breath catching. All she could think about was him—the way he tasted, the way he smelled, the way he felt.

The way he touched her. That mattered, somehow, didn't it? Brynna squirmed beneath him, wanting *more.* "Chance…please…I need…"

What words? What words could she possibly use to describe what she wanted from him?

"What?"

"More. I need more." She wrapped her legs around his waist, putting her body exactly in the position she needed, wanted. "Please."

"Protection."

"Ummm-hmmm. Hurry. Please hurry."

"Your wish is my command."

Brynna laughed. He handled the condom, and then he was there, and she felt him right where she wanted him. "Chance…I'm starting to think you might actually be attracted. Attracted."

He threw his head back and laughed. "Brynna Beck, I think there's a wicked woman inside you, just waiting to break through the surface."

Did she think so? She certainly felt wicked with him.

And then she was feeling far too much to even think.

—

WHEN they were finished, he was holding her, and her heart was finally slowing back to where it should be. Brynna looked up at him.

She had no idea what to say now.

He leaned his forehead against hers. "No regrets?"

Brynna closed her eyes and twined her arms around his neck. "None."

"Are you hungry? I promise no sweet potatoes. Or anything else you can't have."

It sounded so...normal, didn't it? Sex with her lover, and then food. Never mind that they were in an abandoned storm shelter while what had to be a tornado raged above them.

Brynna forced herself not to dream or plan. No ties, just sex with a man she respected. That was it.

That was all they'd promised each other. Brynna wouldn't break her word.

No matter how he made her heart feel.

This moment, this time together, it was just...just...just like the eye of a storm. It would be there for a time, and then everything around it would rise up and erase it. Make it like it never happened.

And that was the way she'd promised him this would be. "Yes. I'm hungry. I need my clothes."

Chapter 18

BRYNNA WOKE THE THIRD day knowing she'd made probably the biggest mistake of her adult life. *Never* had she felt about a man the way she felt about Chance.

That was completely stupid, wasn't it? Nothing could happen.

Nothing forever, anyway.

Not that she *wanted* forever. She didn't. Not yet. Not until she was closer to thirty. Thirty was a good age to be serious about a man, wasn't it? That would give her time to build the career she wanted. To buy the house she wanted.

To learn about the world more, to learn about *men* more. To know she was making absolutely the best decision for herself that she could.

Chance Marshall would *never* be the best decision for her.

He was too wild. Too harsh. Too broken by loss. She couldn't fall in love with him. Even if she believed falling in love over a few days was possible—which she didn't.

No matter that she'd seen people fall that way before. It had been coincidence or anomalies, that was all.

She did not love Chance Marshall. That was ridiculous.

Sex was one thing, wasn't it? But emotional attachment?

She would not let herself get emotionally attached to a man who could never make a future with her.

The sex had been a mistake, hadn't it?

What was she supposed to do when she made a mistake?

Not make the same mistake twice, that was what. Deal with the consequences of that mistake and *learn.* Learn not to *repeat* that mistake.

She'd always been considered a fast learner, hadn't she? Maybe not where social situations were concerned, but in other ways, she certainly had been. Not this time.

Brynna snorted. Next time she was lost in Oklahoma with a

hot guy, she would *not* have sex with him. No matter how much she wanted to.

That was a vow she'd probably be able to keep.

Chance checked the outside as soon as he was awake. "It's cleared. We can leave now."

"And do what?" A part of her didn't want to leave their little shelter. They had been safe there.

Out there, outside, uncertainty waited.

As did her family.

"I'm ready whenever you are." She'd already washed herself up in her little makeshift shower. She'd redressed in some of the clothing he'd found for her that first day. She was as ready as she would ever be, wasn't she?

Out there, whatever *this* was with Chance ended. Their interlude would come to its inevitable end.

She'd just have to deal with that, wouldn't she? They couldn't stay sheltered down there forever.

The storms were over. It was time to get back to reality.

Her family was waiting.

—

CHANCE knew something was on her mind, but he didn't push. Instead he led the way back to the highway. Brynna would talk when she was ready.

If she never was, well, he'd deal.

They'd made each other no promises.

So why did her silence bother him so much? "Bryn, you ok?"

"Of course. What are you going to do when we get to Finley Creek?"

"Check on Elliot. Gabby. Then find the sons-of-bitches who did this to us." His thoughts darkened as he looked at her. The clothes draped her thin body, her hair was a wreck, though she'd tried with the cheap plastic comb he'd found on the second day, and there were healing cuts on her cheek and down her arm.

Not to mention those on underneath the baggy shirt. She hadn't deserved what had happened to her, and he was going

to make those bastards pay.
　No matter what he had to do.
　But he had to find them first, didn't he?
　As soon as he had Brynna safe, he was going to do just that.

Chapter 19

HE'D SPENT TWO DAMNED days combing the countryside for that little bitch. No sign of her.

He wanted to believe she and Marshall were dead, but that wasn't likely. The guy was like a damned cat, nine fucking lives. No, Marshall was out there with the girl. Probably fucking her over and over again, enjoying himself, while *he* was getting rain drenched and tired.

He and Walker were damned near exhausted, but Golden Boy wouldn't let them stop looking. Said it was all their asses on the line if they didn't find that girl or Marshall.

Said it would be all over. All of the last fucking twenty-four *years* of work would be for nothing. Because of that girl.

They had her laptop, but only the computer guy was privilege to that information. And he'd told him the girl had found a lot. Found enough to get all of them fried.

Just another reason to find her.

Walker was cursing as he pulled into the only gas station for miles. "I need to piss. Grab a coffee or something. Some damned food."

"This is ridiculous. Guy and girl are probably off somewhere screwing. Not like they've run to the cops or anything. We'd have heard by now."

No, the only thing they'd heard was the reports of the girl's being missing. She'd become a damned media sensation, which just increased the pressure, didn't it?

Once he found her, he was going to enjoy punishing her for every damned minute he'd had to search the Oklahoma countryside for her.

Oh, he was going to make her pay.

"Call Golden Boy. Let him know we're still out here. Searching. See if he's heard anything." It rankled, taking orders from the man who'd replaced his friend all years ago.

But someone had to organize what needed done. And *he* wasn't as good at it as the younger guy who'd assumed control.

Golden Boy was a fucking manipulative cold son-of-a-bitch, but he got things done.

Kept their little racket going.

The guy hadn't even been twenty when they'd first started working together. But he'd grown even colder, harder, and more evil over the past two decades. And now he had power, and wanted so much more. He'd get it eventually, too.

Nothing much scared *him,* but that damned politician certainly did.

Why else was *he* doing what he was told, still?

No. He'd find her on Golden Boy's orders, but when he had her?

How she died was entirely up to him. And he was going to enjoy every minute of her suffering.

Walker made the call. Now all they had to do was wait.

The Damned Billionaire was about to join them. Sometimes he wished the Damned Billionaire and Golden Boy would just kill each other and end it all. They hated each other that much, though he wasn't certain the two had ever met in person. Funny how that was.

Then he and Walker could divide up what was left and go their separate ways.

That would work best for all of them, wouldn't it?

Too many top dogs around and there was bound to be a dogfight sooner or later, wasn't there?

Chapter 20

CHANCE DIDN'T SEE WHERE they had much choice. Once they reached the highway, they would have to go in the direction they had originally been headed.

Toward the small gas station, they'd almost made it to before. He'd checked his phone periodically; there wasn't any more signal now than there had been days ago when they'd first been out in the countryside.

But there would be a way to contact his brother at that gas station.

He estimated they'd walked close to three miles in the storm from where the intersection was before they'd found the cellar. The gas station had been visible from there.

It shouldn't take them that long to walk there.

But it would be on that highway. Anyone coming up the road would be able to see them. It wasn't a very busy highway, but there could be traffic.

Even traffic of the kind they didn't want.

Chance wasn't stupid; those assholes could still be out there. Waiting.

They had wanted Brynna enough to organize what they had done. What was there to say they wouldn't keep trying? They knew who she was, where she lived, where she worked—it was just a matter of time before they tried again, wasn't it?

If it was him, he'd stick close to where his target had last been seen, and he would wait. Take her out before she made it back to civilization.

Now would be a damned good time to try again, wouldn't it?

They kept walking.

A car passed. He almost waved it down, but one look at his companion changed his mind. He'd rather they walked to help.

Anyone could have been in that car.

"You let them go on by."

"Yes. I don't want to risk those men being in the car."

"Don't you think that's a bit illogical? Wouldn't they be gone by now?" She was frightened, wasn't she? Chance reached out before he thought about it. He wrapped her hand in his and pulled her closer.

He kissed her, then pulled back. In the bright light of the day, he could see the pale-gold flecks in her eyes and the tiny freckles on her nose. Carrot-topped and freckled and, oh, so pretty.

Those men would still be out there looking for her. Would stalk her and come for her when she was least expecting a threat. Would her father and sisters be able to keep her safe?

His father hadn't kept his family safe, had he?

There was no way in hell he was going to let her face those men alone. That meant he was going to stick to this girl-woman like glue, for as long as he had to.

They kept walking.

Eventually, they were close enough to see the intersection in the distance. Chance's pace picked up, and she followed. "We'll be there soon. We'll make a call from that gas station, and Elliot will hop on up here to get us. You'll be home in a few hours."

"A bubble bath. I want a bubble bath. Mel and I share a bathroom now. She has flower-smelling bubbles. I normally don't like them because the scent lingers. But today, I'm going to use as much as I can. I want to smell *nice* again."

"I'm going for a hamburger. And I'll probably never eat green beans again."

"Me, either. I want spaghetti with purple sauce."

"Purple?"

"It's tomato-free. You make it from carrots and beets and seasoning. It doesn't taste that much different from the real stuff. Or at least Mel and Jillian said it doesn't. Mel makes me a big batch of it at a time. Then we freeze it in zipper bags to use later."

"Mel makes it for you?"

"I'm not very good in the kitchen. Mel is. She loves to cook. Your mom taught *her* some, too. Your family was a big part of my childhood, Chance."

"I know. And I'm glad they had your mom and dad. They

were good friends."

"They were." She threw her arms around his waist and hugged him. She grinned up at him, the slight gap between her teeth charming him once again. She'd used the baking soda in the cellar to brush her teeth three times a day. Brynna had such a beautiful smile. "I've forgiven you for dumping that pancake batter over my head."

He laughed. "Good. Although where your sister bit me scarred. I've never forgotten that day."

"Sure, you did. You didn't remember me at all, did you?"

"I did. It was the hair." He touched it lightly. "So orange."

"I know. Of all of us Becks, I'm the only one with orange hair."

"It's beautiful, Bryn. You are. Don't ever forget that."

"We need to keep walking."

They were a quarter of a mile from the gas station, maybe one hundred feet before they were back at the intersection where it all began.

He'd heard the sounds of helicopters overhead, and he knew they were search teams. Hunting for victims of the storms. He'd seen it countless times. He could see them in the distance, but they were too far away to help them. Even if they could. He and Brynna were walking on their own, uninjured and unthreatened. The search-and-rescue teams had to look for injured and in distress first.

A large truck rolled up behind them.

Chance turned, his instincts rising.

Another truck pulled in directly in front of them.

"Bryn…" Chance's hand tightened on her. He held his gun in his other hand. "When I tell you to run, I want you to take off. Run straight through that field until you reach the town."

"Who are they?"

"Just get ready."

Two men climbed out. Chance recognized the heaviest of the three as the man he'd fought with before. "Go! Now!"

Brynna ran.

—

BRYNNA did exactly what Chance told her, but it didn't matter. There was a third man walking across the field. It was the tall man. She had no way to avoid him.

But she tried. She ran as fast as she could, but he had the advantage of longer legs and a stronger body.

He tackled her, taking her straight to the ground. She screamed and fought. "Let me go!"

"No. If I do, they will kill you without thought." He grunted over her and then dragged her to her feet. "I have been searching for you for days, Brynna."

It took her less than ten seconds to figure out who the man holding her was. It was the port-wine birthmark on his neck that did it. She'd seen videos of him before—at work with the TSP and on the television and internet.

The birthmark had always caught her attention. It was perfectly shaped like the state of California.

Less than eight inches separated her from that birthmark now. There was no way she was wrong.

He was the richest man in Texas, which was saying quite a lot.

Handley Barratt was like some superstar billionaire or something. Why would he be out in the woods looking for her?

"Let me go." Brynna pulled against his hold, but he wouldn't budge.

"Keep quiet and keep walking." He turned and looked at her.

He had a beautiful face. He didn't look like he'd be in his sixties, but she thought he was. He might have been a little younger, like maybe her father's age? Brynna wasn't any good at figuring that out.

He was one of the men who'd pulled her from the rental car. One of the men who'd come for her.

And now he had her; what was he planning? "Chance will find me. Find you."

"I'm sure he'll try. He's the relentless type."

"He made me a promise. To keep me safe. Chance always keeps his word. He's going to come for you. And probably kill you."

"You're that sure of him?"

"I am." She kicked out at him, making contact with his shin. He cursed, and his hand tightened on her arm. He dragged her closer until she hovered on her tiptoes. Handley Barratt was around six and a half feet tall, at least two inches taller than Chance. "He's coming for *me*."

He looked down at her for a moment. He shocked her when he lifted a hand and touched her lips gently. "Yes. I suppose he would. Listen, if you want that boyfriend of yours to stay alive, and want to *be* alive when he does find you, then you'll cooperate."

"How?" She had absolutely no intention of doing anything this man said. How could he think otherwise?

"Keep up. Quit stalling. I *told* them going after you three days ago was a stupid idea. Now the entire mob that is the media is on the trail of you and lover boy."

"Why?"

"How the hell should I know? But those two fools seem to think finding you and Marshall and getting rid of you is the smartest use of our time."

And Brynna suspected he didn't agree. So what was he saying? "Why?"

"Are you a broken record? Of course, you are. The autism. I'm sorry. I forgot about that for a moment."

He started walking again, dragging Brynna behind him. No matter how she fought and scratched, she couldn't get him to let her ago.

Until finally, he'd apparently had enough.

He wrapped his hands around her upper arms, lifted slightly, and started shaking her. "Listen, you damned little fool. If they find you, you are as good as dead. They don't think you're much of a threat, and that fool thinks to rape you before he kills you. Do you understand me? I am your only hope of surviving any of this."

"I-I-I don't understand. Aren't you going to kill me?"

"No. Not if I can help it. You're going to go that way, run. As far as those idiots know, you'll escape me out here in the woods. I'm giving you a three-minute head start."

She'd seen his face, though. What did that mean for them? "Aren't you afraid I'll turn you in?"

"I know you probably will. If they'll even believe you. I have ways of making people doubt anything you've ever said in your lifetime. I'll do just that. And hell, who knows? Maybe it's time all of this ended. Came to the conclusion it should have twenty-four years ago. Go. Now. And don't look back."

"I can't leave without Chance." Brynna was afraid to hope, afraid to believe he meant it.

"Marshall's time is over. He's been on borrowed time for ten years. Him and his brother both." He reached out and shoved her slightly. Brynna stepped back to keep from falling. "But you…you don't have to be. You weren't even born when this first started, little girl. Why should you have to lose in it? Go. Before I change my mind. Go, and forget that Marshall bastard. He'll only bring you trouble."

Brynna listened. She ran toward the sun. Where Chance said the road was.

Once she reached the road, she had two choices—head toward the town, or back where she'd started.

Back toward Chance.

She looked toward the town, where she knew she could probably find help, and made her decision.

She turned away.

—

SHE found him. She didn't know how it happened, but Brynna found him. He punched the heavily muscled guy in front of him hard, but the man didn't go down.

The man fighting Chance was the one who terrified Brynna the most. He'd been in her nightmares for the last two nights, and she suspected he'd be there for a lot longer to come.

His big, dark-headed friend held a gun trained on Chance, but he hadn't shot him yet. Afraid he'd hit his partner? Or was he just enjoying watching the bloodshed?

None of the men had noticed her yet. They weren't going to stop until he was dead, were they?

She was just thankful he wasn't dead yet. She scrambled closer, hoping the one wouldn't turn around. Wouldn't see her.

She'd have only one shot at helping Chance. She had to make it a good one.

Brynna looked around, searching for a branch big enough to do some damage but small enough that she could control it.

She found one. She crept up behind the man with the gun

and swung the branch as hard as she could.

He went down without a sound. Other than the sickening sound of the tree branch crashing in to his skull.

The other guy cursed and lunged away from Chance.

Toward her.

"Brynna, run!" Chance yelled it at her.

Brynna ran. Like she had before.

But the muscled man was there. He tackled her from behind and her head cracked against a rock. Dazed, she couldn't move.

It was just long enough for him to get his hands on her.

He had a knife. Where had the knife come from?

The guy who'd touched her before lifted it and jerked his arm down, straight at her heart.

Brynna rolled to the left.

The blade sank into the skin under her right arm, sliced through her skin and didn't stop until it hit the hip bone.

Brynna screamed and screamed.

Chance knocked the guy off of her and punched him. And punched him again.

Finally, the man jerked to his feet and ran off into the woods.

Then Chance was there, leaning over her. "Baby, no...Bryn. I told you to run. To get away. Why didn't you listen?"

"I couldn't leave you behind." She touched his cheek, trying to ignore the burn. The pain. She pressed a hand to her ribs and pulled it away.

Bloody. "Chance...I hurt. He cut me. The other side. And it went deep."

"I know. We're going to get it stopped. I have that damned duct tape in my pocket. We'll get the bleeding stopped, and we'll get you into town. Get you fixed."

"It was Handley Barratt."

"Who?"

"The guy in the field. His name is Handley Barratt. He's the billionaire. He took me away, and then he let me go." She gasped and coughed. Her chest hurt. Her lungs hurt. Everything on her hurt right then. "Chance...I...I didn't think you could fall in love with someone so fast."

"What are you talking about? Of course, you can."

"He said that guy was going to rape me. That they were

going to kill both of us. Except he didn't want to." Brynna turned her head. She could see the man who had had the gun's head.

His skull. There was blood everywhere around him. Had she done that? "Is he dead?"

"I don't fucking care. I'm more worried about you." He had his shirt off and was cutting it into strips like they did in the movies.

Brynna loved his chest. She'd never seen one more perfect. He wrapped the strips around her like he'd done once before. More tape covered the cloth. She hoped it would work better this time. "Chance…if I bleed to death, will you tell my sisters and Gabby that I loved them. Tell my dad he was the best dad in the world, and I've always known it. And Carrie…tell her I wished I knew her longer."

Chapter 21

BRYNNA DOZED OFF IN HIS arms. Her head hurt from where she'd hit it on that rock, and her side was lit on fire. It was easier to use sleep as an escape.

When she woke, Chance was talking to someone. A man's voice that Brynna didn't recognize answered.

"Get her in. There's a bed behind the passenger side. And in that cabinet right by the door is a first aid kit. I don't know how much good it will do you, but it's something. I'll get this rig fired back up. We'll get her there, son. I promise."

"Thank you." He sounded so worried, so afraid. Brynna tried to push her eyes open, but it was too much effort.

"You're the ones been on the TV and radio, aren't you?"

"I'm sorry? We've been without cell service or television for almost three days."

"That girl's been plastered over every place. She autistic?"

"Somewhat."

"Then that's her. Every time you turn on the radio, they're blasting something about some young autistic girl missing with an ex-Texas Ranger."

"That's me."

"Speculation is that you were murdered over some old case."

"We weren't. But we were attacked several times. They hurt *her* simply because they could."

"Get her fixed up, then go after your demons. Only way to do it. Saw one of her sisters on the news back at the Flyin' Truckerville Stop about one hundred miles back. Pretty redhead with a crutch. About a mile of curly red hair, that one."

"Brynna's is straight. Most of the time. When it's wet, it curls."

"She's a pretty one. Can see why you look about crazy over her. How's she doing?"

"I'm ok," Brynna said, though she didn't open her eyes. Chance leaned over her—she could feel his breath on her face.

"Baby, how do you feel?"

"Like someone stabbed me. Where are we?"

"We're in a semi-truck headed back home. We're taking you to the hospital. You remember what happened to you?"

"Yes. Take me to Jillian, Chance. She'll be able to deal with Daddy. Promise. Take me to my sister."

"I promise."

Chapter 22

FOR AS LONG AS HE LIVED, Chance would never forget the debt he owed to Meryl Wanamaker from Peabody Street, Lofton, Indiana. The trucker drove them straight to Finley Creek General at a decent rate of speed.

He'd been repairing his truck on the edge of the on ramp when Chance had hit the highway, Brynna in his arms.

The older man hadn't hesitated to offer help.

Chance would never forget the guy.

Wanamaker dropped him off at the emergency entrance, and Chance carried Brynna inside, yelling for help.

Doctors and nurses rushed toward him. They pulled her from his arms and laid her on a stretcher.

"Dear heavens," one of the nurse's said. "It's Jillian's sister!"

Brynna opened her eyes. "Chance?"

He grabbed her hand. "I'm here, baby."

"Ok. Hospital? I hate hospitals. Hate them. Stay with me."

"You know I will."

They wheeled her away. Chance did everything he could to stay with her as long as they would let him.

He didn't speak to anyone other than to demand answers until his brother was there.

Elliot was speaking to the other people in the room. Chance wasn't even certain *how* he'd gotten to the room to begin with.

Chance didn't give a damn about what they were saying; he just wanted to know how she was.

"All this is just great, but how is *Brynna*? Tell me…how is she? The blood…?" Chance looked at his hands. He could still see the red, couldn't he? He rubbed his palms against his pants. There was nothing there. It was all in his head, all in his heart.

The hospital admin looked at him with compassion on her face. She'd told him…told him she knew Brynna. Would make sure she was taken good care of. "Mr. Marshall, I told you. Next of kin. It's up to them to give out the information. Not me."

Chance looked around. There were other people there, people there for Brynna. Gabby was right there. His brother.

Kevin Beck and a host of redheaded women. He looked at them, one by one. They were all about the same height as Brynna. They all had varying shades of red hair.

And tear-filled light-brown eyes.

Eyes that looked at him, asking *why* he hadn't kept their sister safe.

Her father was at the center of his daughters. "I'm her father. How's my daughter? You can share with all of us here."

"She's still in surgery. There was some damage from the knife, but it was mostly superficial. The biggest concern was the bleeding. She did have to have a transfusion. And to combat infection, they've put her on strong antibiotics. She's responding well. Very well, actually. She'll be out for a few hours—most likely until morning. I've pulled some strings. I can't get just anyone back there to sit *with* her, but Jillian is cleared since she routinely works the surgery floor here. I thought it might be best for Brynna not to wake up in the hospital without a familiar face nearby."

The smallest woman nodded. Chance looked at her quickly, light-brown eyes, long, dark-red hair. Same gap between the front teeth as Brynna. Brynna's *family*. He turned away—he couldn't look at any of them again. "Of course. Thank you. Fin, I owe you one."

"No thanks necessary. I owe Bryn a few myself."

Chance couldn't take it; not all of them looking so much like *her*. He walked out.

—

"CHANCE?"

Chance turned. He hadn't realized his brother had followed him. "She's going to be ok. She's not going to die."

"That's what they say."

Chance looked up when rain fell on him. He stepped back

under the awning. "You'll need my shirt. Damn it. It's got DNA. You'll need it with someone like that sonofabitch. Can't let it get any more degraded than it has."

"What happened out there?"

Chance removed his shirt and tossed it to his brother.

"Chance. Tell me." Elliot grabbed him and hugged him. Chance tolerated it for a moment. "Don't scare me like that ever again."

"Get off of it, Elliot. I'm alive." He was. Perfectly fucking fine. It should be *him* in there. Not that girl-woman, who had plenty more redheaded sisters wet-eyed over her.

They'd looked so much like her, hadn't they? Every last one of them.

"Almost three days, Chance. While I thought my brother was dead. I get a hug, whether you like it or not."

Chance heard Elliot's pain in his voice. *He* was all his brother had, wasn't he? If their roles had been reversed, he'd be just as upset as Elliot. "Sorry. Sons-of-bitches didn't make it easy. We had to rabbit out of there fast. We holed up in an old camp storm shelter a few miles from the intersection. Just waited out the storm mostly. Barratt and his friends caught us again on the way out." Chance would find them and make them pay one by one for every drop of blood Brynna had lost. One by one.

"Barratt? Houghton—the billionaire's son?"

"No. The billionaire himself. She got away from him while I was otherwise occupied. You'll have to ask her—when she wakes up." She should have kept running. She never should have come back for him. Why had she?

"He the one who stabbed her?"

"No. Another big bastard. I don't know his name. But I'm going to find him. For her. She'll never feel safe as long as they're out there." Brynna deserved to be *safe*. He'd do whatever he had to for her to be *safe*. For as long as it took. "I made her a promise that I would keep her safe, Elliot. And I'm going to keep it."

"We'll get them. Do you know why they were on your tail? Were they? Or did you stumble into something? Possibly the grand jury issue? Were you followed?"

"They weren't after me, El. They went for *her* first thing. Her laptop. They wanted what she had. What she knew. And they wanted her." Had wanted *her* from the beginning. Why? What connection other than that damned video could Brynna have to whomever had killed his family?

"Which was?"

"She ran the video taken ten years ago through some video software program she's designed. And found something. Something new. This is about her. And it's about Gabby. And it's about us." He'd been hunting the men responsible for his family's deaths for ten years and had never gotten close, but now…now it had gotten a hell of a lot closer. To *him*. To Brynna and Gabby. The two women in the world that Elliot and Chance would do anything to protect—it had to mean something that Gabby and Brynna were still a part of this, didn't it? That *Brynna* had been their main target. Why?

Who had known what she'd found on that video? Known it quickly enough to orchestrate all of this?

Three men did not wait around the Oklahoma countryside for three days waiting for a woman if she didn't have something they desperately did not want found. Not men like Handley Barratt.

What was it?"

"She didn't know." Or she wouldn't tell him. Wouldn't violate TSP protocol enough to share. "She was coming back to have Gabby—and Russell—take a look."

"No. Not Russell. And this goes no further than you and I. No one outside of the inner circle. You, me, Gabby, the Becks, Erickson. That's it. We can tap Journey and Foster if needed. No one else."

Elliot was closing ranks. His brother, who had always pushed that the TSP was the way they'd find their answers. What had changed his mind *now*? "Why?"

"Because Brynna is isolated, practically sheltered as much as Gabby. *More* than Gabby in a lot of ways. *If* someone was after *that* girl—they were Texas State Police, Chance. It was the only way they learned of *her*. Most of her work has Russell's name on it. She never even testifies before the grand jury."

Chance grabbed Elliot's shirt front as what that meant hit him fully. Someone who *knew* Brynna, knew her and was in her contained world, had done this to her. Someone had betrayed her. Her. Brynna, who had probably never done anything to hurt anyone in her life. His anger threatened to boil over. "Then *you* find the rat on your ship, big brother. *Before* I do. Because I plan to kill him when I do. They *touched* her, El. And that one guy—he wasn't just going to kill her. He was going to *force* her first, *rape* her. She'll always have the memory of that threat. Of his hands on her body. He's going to pay for that. You get my drift? Him—I'm going to find and rip apart with my bare hands. One cell at a time. Just for her." No one had the right to make her feel that afraid. No one.

Chapter 23

HE SAW THE SISTERS ON the news first. That's when he realized where the damned bitch had ended up. Safe and secure and back with her family. With that damned Kevin Beck. Bet the guy had his daughter surrounded with two dozen cops, ready to fry any guy's ass who got too close.

One of Beck's daughters, the crippled one, was giving a speech about how grateful they were to the TSP for protecting her sister. Beck had four of his five daughters right there on the news next to him. Only one missing was the damned one *he* wanted.

He snorted. It hadn't been the TSP; it had been luck that got that little bitch away from him. That and her damned knee. He never would have thought she'd be one to fight back.

And *he* had more experience than most men on making a woman cower before him in fear. Some fought, which he enjoyed the hell out of.

There was nothing like holding a woman down while he sliced her to ribbons, knowing she'd fought as hard as she could and he was still strong enough to subdue her.

Would the little redheaded bitch fight him again when he had her? She'd escaped him *twice* now. He'd get her again. One way or another.

And he *would* have her again. It was just a matter of time.

After that, who knew? He may go after those sisters of hers. Starting with the little one right there. He watched her, dressed in her pale-blue scrubs, until the newscast ended. Yes, he'd enjoy having her under his knife sometime, too.

It was just a matter of time.

Chapter 24

SHE KNEW WHERE SHE was the moment she opened her eyes. How could she not? Hospitals had a nasty chemical smell all of their own.

Brynna shifted on the bed and cried out when a fiery rush of pain went through her side.

Someone moved closer. Brynna shifted her gaze slightly to the left. Blue eyes behind purple glasses looked at her like she was a bug under a microscope.

Gabby. Brynna fought the urge to cry when she looked up at her best friend—one of her only friends, actually. Seeing Gabby, wonderful, goofy, neurotic Gabby, made it clear once and for all that she was safe. That whatever had happened to them *out there* was over. "Bryn? It's ok, I'm here."

"Gabby, this really happened, didn't it?"

Brynna lost her battle with the tears. With everything she felt, and everything that had happened to her, with Chance. Chance.

Mel came in, and then they were all acting like blubbering morons.

Usually it was Gabby acting like the blubbering moron, but this time, this time it was her, and Brynna didn't know how to stop it.

Didn't know what she was supposed to do at all.

After a while, she leaned back against the pillows and tried to get some sort of rest. She hurt. No doubt about that. But it was more than that.

She'd thought she was ok with what had happened between her and Chance, but she shouldn't hurt like this. Shouldn't worry about him, shouldn't want him right there beside her.

Maybe it was because they'd been together for hours on end. Maybe it was the pain medication they'd obviously given her. It was only supposed to be no strings.

She had to remember that.

The hours in the hospital blurred together and turned into at least a day. Mel stayed with her most of the time; Jillian and their father had been in and out.

The next afternoon, she was feeling good enough to sit up partially. And to pester the woman sitting in the chair next to her bed. Mel was writing in a notebook—Mel had always liked writing—and practically ignoring Brynna's snipping and snapping.

She was just doing it to annoy her sister—and entertain herself. When Mel had been in the hospital for the first time, she'd snipped and snapped at anyone around. And they'd let her—to keep her focus off of what she was going through.

Mel knew exactly why Brynna was pestering her, didn't she?

A rush of love for the woman who had been there for her every day of her life hit her. A bit of strength she hadn't known she had stiffened her resolve to get through all of *this*. To forget that *she* had been the one to forget for a little while that what was between her and Chance was only sex. That it had ended the moment they had left that cellar behind.

She would get through this.

And almost as soon as she made that resolve, people walked through her door.

Gabby and Elliot…and Elliot's brother.

She forced herself to greet him just as blandly as she did Elliot. It wasn't easy. She hid her instinctive reach for him by grabbing the stuffed bear that had been sharing her bed.

She made it through the chitchat somehow, not really certain what she said or what anyone else did.

Until he stepped up right next to her and glared.

She had no clue what she'd done to him now.

—

CHANCE felt like a rank bastard when her pretty, laughing face fell. She looked away from him and wouldn't look back.

"So what are you three doing here?" Mel asked, bluntly.

"What's happening?"

He hadn't meant to hurt her. He leaned a little closer to Brynna—her hair smelled clean, fruity, and had been brushed and braided neatly.

"We need to know what Brynna found on that video that sent her heading back to Texas so quickly."

The women talked for a moment, but Chance didn't hear exactly what was said. Until Brynna shifted on the bed, and Gabby moved closer, almost blocking Chance against the back wall.

"I'm ok, Gabs. I promise. I promise. I am *ok.* So are you. So is Mel. We are all ok now." Brynna reached for Gabby.

"Then we can do this," Mel said. The three were connected. They loved each other. Belonged to each other.

It had been a decade since *he'd* felt that type of belonging.

Brynna shifted in the bed, then winced. He was close enough to see how she flinched. He wrapped his hands around her shoulders without thinking that maybe she wouldn't want him touching her and guided her down on the bed. "Damn it, Brynna, don't hurt yourself."

She looked up at him quickly, then looked away. Chance didn't want to let her go.

She explained what she had found on the video, and he listened quietly.

He didn't understand half of what she'd said, but the rest of the room did. He'd catch up later.

Brynna grabbed for her blanket to pull it around her shoulders. Chance did it for her, needing to touch her once more.

Damn it, he'd spent *days* touching her however and whenever he wanted to. Why did he expect it would be easy to just forget that?

For those days, those hours, this woman had been *his.*

He'd done a piss-poor job of keeping her safe, hadn't he?

She was wilting; how much longer would she be able to push herself? She needed to rest, not worry about killers. He shifted until he was behind her. She leaned back against him, almost instinctively.

Hell, the least he could do was hold her up for a little while, right?

He knew he was lying to himself from the get-go. He

just…wanted to hold her for a little bit. "Maybe it wasn't just what was found on her laptop," Chance said. "Maybe they were just not wanting someone looking at the files at all."

"But by harming her, that was bound to draw attention to what she was working on," his brother said. "And it was Gabby's laptop. How do we know they didn't somehow track the laptop to find you?"

"Is that even possible?" Mel asked. "I mean, that quickly?"

"I don't think it would have been necessary." Brynna shifted again, her pain obvious. Chance fought the urge to touch her hair, to pull her tighter against him. Holding her like this was one thing—he wouldn't let himself do anything more. "They probably traced my phone."

"But why did they focus on you? Instead of Gabby?" Elliot asked.

"Because I had Gabby's laptop and had signed out a zip drive that had the videos from that night on it. *My* name was right there in the evidence log. Anyone at the TSP could have seen it. Could have known I was in St. Louis, and could have found me with my phone. Gabby and I use cell phones to track suspects all the time."

Gabby nodded. "So you think it wasn't because it was my laptop."

"It was the zip drive. With copies of the exact originals turned in from your old laptop ten years ago. It was still in the original envelope, sealed, with the original date. I made a copy of it at the evidence desk using one of the TSP-issued drives. I signed for it, like we do everything, and told people where I was going. It was blocked off of the CF schedule three weeks ago. I even told Daniel McKellen that I was going to be up there. And when I expected to get there. I texted him when I got there, too," Brynna said. She looked up at him for quick moment.

"Why the hell for?" Chance asked. He'd met McKellen. The guy was about his own age and seemed decent. But why would the guy have cared where Brynna was?

Chance looked down at the woman in his arms, and he knew why McKellen was interested. How could the man not be?

McKellen wasn't the kind of guy a woman like Brynna needed, though. Did she realize that?

"Because he's a friend and he was worried." She finally looked up at him fully. "He wants to be a whole lot more."

Chance stared at her. "If he's not the son-of-a-bitch who hurt you."

Temper flashed in light-brown eyes, and she glared at him. "He isn't. He's just a nice man who wants to get to know *me* better. He gave me flowers the day I left, you know. Those pink balloons right there are from him, too. He knows I like pink."

Flowers, balloons. Damned bastard was trying to get her attention, wasn't he?

What pissed him off the most was that *he* didn't have a right to tell her what had sprung to his lips. That no other guy was ever going to get to know her more. That no other man would ever have that right.

Because they hadn't agreed to those kinds of strings, had they? He'd would just have to deal.

Chapter 25

BRYNNA HADN'T BEEN ALONE with her father five minutes before the intercom started buzzing and a calm voice came over the loudspeaker advising everyone to stay in their current locations unless absolutely necessary, that the hospital had entered a lockdown procedure, and that new information would be forthcoming.

Brynna looked at her dad. "What's going on?"

"I don't know. I'm going to call your sister. See if she and the rest got out of here ok."

His worry was hard to miss. Brynna thought he looked like he'd aged overnight or something.

She stayed quiet while he tried Mel's phone. His face tightened, then he tried again. And again. "She's not picking up."

"Go find her."

"I'm not leaving you here alone, baby. Mel's probably in an elevator or something."

Or something. So why did Brynna feel so tense all of a sudden? The intercom kept up with its monotonous edict, but Brynna tuned it out.

Her father paced for the next ten minutes, and she tried to tune that out as well. It wasn't as easy. Her father closed the door and stood by it, watching out the thin glass window, as the hospital staff congregated in the central nurse's station.

"Dad, is Jillian still on the clock?"

"For a few more hours." His tone was grim. "I'm going to step out into the hall. See if I can find out anything."

"Don't worry. I'll be right here when you get back." Helpless and stuck while the world went on around her. Where were her sisters, and why did she get the feeling *something* bad had just happened to one of them?

HER dad came back in, and this time he wasn't alone. Chance was behind him, and he looked like he'd rolled around in the parking lot or something. There were two nurses behind him.

"Chance? What's going on?" Was that a scrape on his cheek? "Where's my sister?"

He stepped up to the side of the bed. "Don't freak out, first. She's safe."

"Where is she, and where is Gabby?"

He wrapped his hand around her shoulder lightly, and he turned her to look at him, as the nurses started unhooking the monitors next to her bed. "Your sister is downstairs in the ER getting looked at. Just to make sure she's ok. Gabby is with Elliot; he's getting his shoulder sewn back up."

"Why? *What is going on with my sister and Gabby?*" She started to fight against his hold. She figured out why he was touching her real quick when he held her in place while the nurses pulled the tubes jammed into her hand out of the stints of her IV. "What is happening?"

"Look at me, babe." He leaned down until all she could see was the green of his eyes. "Someone took a few potshots at us as we were leaving the hospital. Elliot got nicked, but he's going to be just fine. Dr. McGareth is sewing him back together. I landed on Mel's ribs pretty hard when I knocked her out of the way. They are just keeping her as a precaution, to make sure there isn't any extra damage to be worried about. But she was talking and complaining, so I know she's all right, got me? As for you...they are moving you to a room without windows. And putting Mel in here with you."

Brynna reached up for him, then dropped her hands back to her lap. She *wasn't* going to touch him. Seek comfort from him. It wasn't his job to comfort her anymore. She pulled back against the pillows as one nurse did something to the wheels and scooted the bed closer to the door. Brynna looked at her father. "Daddy?"

"I'm heading down there now. Jillian's going to bring Mel up and get her settled herself."

"Don't forget me up here. I need to know Mel's ok. Need to. Need to. Need to."

"Don't flip, Bryn. She's going to be ok." Chance stepped back as two orderlies walked into the room. They pulled the bed the rest of the way to the door.

Brynna did the only thing she could. She closed her eyes and leaned back against the pillows.

She didn't open them again until she was pushed into the new room and the bed put into place.

She opened her eyes and took a look around.

The walls were yellow.

Chapter 26

JILLIAN'S BEST FRIEND LACY was a doctor at the hospital and had been working in the ER when Mel had been brought in. She was with Jillian and Mel when they wheeled Mel in an hour after Chance had come back to tell them what had happened.

After he and her father had insisted the hospital move her to an interior room.

The hospital moved Brynna quickly.

Brynna was still trembling at what had happened. At how lucky they had been that Mel and the rest hadn't been hurt.

Mel wasn't talking much when they got her into the bed. She was pale and hurting, though. Brynna couldn't miss that. She waited until they had her sister sit up in the bed, then slipped out of her own.

It took more energy than she'd like to cross the small room and slip into the chair next to Mel's bed.

"Well, this is a crappy way to end the evening, isn't it?"

"How badly do you hurt? What happened out there?"

"Someone took a few potshots. Gabby and Elliot were close enough to the doors, but Chance and I were a bit more exposed." Her sister was obviously struggling to speak. Like she had before. Sometimes Mel had trouble breathing, not so much from missing part of her lung, but from muscle weakness. She'd suffered a lot of damage when the bullet had entered her left side and torn through her lung. If she hadn't been knocked out of the way that night, she would have been dead. Everyone knew it. Brynna had never forgotten that. "Chance knocked me out of the way, but he wasn't exactly gentle about it. There wasn't time to be gentle."

"No. He's not exactly gentle, is he?" Brynna wrapped her hand around her sister's, as Jillian came back in the room and covered Mel with a blanket. Jillian glared at Brynna, then back at Brynna's empty bed. "In a minute, Jillian."

"ASAP."

"So how badly is Mel hurt?"

"She's just staying overnight as a precaution, Bryn. They want to do a few X-rays in the morning. And a few other tests. Just to make sure there wasn't too much damage to the area around her lungs."

"Lung and a half," Mel said.

"Lung and a half," Jillian amended. "What is going on, you two? How much longer do we have to be afraid?"

Mel reached for Jillian's hand. Then they were connected, the three of them. "We'll figure this out, Jillian. I promise. We'll get through this, like we have everything else. We're Becks, after all. Nothing is going to keep us down for too long. Nothing. Remember that."

Chapter 27

MEL GOT LUCKY. *SHE* got to go home around noon the next day. Brynna wasn't so fortunate. They were going to keep her one more day because she was showing signs of infection.

They switched her antibiotics out for some stronger, then told her the best thing she could do was rest.

It was all she could do not to snarl.

Jillian was going to drive Mel home. Then she was returning to work the evening shift. She'd talked to Gabby on the phone earlier, and her friend was scheduled for the ten o'clock shift at the TSP, along with Elliot.

Brynna's father was off somewhere talking to some of his cronies about who might be responsible for the Marshall murders. And Syd was at school.

She hadn't dared ask where *he* was.

Everyone was doing something productive but her.

Mel had snagged the spare laptop Gabby had brought her and taken it while Jillian was helping Brynna take a shower in the small bathroom.

Before Brynna realized the laptop was missing, her sisters were gone.

Damn them. She was so going to get even with Mel, as soon as she was out of this yellow-walled hell.

She grabbed the remote as another nurse came in and took her vitals.

"Some of your sisters are on the news again," the nurse said. Brynna thought her name was Annie something or other. She'd seen her with Jillian a time or two. "Channel 7. Jillian and your older sister, I think."

Brynna watched Mel frown at the reporters. Her sister was irritated, wasn't she? She hadn't mentioned anything about a press conference before she'd left. Had they been ambushed outside the hospital? Brynna thought she recognized the parking lot where her father would often drop Jillian off before her shifts.

"Is it true what happened to your sister and Chance Marshall has to do with the Marshall murders? There's some speculation that she stumbled onto some crucial new evidence in her work with the TSP."

Stumbled onto? Please. Brynna knew she was a better computer forensic tech than that. What she'd *found*, she'd done with *skill*. Stupid reporters.

Mel glared. Oh, Mel really was mad, wasn't she? "What we know at this time is that my sister and Chance Marshall were attacked by a trio of men in a stolen vehicle. As far as we know, the attackers were simply trying to cover their tracks and preserve their own hides. Any other questions about that should be directed to the Texas State Police."

"Does this case have anything to do with who shot you, Ms. Beck?" some stupid man in the front asked.

Of course, it didn't; Mel had been shot in St. Louis when a madman was targeting Ari's older sister Paige. Mel had been with Paige on their way to the hospital when Carrie was giving birth to baby Maddie. It had nothing to do with *now*.

"Of course not. The men responsible for shooting me are in prison, where they belong. Now, I'm sure you all understand, but standing here is rather painful for me, and we need to get back to our sister."

Her sister was hurting; couldn't they see that? Mel hurt anyway from the damage done by the bullet. And she'd been bruised when Chance had knocked her out of the way the night before. She needed to be resting, not in front of the media.

"Rumor has it Handley Barratt of Barratt-Handley Enterprises is directly involved in the attack and the Texas State Police is looking for him. Is this true?"

How did they know that? Brynna thought Elliot said they were keeping that quiet?

"If the TSP is looking for someone, shouldn't you be asking the TSP? I'm hardly out there looking for anyone. I'd probably fall over if I tried."

The crowd laughed. Brynna didn't. It always upset her when Mel joked about what had happened to her, about what she could or couldn't do now. Her father had told her it was

Mel's way of dealing with what happened. Brynna didn't understand it. But she'd never said anything to Mel about it. She didn't want to hurt her sister's feelings, if she did.

Another reporter stepped closer. "Ms. Beck, if the Barratt family is involved, is there anything your family wants to say to them?"

"Only that we have complete confidence in Elliot Marshall and the rest of the TSP. Whomever was involved in the attack on our sister will get what they deserve. It's just a matter of time. Thank you, ladies and gentlemen. But we really do need to get back inside."

Brynna hoped Mel was right. Hoped that they found those men soon. How much longer could they all go on like this? She wanted her *normal* back.

Hospitalizations and press conferences weren't her normal at all. How much longer could she *deal*?

Chapter 28

HOME. BRYNNA HAD NEVER been happier to see the house at the end of their street that had stood as her sanctuary for as long as she could remember. It was now painted a light gray, with shutters that were in need of an updated coat, but it was home.

Her gaze slid to the slightly larger house across the street that she was one day hoping to buy. If the computer software she'd designed for Lucas Tech sold for high enough, she would be able to do it. If the house didn't sell before she could get it.

It seemed weird to remember the goals she had in place. Weird to realize that other than what had happened to her out there, *nothing* about her future had truly changed.

She wanted that house. Wanted that signal to herself that she had finally gained control of her life in every way possible. It was a sign to her, one that told her she had finally grown up.

She certainly felt like she had. She felt like she had aged three decades over the last week or so.

Her father reached into the back of the SUV and helped her out. He was hovering, wasn't he?

A dark SUV pulled in behind them.

Brynna drew in a sharp breath. Her father looked down at her.

"I'm ok. I just…wasn't expecting him so soon. I figured he'd be busy with Elliot."

"Baby, did something happen between you out there? Something that you're confused about?"

Brynna looked at her dad—*he* would never see her as fully grown, would he? "I know what happened between us, Dad. And I'm ok with it, I promise. But as long as he's here, isn't it a reminder of what happened?"

"I can make him go."

She thought for a long moment as the man in question in

climbed out of the SUV. "No. He needs to do this. To finish this thing with his family's murders. If I can help him, I'm going to. If…if it was my family…I would be just like him. He's hurting, Dad. And I think he needs to see a *family* again. Or he's going to be hurting forever."

"You have always been one of the wisest girls I've ever known. I'm glad you're my daughter, Brynna."

"Well, I can't think of a better family to be a part of." It wasn't cheesy emotion that drove her to say it, but honest belief.

She had one hell of a family. A rush of grief for her mother had her turning back toward the rear of the house. Where the roses her mother had loved waited.

Home.

It was where she belonged.

"Daddy, I want to go inside. I want my own room. Can you…deal with Chance for a little while for me?"

"Consider it taken care of."

Chapter 29

CHANCE REMEMBERED THE Beck house from his childhood. He'd been there before, after all. It had changed color over the years—it used to be a light mint green with dark-green shutters. Flowers were everywhere. A *Welcome Home, Brynna* sign waited in the yard, written in a feminine hand. One of the younger sisters, probably.

The sun reflected off carrot-red hair and drew his attention to the porch.

Brynna.

He hurried to her.

Her father stopped him on the porch, just as the woman in question pushed the door open and stepped inside.

"Marshall? You and I need to talk for a moment."

Chance tensed. "About what?"

"About my daughter. I'm not a stupid man, nor am I blind—I know something probably happened between the two of you. I'm not sure how it couldn't have. But whatever it was, my daughter needs to heal. She needs peace. And she needs you not to upset her. If you can promise me that, then you are welcome to stay here and help me keep her safe. If not, well…Daniel McKellen is more than willing to help. He'd be here in a heartbeat—all Brynna has to do is ask."

McKellen again. The thought of the other man just pissed him off. Chance knew it and accepted it. And he knew the reason. "All I want is her safe and whole. I won't stop until I can guarantee the threat to her and her family is removed. You have my word on that."

Chance looked at the man who had been his father's close friend and felt himself opening up in a way he hadn't in a while. "There's something about your daughter that makes me *feel* again, Beck. And I'm not sure what I want to do about that. But I know I'd cut off my arm myself before I ever do anything to hurt her. So she's probably better off with *me* staying as far away as possible. But...she *has* to be safe. She has to. If that means my body between hers and whoever is out there, then so be it. You won't let me sleep in the house, then I'll damned well sleep on the front porch. Or the back. Or in the tree in the front yard. Whatever I have to do."

Kevin stared at him a moment, from the eyes his daughter had inherited. "I know. Come inside. We have a guest room just down the hall from Brynna's and Mel's. You're welcome to it as long as you need."

Chapter 30

THE THIRD DAY AFTER SHE'D been released from the hospital, Brynna was about to go nuts. She was able to move around quite a bit easier than she had been, and she was ready for normal to come back to her world.

It didn't help that she had a never-ending roster of babysitters watching every move that she made. From her father down to Jillian's friends Lacy and Ari, *someone* was always with her.

They were taking two-hour shifts sitting with her. She appreciated it—she truly did. But Brynna *liked* being alone.

The worst of the lot was currently sitting at her dining room table, watching her where she sat on the living room couch. The house was open concept, and unfortunately, Chance could see every move she made.

If he was watching. He seemed to alternate between ignoring her presence and staring at every move she made. *Micromanaging* every move she made. He was driving her crazy, and she was going nuts from boredom, too.

She finally got sick of the inactivity and grabbed her new laptop out of her bedroom. It was a present from Carrie and Sebastian and had been delivered by special courier the first afternoon she'd been home.

Brynna had almost cried when she'd opened it.

She sat it on the opposite end of the dining room table from *that man.* Brynna was going to make herself useful somehow. Even if it was only on finishing the coding she was still trying to figure out for Lucas Tech. Elliot dropped Gabby off early, and the two of them spread notebooks and laptops over the table until Chance looked up and glared at them from the files he had spread out in front of him.

Brynna smirked at him. Having him *there* but not having him in the way she wanted was making her feel a bit contrary.

She worked with Gabby for several hours until her stomach got the best of her.

Brynna went into the kitchen quietly and grabbed a bowl and the box of cereal. It wasn't the best lunch, but it would do. She wasn't the greatest of cooks, after all. Mel and Jillian usually handled meals; Brynna and Syd dealt with cleanup.

"What are you doing up? I can get that for you. Get your ass back in that chair. Better yet, the couch." He barely looked at her as he gave the order. "Now. You need a break."

It was *her home,* not his. "I've been sitting for three days. I'm not used to doing nothing. And look—the stitches are half healed." She yanked her nightgown up enough to expose the area beneath her blue sports bra. Brynna hadn't bothered with constrictive clothing since she'd gotten home from the hospital—today was the first she'd bothered with a bra and a pair of loose cotton sleep shorts. The nightgown was light cotton and covered with Mario and Princess Toadstool. "I am certainly capable of getting up out of the damned chair. I don't *need* someone to wait on me hand and foot."

Chance's gaze went straight to her stomach, then rose to the sports bra above. "Pull your damned shirt down."

"*Quit* telling me what to do! We are not lost in the wilderness anymore, in case you've missed it. This is *my* home, and I make my own choices!" She busied herself with pouring rice milk over the Cheerios. "Why are you even here?"

Mel and Gabby looked up from where they were sitting at the dining room table. Mel had her own notebook spread in front of her. Brynna suspected her sister was writing stories of some sort—from the glimpses she'd had of her sister's notebooks that made the most sense. Her sister had always been gifted with words. More than that, Mel *understood* people and emotions so much better than a lot of people.

Mel used to write horror stories in high school to entertain herself. She'd read them to Jillian and Brynna just to scare them.

Her sister hadn't written much in the past five years, as far as Brynna knew. Until she'd been shot, anyway. Now Mel was rarely without a notebook of some sort. Just like Brynna was rarely without a computer. She just didn't think Mel was ready to share her writing again; not yet.

"I'm here because some bastards are out there who think

nothing of shooting at me and Gabby and my brother and your sister. I'm here to keep you safe."

"I didn't ask you to be here." She sprinkled sugar liberally over the cereal. "Why don't you leave? Go play with Elliot."

"Bryn—" Mel said, and Brynna looked at her sister. Mel shook her head side to side. "Play nice."

"I am being nice. I don't want him here…*telling me what to do*. It was one thing when we were stuck together or running for our lives for him to be in charge. But this—what I do with the rest of my life is *my* business, not his."

Gabby stood. "Why don't we make brownies? Chocolate makes everything better. I'll even make them allergen-free, Bryn."

"Brownies would be wonderful," Mel said, her eyes still on Chance. "In the meantime…"

Brynna took a scoop of her cereal and ate it, leaning against the counter. "I need a break. I *need* to get outside. To get away from everything."

Chance stepped closer. "You aren't stepping a foot outside, damn it. If you do, I'll spank you myself."

"Whoa, boy," Brynna heard Gabby practically squeak. "This is so not going to end well."

Brynna looked into dark-green eyes and carefully placed her cereal bowl on the kitchen island. "*You,* Chance Marshall, have no right to tell me what to do *at* all. It is not your place. You are not my father, my brother, my boss, or anyone else to me. *I make my own choices.*"

She didn't know why she did it—she certainly had no intention of going outside. She was still dressed in pajamas— clean ones, yes, but pajamas, after all. And the knowledge that someone *had* shot at her sister and Gabby was still right there in the front of her mind.

But something inside her rebelled at the idea of Chance giving her orders when she hadn't given him that right; it angered her beyond anything she had ever felt before.

"Damn it, Bryn! I know that. Until you make stupid choices." He stalked her around the kitchen island.

"Don't call me stupid, you ass!" She grabbed the first thing she could reach and tossed it right at his head.

Cheerios went everywhere.

Mostly they clung to his head and shoulders. He blinked

and one oat "O" rolled down his cheek. Had it actually landed in his eyebrow?

Brynna's eyes widened, and she backed away until the counter was right at her back.

Gabby and Mel booked it out of the room as fast as Mel could book.

Chapter 31

CHANCE STARED AT THE crazy carrot-topped woman while he tried to grab control of his temper. He licked his lips—rice milk had a slight peculiar taste.

He was vaguely aware of the other two women leaving the room as he stalked around the kitchen island that had caught most of the raining Cheerios.

The main thought in his head was to catch that woman and spank that skinny little ass he loved so much until it was as red as her hair.

Only big, pale-brown eyes and a mouth that trembled stopped him. "Chance…I…"

"You are a menace to everyone who knows you." Chance knocked Cheerios off his shoulders and ran one hand over his sopping wet hair. She lifted one small hand and brushed at soggy oat cereal until a clump of it fell off his chest. "Do you get off on causing problems for the people in your life?"

"I'm not a menace, and I don't cause *problems* for the people in my life. *You* aren't really *in* my life that way, remember? We agreed—" He didn't miss the hurt that skittered across her face. "I *don't* cause problems for my family anymore!" She put both hands against his chest and pushed him back. "*You* are not in my life anymore. *It was just no-strings sex! You have no right to try to control me!*"

She pushed again as she yelled the last.

Chance wrapped his hands around her upper arms gently. She looked up at him—and that's when he realized. Whatever he'd said had hurt her. Deeply.

"Bryn…" He lifted her before he thought, placing her right on the kitchen island, smack dab in the center of the dripping milk. "Babe, I didn't mean…"

"What do you want from me, Chance? You confuse me. I thought we agreed we were *both* going to be ok with just the no-strings thing. But you're here, and I see you looking at me, and it makes me want...I'm not good at figuring out what people want from me. Especially men. It took me a few months to realize Daniel—Commander McKellen—wants more than just friendship. If *Gabby* hadn't pointed it out to me, I never would have figured it out."

"Stay away from McKellen. He's not the kind of man you need." McKellen was too hard, too rough for the likes of Brynna. She needed a good man, not a cop. Maybe a teacher or a doctor or someone who didn't see the darker side of life and drag that back home to her.

She needed a pretty house and a pretty family, complete with three or four pretty children and a floppy-eared dog trailing after her.

She needed anything but him.

Yet as he pulled her against him, crushing sloppy cereal between them, he knew the truth.

He needed *her*. More than he'd needed anyone ever before in his life.

More. He wanted her more than he'd ever wanted anyone. More than he ever would.

Chance lowered his head and pressed his lips against hers. His *Brynna.*

Chapter 32

SHE DIDN'T WANT TO WATCH the video of the Marshall murders again. But she, Gabby and Mel knew the answers to why the men had tried to kill her in Oklahoma in the first place were on that video.

And wasn't it better to do it when Elliot and Chance weren't around? When they wouldn't be upset by what she had found?

Not to mention she wanted other opinions, especially Gabby's and Mel's. Brynna curled up on her double bed, her laptop in front of her. Gabby was on her left, her sister on her right. She would never forget that night. It had shaped all of them. And if she and Mel and their father had been five minutes earlier getting to the Marshalls' that night, they'd probably be dead as well. "We weren't supposed to be there that night, either."

"No, but the three of *us* were going. For Sara," Mel said. Sara had called them, asking for them to come over for a sleepover after her older brothers had cancelled on her birthday plans. So they'd agreed to go. It had been that simple.

Thank God they hadn't made it there five minutes earlier.

Brynna had always felt a bit guilty for feeling that way.

"I was just waiting for my mom to get home from work to drive me," Gabby said.

"*We* were five minutes away. But Brynna threw a fit at the last minute. A ten- or fifteen-minute fit. She saved our lives that night. I've never forgotten that. How...random our very lives were in that moment."

"Why did you throw a fit?" Gabby asked.

Brynna thought back, remembered. Remembered the sudden horror and fear that had filled her as they'd turned off of Barrattville Road that night. There had been a gas station five miles from the Marshall homestead. Their father had pulled in there to try to calm Brynna down. They'd been parked when the sirens had come. When they'd learned...

"I don't know. I remember just sitting in the back seat and thinking that we couldn't go there. That we needed to be at home with Jillian and Syd and our mom. I wanted my mother so badly. By the time Dad had me calmed down, Mel was inside the gas station, and sirens came. After that, I just remember Jarrod carrying me inside our house."

"Dad followed the responders. We knew...when they turned off at the Marshalls' driveway that it was something bad. Dad handed us off to the first patrol officer he saw. It was Jarrod," Mel said. "He was twenty-two and grass green. It was his first week on the job. First time he'd ever seen a murder scene."

"When...when dad realized they were all dead, he yelled at Jarrod to get us out of there fast," Brynna said. It had been the first time they'd met Jarrod. That night had connected them all somehow. Her and Mel. Gabby. Jarrod.

"That night was when I decided to follow Dad into the TSP—as soon as I could."

"And she recommended *me* to Benny after I got my associate's and decided not to go on for my bachelor's. I already knew more than my professors at that point." And she'd been so lost. She'd known she wanted computers but hadn't wanted to make a bad choice. A random one. But if she hadn't made that choice she probably wouldn't be sitting there between *Gabby* and Mel, would she? No.

She wouldn't have her best friend. That thought mattered, didn't it?

"That night changed *all* of our lives, didn't it?" Gabby looked down at Brynna's laptop. "*We* were going to be there. Chance and Elliot were supposed to be there, too. The five of us could have died, as well."

"Sara and Anne would not have wanted us there. They would have wanted us safe." Brynna knew that for a fact. Anne Marshall would have wanted her and Gabby and Mel *safe*. No matter the cost. And she'd want them safe now. Would want Elliot and Chance safe always. Shouldn't the three of them do their part to make sure that happened? Brynna opened a search box and brought up the videos. "But they *would* want the answers so none of us get hurt again. None of us."

Gabby nodded, slowly. "They'd want *all* of us safe. We're

not safe now. Not like this. Not living with this constant fear, these shadows."

"Chance isn't safe. He's not going to ever stop. And I'm terrified they'll catch him and kill him." Her nightmare, wasn't it? She knew how determined he was. More so than ever now that Oklahoma had happened. Chance wasn't ever going to stop, was he? No. He'd follow those men until he had them—or until they killed him. She just knew it. "So how do *we* find the answers first?"

"By using our heads. Our skills. Even our hearts," Mel said. "Combine what we know has happened now with what happened then. We knew the vic—victims really well. We may have been children when we did, but we were never stupid. So load the damned video, Bryn, and let's do this. Together."

"I have two videos. The altered one and what I think is the original." She had everything she'd worked on in St. Louis thanks to Carrie. It was just a matter of finding the words to show everyone else what she had found.

"Then we watch them both." Gabby reached over and brushed the mouse. Clicked.

The video started to play.

—

BRYNNA paused the video.

Gabby hit the button again after they'd blown their noses and wiped their eyes. "Let's do this."

Brynna watched as the people they had all loved were killed. Sara first. Then Slade and his mother at around the same time. They killed Chance's father last. After he'd watched the others.

Brynna knew it was just to hurt the man who looked like Chance and Elliot. Just to hurt him. How could someone do that?

Someone looked right into the webcam. Brynna fought the urge to back away from the laptop.

It was him.

The *fifth* man.

He said something into the camera. Brynna had missed

that, hadn't she?

"Rewind that last part, Bryn," a weepy Mel said. "We need to know what he said."

Gabby was the one who figured out what the man said— *Fuck it all, Gabby.* The fifth man had called Gabby by name.

The man knew who Gabby was from the very beginning.

Brynna stared at the screen, as Mel lurched into the bathroom and vomited. Gabby wasn't saying a word. "I *knew* the fifth man said something. But I couldn't figure out what. I think I was more focused on *who* could erase a man from the file completely. I didn't realize…"

She should have realized. Should have told the others. Was it significant that he'd known who Gabby was? What did that mean?

"It wasn't completely," Mel said from the bathroom. "You could sometimes see the shadows."

"That's because the tech ten years ago wasn't as good as it is today. If we hadn't already known, we wouldn't be predisposed to look. I never could remember how many men because they weren't always visible at once. I think I blocked out that man at the end." Gabby straightened on the bed. Brynna finally looked at her friend. Gabby was pale and looked sick. She worried the other woman was going to be next to lose her lunch.

Mel sat down at the desk chair and looked at Brynna and Gabby. "You were traumatized. Hell, so were we—and we didn't see anything. Except for Slade being loaded into the ambulance. Brynna practically went catatonic, Gab. For the whole next week. It was her first exposure to death at all. Except for a hamster or cat. Mom and Dad kept her sheltered from anything like that."

"Mine, too." Gabby wrapped a blanket around her shoulders. "So. The fifth man knew *me* by sight ten years ago. What do we do now?"

Chapter 33

"SO THERE WAS A FIFTH man?" Chance had watched the video of his family's murder more times than he could count. *He* had never seen a fifth man.

He thought.

Brynna glared at him. She lifted her nose in the air. Chance fought a smile. How many times had she looked at him just like that in the cellar? His body tightened in remembrance—the last time she had, he'd stripped her naked and had her gasping for breath beneath him. "I wasn't wrong when I said so before. There was a fifth man and a very sophisticated bit of editing. You can see him occasionally, even in the altered video. *If* you know where to look."

He'd insulted her skills, hadn't he? Brynna, who prided herself on being one of the best. Damn, he wanted to kiss her again. Right there on those soft pink lips. He knew how she tasted; he wanted to taste her again. And again. "I'm not doubting you. I'm verifying."

"Uh-huh. Anyway, how does this help us?"

Us? Brynna wasn't getting anywhere near the bastards again. Not if he had to lock her in her damned room. "*You* not at all. I think your participation is over. I think you, Gabby, and the rest of your family need to get out of town for a while. I have a cousin with a large spread eighty miles from here—complete with armed cowhands, if needed. He's already agreed you could stay there. Let Elliot and I finish this."

Brynna stared at him like he'd grown two heads. "Not happening. I'm going back to work Monday when Gabby does. I want my *life* back. I have goals. I'm not going to hide."

"Screw your goals. I want you *safe*. As far from these bastards as I can get you." As safe as he could make her—because *she* was the one woman who meant the world to him.

He'd agreed to no strings. He'd agreed, but that didn't

mean he wouldn't keep her safe. Chance almost told her that, but he didn't.

Cheerios made an impression.

"I make my own choices, Chance. Not you." Stubborn brown eyes looked at him.

Chance looked at her, at the low-cut, pink T-shirt that clashed with the carrot hair she'd braided in two childish braids. A green sports bra, similar to the one she'd worn under her gown that morning, was just visible where the shirt had slipped off of one lightly freckled shoulder.

He had kissed every one of those freckles, hadn't he?

"Don't start, you two. We're not having another food fight in here tonight. It took Gabby twenty minutes to get all the wet Cheerios up this afternoon," Mel snarked at the two of them.

For the first time in a while, Chance felt actual embarrassment when the people in the kitchen looked at them.

Gabby giggled.

"Ok, apparently I've missed something," Elliot said.

"Never mind." Brynna stood. Chance watched her walk toward her older sister, her irritation clear in the twitch of her hips as she stalked away. He loved watching her walk when she was angry. Brynna might not *speak* expressively, but she threw her whole body into how she felt at times. "How much longer until the spaghetti?"

"A few more minutes. You going to make purple sauce?" Mel asked. She touched Brynna's shoulder. Chance didn't miss the connection between the two.

"I'll warm some up in the microwave for me."

Chance watched Brynna grab a stack of glass plates out of an upper cabinet. He didn't like how she favored her injured side when she stretched. The girl-woman was *hurting*. She looked at him. "I suppose *you're* staying, too?"

Chance nodded. He hadn't planned on it, originally. But they needed to discuss what had been on that video. And after what had happened between them that afternoon, he…needed to see her. He couldn't explain it; he just needed to. And he needed to find a time to talk to her about the stupid idea she had of going back to that damned TSP. "I want you to show me everything you found after we eat." It was as good as an excuse as any, wasn't it?

And he wanted to know what she had found.

"Of course." There was something in her eyes, something that told him whatever he'd said had hurt her. Again. Damn it, did he do anything but hurt her?

"Give me those." He took the plates from her. He needed something in his hands before he pulled her closer and just held her. Damn her, she made him want things, didn't she? "Sit your ass down."

"I'm not helpless. And you don't have to curse all the time." Did she stick her little nose in the air at him? Again? He clenched his fists on the plates before he did something stupid—like lifted her off her feet and plopping her right back on that kitchen island and kissed her senseless.

"You're stubborn, hardheaded, and contrary." Beautiful, sexy, everything a man could want…

Kevin coughed. Chance looked over at the older man.

"You forgot obstinate and determined," Brynna said, haughtily.

The door opened, and Brynna's younger sisters walked in. Mel tossed lettuce at one of them. "I think you know what to do. Syd, drinks."

"Crud, Mel, at least let us take off our jackets," Jillian said, juggling the lettuce expertly.

Chance welcomed the distraction. He needed to get away from Brynna before he kissed her right there in front of her entire family. Before he told her just exactly how he felt about her rushing back to work. She needed to stay home and rest. Stay home where *he* knew she was safe. Selfish of him, but that was how he felt.

But he also knew he didn't have a right to tell her what to do with her life.

Like she'd pointed out with a bowl full of Cheerios that afternoon—he'd agreed. No-strings sex didn't mean those kind of ties. He had to accept that, didn't he?

He set the damned table.

It was his first real dinner with the Becks. Elliot sat at his right, Gabby on his brother's side. He sat close enough to smell the fresh clean scent of Brynna's shampoo. Close enough to brush against her shoulder. Close enough to trick himself into thinking that this was where he belonged.

It shocked the hell out of him when the family said grace

before they ate. It shouldn't have. His own family had once had the same tradition.

The simple act, holding hands with the people next to him, overwhelmed him. Made him remember.

Made it hard to release the small, pale hand in his. Brynna pulled away first.

He felt the withdrawal clear down to the bottom of his soul.

The Becks were damned lucky to have each other, and he could tell they all knew it.

And they were more than willing to let him and Elliot in. All they had to do was be brave enough to accept it.

He'd never felt more like a coward in his life.

Chapter 34

THE TSP LOOMED RIGHT IN front of them as Brynna walked in to the building with her father beside her the next morning. Chance had pulled her aside after dinner and told her his opinion of her going back to work. The argument had ended with them in a draw. And ended with her staying up most of the night thinking. She couldn't let *him* keep messing with her thoughts this way. She couldn't

Brynna stared at the familiar gray-brick building with both longing—and apprehension. People were going to want to talk to her, greet her, and ask probing questions they had no real business asking, weren't they?

She tightened her hand around her bag. She had extra memory cards and zip drives. She was going to copy everything she could off the TSP servers.

She hadn't told anyone else what her plan was—just the woman waiting inside.

Gabby was going to cover for her while she did what it was she had to do. They'd worked out the details in a private moment the night before.

They were dealing with the past; it only made sense that the answers were hidden in the files somewhere. The *old* files. The ones she and Gabby had been tasked with scanning into the TSP database the first year Brynna had worked for the TSP.

That database was going to be copied completely by the time she left that afternoon. The details they needed were in that database.

Brynna was determined to find them. It was the only way any of them were going to get their *normals* back.

She was stopped in the computer forensics lobby by a friendly face, at least. But she had a sneaking suspicion that Daniel—Commander McKellen—had been waiting for her to walk in.

She'd always liked looking at him. He was eleven or twelve years older than she was, and that had been a little weird for her at first. She'd never had anyone that much older than her interested in her before. Mostly, her previous dates and relationships had grown slowly with guys she saw every day. She didn't see Daniel *every* day, though. And he'd been interested almost from the very beginning. But when they'd worked together the first few times, he hadn't made her feel like she was young and naive. And they'd discovered they liked talking to each other.

It had taken her months to figure out that he wanted to do more than talk with her.

Brynna knew herself well. She'd shied away, not because she didn't like him or wasn't attracted to him—she definitely could be—but because she hadn't wanted to be involved with someone *right now*. And she hadn't wanted the complication of having a romantic relationship with a superior. It was far too complicated for what she wanted from her life right now.

She hadn't wanted a relationship with a man at all. And she'd been happy with that decision. Chance had changed all that, hadn't he?

Now she didn't know *what* she wanted. From anyone, including herself.

"Brynna, it's good to see you here today. How are you feeling?"

"I'm fine, Daniel. The stitches came out a few days ago. I can't run a marathon, but I'm ok to be here." She looked into his dark-brown eyes, and it felt weird that they weren't green.

Brynna knew that wasn't the least bit fair to Daniel.

Gabby had stepped closer to the entrance to the annex to give her and Daniel a bit of privacy.

He was tall, just as tall as Chance, and just as fit. His hair was a few shades lighter than Chance's. His face was more handsome than Chance's.

Chance. She *had* to stop thinking about *that* man all the time, didn't she?

"Good. I'm hesitant to ask since it's your first day back, but would you like to go to lunch with me? To celebrate your return? Just the deli on the corner and if our schedules coincide?"

"Daniel...I..." Why not? Why shouldn't she? Chance meant the no-strings, despite this weird thought he had that he controlled what she did now. Maybe it had been her feelings on the *strings* that had changed rather than her feelings for the man? Maybe she was almost ready for strings with someone, after all? "You know, I think I'd like that."

"Great. I have a meeting with Chief Marshall at one, but we should be finished by two. I'll text you when I can." He smiled down at her, a truly handsome smile that had her own lips lifting in return. "I can hardly wait until lunch. It's really good to see you around here again. The TSP just isn't the same without you."

Brynna felt a warmth in her stomach as she watched him walk away. Chance might not want strings with her, but...other men would, did. If she was ready for strings, she could find them.

Gabby held the glass door to the annex open for her, where she'd come to meet Brynna and her father. "He *really* has it bad for you. He was almost as upset when you were missing as Jarrod."

"I like Daniel. I almost wish..." This was Gabby, the one person other than her sisters with whom she could speak the truth. "I almost wish I had said yes when he asked me out months ago. Maybe...maybe I wouldn't have been in St. Louis then. Maybe...what happened to me and Chance wouldn't have. Maybe I wouldn't *feel* like this."

Gabby looked at her for a moment. "I'm sorry. I know you're hurting, and not from your stitches. I think he cares for you, no matter what you've decided between you."

"But that's not ever going to be *enough,* is it? He cares for me, but he won't do anything about it." Even after the kiss on her kitchen counter, Chance had said *nothing.* Nothing real.

He'd just cursed at her, kissed her, then bolted out the back door and stayed gone for hours.

When he'd returned for dinner, it had just been more of the same. More discussion of the *who* behind everything that had happened. That was practically all that their worlds had been centered on for *days.*

Brynna was starting to drown from the sensory input of it all.

"No. I can't see where it would be." Gabby had a strange

expression in her own eyes. One that made Brynna suspect her friend was just as conflicted by Chance's brother as Brynna was with Chance. "They don't make anything easy, do they?"

"Not at all."

"This isn't helping us. We need to get inside and get going. I want to go over that video again and again. I want the answers, Gab. And I want this *finished* so that I can get on with my life. And then...when lunch comes around, you will go upstairs with Elliot, and *I* will go with Commander McKellen, and he'll buy me a nice lunch and flirt with me. And maybe...maybe he'll ask me out to dinner or to a movie again, like he has before. And this time, this time, *I will say yes.*"

Gabby stared at her for a moment as they walked past Benny's closed office door. "Just don't do anything too crazy because you're conflicted over Chance Marshall. That won't be fair to you—or Commander McKellen."

"No. It wouldn't be. I won't hurt Daniel. But...maybe I shouldn't be afraid of romance any more. Maybe...maybe *I* should at least try."

"Maybe. Hey, Bryn, we'll figure this out, you know? Both of us. We'll do it together. And *then* maybe we can somehow get Jarrod to act on his crush on Mel. We'll do *normal* again. I promise."

Brynna surprised both of them when she threw her arms around her best friend and hugged her.

Chapter 35

BRYNNA YANKED THE FINAL memory card from the computer and shoved it into her pocket with the other six. She had everything, didn't she? She resisted looking toward Benny's office as guilt hit her. What she was doing was so far outside of protocol Elliot would probably fire her as soon as he found out what she was doing. Of course, that would mean he had to fire Gabby, too, didn't it? She turned around to look at Gabby. "What? Sorry. Guess I'm nervous. Aren't I?"

"I think we both are. What if it wasn't Handley Barratt who had the video altered? Isn't he super tall? None of the men on the video were that tall, were they?" Gabby asked.

"No. He was at least six five, Gab. Taller than Chance." They'd used what they knew of the Marshall family to estimate the height of the killers on the video. None had been as tall as Handley Barratt.

"So if *he* wasn't one of the men on the video, why would *he* erase the fifth man?" Gabby asked.

Brynna's mind ran over all the people *she* knew capable of that technology. People who had even a brushing acquaintance with the TSP. It was an extremely short list. "Someone else did it."

"Someone who could access the file *from* the TSP. Someone who could do that ten years ago—and someone who could know that *you* signed the zip drive out now. Who knows Elliot is back and with *me*. Someone with the skills to alter a video like that," Gabby said slowly.

Brynna's mind centered. Only *their* department. Only theirs. And that person had known what *she* was doing in St. Louis, hadn't they? Hadn't *he?*

Brynna and Gabby jumped up, almost together. "We need to get to Elliot *now*. Let him know."

Gabby turned toward Benny's office. "Bryn—there's only

one who would have known *me* ten years ago like that. Just one, who has known *everything* you and I have done since Elliot came back. We need to get upstairs now."

Benny came out.

That's when Brynna *knew*. "Benny, what are you doing?"

"I'm sorry, girls. I am so sorry."

Benny held his cell phone in his hand. He pushed a button.

Brynna screamed as the world around them exploded, as she was lifted off her feet and thrown.

Chapter 36

WHEN BRYNNA OPENED HER eyes, Benny had his hands wrapped around Gabby's throat. Benny. It had been Benny all along. Why hadn't they seen?

There was a gun nearby. Why was there a gun? Was it loaded? Brynna screamed, Benny looked right at her. They needed that gun, needed it, needed it. "Get the gun, Gabby! Get it!"

Gabby needed time to get it, didn't she? And that meant… "You'd better run, Benny. They're coming for you!"

She struggled to her feet.

Benny grabbed her, and her shirt ripped. He knocked her to the floor, and she cried out.

Benny loomed over her. Brynna kicked at him. Then she saw it—the gun. She kicked, sending it to her best friend. "Gabby!"

Gabby screamed. Brynna screamed.

"You're a bastard, Benny!" Gabby yelled, heaving wood at him.

Benny kept coming, right at Brynna. Benny wasn't going to stop until they were all dead.

Brynna screamed again.

Benny backhanded her, and Brynna fell. Fire ripped through her. She couldn't breathe. She looked down and saw the blood.

Saw the metal rebar sticking out of her side. Felt the fire again and again and again. Darkness almost took her.

All she could do was lie there and fight…to breathe. Gabby was yelling. Gabby.

Brynna had to get up, didn't she?

She tried, but her body wouldn't cooperate. Mel's face flashed into her mind, warring with the darkness that was threatening to smother her.

Mel hadn't given up.

Brynna wasn't going to either.

She pulled her legs up beneath her and tried to move…just as Gabby pulled the trigger.

Then all Brynna saw was the blood.

Chapter 37

CHANCE WAS RUNNING, AND he knew it. Elliot had known it, too, when he'd called him before he'd taken off.

"You're not going to be able to run from her forever, Chance. It's not fair to either of you."

"We agreed, El. No strings. Just casual. And she told me...told me that's what she still wanted. That I *confused* her too much. What am I supposed to do, to think?" To feel as he'd held her hand while her father said grace, *grace* of all things. It had *felt* like he was right where he was supposed to be. But that was a damned lie.

What was he supposed to feel?

He did not want strings. Of that he was absolutely certain. Why was he struggling with that?

"Kevin brought her to work a few minutes ago."

"Keep an eye on her."

"I will. No matter what happens between you two, Brynna will probably be a part of my life, Chance. As will the rest of the Becks. She and Gabby are very close. You know that."

"I know." Of course, he did. "I...I'm just going to hunt down that bastard Barratt. Keep him from hurting her again. After that..."

"Then what? What will happen if we catch the guys responsible for Mom and Dad and the kids? Then what? What if it's next week? Next year? Ten years from now? Do you expect Brynna to wait?"

"No. She shouldn't wait on me."

"So you don't love her. It was just casual. Then you probably are doing her favor, but even I can see the mixed signals you've been giving the girl, Chance. You're not doing either of you any favors. But, little brother, are you really willing to pass up this woman because of this quest? I know I'm not willing to pass up Gabby. Something to keep in mind."

Chance had disconnected a minute after that.

His brother spoke the truth.

Chance sighed, then looked at the Wichita Falls skyline just visible in the distance.

He was a damned coward, and he knew it.

Chance turned on the radio to drown out the sound of his own head telling him he was a fucking idiot.

He should be there with Brynna. He'd finish his business with the old colleague of his father at the TSP Academy in Wichita Falls, then he'd get his ass back to the Finley Creek TSP.

He'd stay by her. No matter what she said.

The radio went into emergency mode. Chance listened with only half of his attention.

"We have just received word that the Finley Creek post of the Texas State Police has just been the location of some sort of detonation or explosion. Sources are claiming there are survivors trapped inside. At this point, we do not know if it is an act of terrorism. We will bring you more as we learn it."

Chance turned his SUV around and shoved the pedal to the floor.

He wasn't wasting time messing with his cell phone. Brynna needed him.

She needed him.

Elliot needed him. Gabby needed him.

Dear God, were they even alive?

Chapter 38

GABBY WAS THERE. "Brynna..."

"I'm bleeding. I'm hurting. But I'm alive, Gab. We're alive. And he's...he's dead, isn't he?" Brynna fought the panic, but it was hard. She had to deal, she had to, she had to, she had to!

"Where's the blood? Where are you hurt?" Gabby's hands were gentle when she turned Brynna from being able to see Benny. What was left of him. It didn't matter; if she lived, she would never forget what he looked like. Red. It was red. Everywhere was *red!*

Brynna's hands were already there. She was going to bleed to death before help came, wasn't she? "Here. I...think...it's deep. And it's really bleeding. Bleeding. Metal went through my side. I'm bleeding really badly, Gabby. And I'm scared. Scared. Scared. Scared. I want to get out of here."

"*Stop*, Bryn. You *can't* panic right now. You can't. I can hear help. I can hear Elliot. He's coming for us. He's coming. You can't twig out, Bryn. I...need you to stay right here with me until Elliot gets here. With me, ok." Gabby was trying to stop the bleeding, but they both knew it wasn't going to happen.

She was going to bleed to death, right there with Gabby by her side, wasn't she? After what had happened to Gabby...

No! She couldn't do this to her friend. To her family. She couldn't. "I love you, Gabby. Have I ever said that? When I thought he was killing you...it was just as scary as when Mel almost died."

"I know. I felt the same. You're my best friend, Bryn. And I love you. We need to get out of here so we can tell Mel that, too. Mel is probably on her way here to get us out of this, but I think—I think we should save ourselves this time. Just to prove we can, you know?"

"Why did he do it? He was our friend for years, wasn't he?" She wouldn't think of Mel or Jillian or Syd or Carrie. Or baby

Maddie or anyone else. She *had* to focus on helping Gabby get them both out of this.

"I don't think he was ever anyone here's friend. I think he was just out for what he could get. And you and I—we had skills he wanted. And he used us. Watched us."

"But not anymore." Because Benny was dead.

"No. Not anymore. *We* stopped him. Together."

Brynna couldn't *think* any more. She needed…she needed to rest. Just for a moment.

Chapter 39

WHEN SHE OPENED HER eyes again, Gabby was ripping the sleeve off her own shirt. "I'm going to tie this around you as tightly as I can. Can you crawl, Bryn?"

"I don't know." Even the thought of it made her want to puke.

"We'll need to get you out of here, most likely on a stretcher. I don't think we can wait for them to make a larger opening."

Brynna closed her eyes again, as Gabby moved around her. She couldn't focus. She couldn't.

"I'm going to get us out of here, Bryn. I promise. See this board there? I'm going to get you on it. Do you think you can help me?"

Help her? She wanted to. She really did. But...she felt so sick. The fire from her side had spread to her back and shoulders and...everywhere.

Gabby was there again. "We'll slide you right out. Think how proud Mel's going to be when we get ourselves out. No waiting around to get rescued. I'm tired of being a weenie; fear robs us of the world, Brynna. That's what Mel says. No more being big chickens, Bryn. We're going to get out of here."

We're.

Gabby wasn't getting out of there unless Brynna did. Her friend would not leave her. She knew that. Gabby wouldn't leave her any more than *she* would leave Gabby. They both knew that.

And they weren't in a stable place, were they?

There were holes in the ceiling above them. There was broken glass and sheared wires and *hell* all around them. The longer they were in there, the more at risk they both were. The more at risk *Gabby* was. The building could come down on the both of them at *any* moment, couldn't it? Brynna pulled in what oxygen she could. "Then let's get out of here."

Somehow, when Brynna was out the last time, Gabby had fashioned something like a stretcher from the supply cart and an Ethernet cord. Brynna knew what her friend wanted.

She pulled herself to her knees and climbed on. What else could she do?

"We're coming out right now!" Gabby yelled.

Brynna couldn't help it; she cried out. She moved her foot. She could *do* this! She could. She *would!* She put her foot on the ground and gave a push. The cart shifted two feet or so.

She *could,* she *would,* do this. "We'll do this, Gab. Make Mel proud."

Gabby dragged her to where the door used to be. It wasn't all that far away from where she had been standing when the world caught fire, was it? Brynna helped when she could. She helped even when she thought her heart was going to just stop, when she couldn't breathe, when the pain got so overwhelming she lost what little breakfast she had eaten that morning.

Gabby kept pulling so Brynna kept helping.

The rescuers outside the lab had made them an opening.

Gabby turned that opening into a tunnel, one foot at a time.

Brynna couldn't see anything but darkness. Debris scraped against her face, and she turned her head.

Then the darkness was more than just the absence of light. Brynna fought to breathe as Gabby fought to get them both toward the tiny opening at the other end.

And then Brynna wasn't breathing at all.

Chapter 40

CHANCE ARRIVED AT THE TSP too late. He was met by Det. Evers outside the secured area. "They took Gabby and Brynna Beck to Finley Creek General, Marshall."

"They're alive? They were in there, weren't they?"

"They were alive when they left here." The other man hesitated. "Beck didn't look good, Chance. I'm not going to lie to you. There was a lot of blood."

Chance's heart stopped then. His lungs seized. He forced air in. "But she was alive."

"Yes."

"What the hell happened?"

"Bennett Russell. There're rumors he rigged the place to go. We're going to get people in there for sure. Haldyn Harris is working on getting us video from their department, but it looks like everything on the servers has been destroyed."

"I don't care. I'm going to the hospital." He paused for a minute. "My brother? Who else was hurt?"

"The chief is fine. The rest of what we have are superficial. Russell waited until it was just the three of them in there." Evers looked over at the crowd as a woman wailed. Chance followed his gaze.

"Shit. Russell's family," Evers said. "Someone's going to have to tell them."

"It won't be me. I'm going."

"Keep us informed here. Gabby and Brynna…well, they're ours even though they stuck to themselves down there, you know? They didn't deserve *this*."

Chance looked at what remained. A third of the annex where Brynna and Gabby spent their time had collapsed in on itself. Smoke still billowed.

The hell Brynna had gone through hit him hard, and he fought to stay on his feet.

He had to get to her. He had to.

When he got to the hospital, there were people everywhere. He jogged over to that damned McKellen. "How is she? Where is she?"

McKellen looked at him for a moment. The other man ran his hand over his face. Chance saw the raw scratches on the man's hands. Foster was beside him and had similar marks. It was Foster who answered. "She's upstairs in surgery. Entire family is up there."

"She's alive?"

"Yes," Foster said. "But...she was impaled, Marshall. We don't know how bad the damage is."

"How did we miss it?" Chance asked. "What in the hell happened?"

"Only Gabby has those answers. I'm headed up there now."

—

THE sight of her sisters weeping terrified him, made him fear she was already gone. His brother was there, but there was no sign of Gabby. Where was she? He looked at his brother. "Where's Gabby?"

"Still being examined. I came up here to get an update. We're still waiting."

Chance nodded. He stepped into the hallway while Foster spoke with Brynna's sisters. His brother followed him.

"What happened, El?"

"At this point all I know is what Gabby told me. But it wasn't much."

"How badly is *she* hurt?"

"A lot less than Brynna, Chance." Elliot put his hand on Chance's shoulder. "She probably has a concussion, and she was bleeding in a few places. I don't know. I—"

"You need to get to her." How his brother felt was right there. Chance hurt, too. For Brynna, for Gabby, for himself and his brother. "What about Bryn? Straight answer, El. I need to know the truth."

"She wasn't breathing when Gabby dragged her out of the debris, Chance. She had been impaled, but it wasn't a large piece of metal. I saw it for myself. They got her breathing again. Then we were here. That's all I can tell you. But…there was a lot of blood. I just don't know anything else. I need to get to Gabby. She's going to want to be up here, if possible."

Chance looked up, and there Gabby was, being pushed in a wheelchair by Lacy.

Elliot went straight to her.

And then Gabby was telling them exactly what hell they had gone through at the hands of Bennett Russell.

It almost didn't register that Benny, a man who had been at his high school graduation, who had helped him clean his first fish, had been one of the men who had killed his family.

Why did it matter *who* anymore in that moment? All that mattered was Brynna.

—

NO one spoke to him while they waited. Only his brother. Chance looked over at Elliot. He was splitting himself in two, giving half his attention to running the damned fucking TSP *and* trying to take care of Gabby, who refused to return to her own room until they knew about Brynna.

How was his brother still *sane*?

Why had he taken off the way he had that morning? Why hadn't he stayed close?

Why hadn't they fucking considered that Bennett Russell was close enough to Brynna and Gabby to know everything they did? Why hadn't they considered?

Jillian was crying next to him. Syd…the kid was in total shock and not saying a word. Mel was pacing, prowling the waiting room with awkward steps.

Kevin had called the oldest sister; she'd be there as soon as a friend could fly her there in a helicopter.

Mel paced some more.

No one tried to stop her. Someone should. She was going to hurt herself, didn't she realize that? Wear herself out.

Chance stood up. Everyone looked at him. Why were they looking at him? "Mel, sit. I'm going outside for a while. El?"

"We'll find you. You want me to go with you?"

"No. You have Gabby." Gabby, who needed his brother beside her, strong and protective.

Elliot, who had been there to dig her and Brynna out. Elliot, who would keep her safe.

Chance was going outside. He needed to clear his head. Now.

"She'll be in surgery for a while, Chance," Jillian said, wiping her eyes. "We'll find you when we hear."

He nodded. He didn't know what else to say. Jillian surprised him when she wrapped her arms around Chance's waist and hugged him.

It was too much. *Family* was too much for him right then. Her family.

Chance prowled around the hospital, ending up in the small chapel.

He had a lot of thinking he needed to do.

Kevin found him there fifteen minutes later.

Chance couldn't look at him. He'd promised to keep the man's daughter safe.

"The doctor will be out to give us an update soon. I know you want to be there." The older man was silent for a long moment. "We should have considered Russell. I should have stayed this morning when I dropped her off. We should have convinced her and Gabby to quit the TSP. There's a lot of should haves, aren't there?"

Chance just nodded. What could he say to this man?

"There are a lot of should haves we have to think about. But even more *what-nows?* Let's get back up there, find out how my baby girl is doing. I know she'll be looking for you when she wakes up. She'll need *you* to be there more than anyone."

"Kevin, I…" Couldn't do it. Couldn't love someone ever again. This…he could not do *this* ever again.

How many hours had he spent in this *very hospital*, waiting on word of Slade? He'd come to this chapel the hour before he and Elliot had made the decision to let their baby brother go. *He* had been the one to convince Elliot to let Slade go. To let it end. Would he ever forget that?

Or forget that he sat here waiting on word of his Brynna? What if Kevin and her sisters were faced with that same question? Could he sit back and just let them make the decision to let his Brynna go?

Chance just couldn't let himself be hurt like this again.

But he *had* to know how she was. "Let's go."

The doctor met them in the waiting room a few minutes later. Chance listened to what the man had to say, trying to process it all somehow.

The doctor was the same one who had treated her before, wasn't he? "Brynna is a remarkably strong young woman. I won't lie—we did have to give her a hefty transfusion. And we almost lost her on the table once or twice. She'd lost a lot of blood, had been deprived of oxygen for a few minutes, her lungs were full of debris from the explosion, and with the infection last week, today was very tricky." The doctor looked around the room, his gaze lingering on Jillian for a moment. "We did remove her appendix because it took the brunt of the injury. She's still under sedation and will be at least until the morning. But barring any unforeseen complications, she should be just fine."

Chance breathed a sigh of relief. Of gratitude to whomever was listening above.

But the doctor wasn't finished. "*However*…she's going to have to be watched closely for signs of infection and for pneumonia from the debris in her lungs and chemical burns. She did inhale a bit of insulation, as did *anyone* who was in there today."

The doctor leveled a look at Gabby. Chance looked at her; he hadn't really *looked* at her since he'd made it to the hospital, had he? He did now, needing to see for himself. She would be hurting for a while, but…she'd recover. His brother hadn't lost her; *they* hadn't lost her. "In the meantime, we're going to keep her quiet and let her body *heal* from all she's been through in the last few weeks."

Chance's knees gave out, and he sank back down into the chair as the conversation continued around him.

Brynna was going to live. She was going to live.

They hadn't lost her after all.

Chapter 41

BRYNNA KNEW WHERE SHE was *before* she opened her eyes.

She called for *him* before she remembered. But Chance wouldn't be there. Would he?

A hot hand wrapped around hers. "I'm right here. You're safe now. But you're back in the hospital. Open your eyes. Look at me."

He wasn't taking no for an answer, was he? Brynna opened her eyes.

There he was. Safe. "Chance? What...what happened?" Brynna turned her head and looked around. She was back in the hospital, wasn't she? And there was someone in the second bed.

Someone she recognized.

Gabby.

Memories came rushing back. Benny. The explosions. Fighting Benny. Gabby. The rubble.

"I...remember. Benny?"

"Killed instantly. He'll never hurt you or Gabby again." He pushed the hair out of her eyes and brushed a finger over the bandage on her left temple. "You hit your head pretty hard. How much do you remember?"

How much? "All of it. Every detail. I don't think I'll be able to forget."

"You'll have to give a statement eventually."

"I will. Is Gabby ok?" She'd never forget how her best friend had pulled her through the rubble. If it wasn't for Gabby, she'd be dead.

Brynna knew that.

"She's going to be fine. Bumps, bruises. Pneumonia from the dust in the rubble. But...she's going to be fine."

"Was anyone else in the building hurt?"

"Marti, the receptionist. She was cut by some flying glass. The mayor cut his arm helping Elliot dig. Foster, McKellen, Erickson all have scratches and strained muscles from digging you and Gab out. Other than that, no one. Benny knew what he was doing, babe. He hurt who he meant to."

She tried to nod. It didn't go so well. "Benny's family? Nora and the girls, his sons?"

Chance hesitated. "Brynn, whomever Benny was working with, they took his daughter Alyssia to force him to do what he did. They haven't found her yet. They probably won't. Not until it's too late."

Horror filled her. Brynna *liked* Alyssia. The other woman was studying to be a child psychologist. "Find her, Chance. Someone needs to find her. She's not like our family. She won't have people out there looking for her like we did. Just her dad, and he's dead. She'll be out there all alone. She doesn't deserve…"

"Neither did you. Or Gabby. Or Sara. Or anyone else these people have hurt."

"But we can make a difference for her. Just…you and Elliot need to find her. Please."

Why did it matter so much to her? Alyssia's father had killed Sara and her family. Had hurt Brynna. Gabby. So many others. Why should his daughter matter?

Because Alyssia wasn't her father, no matter what the man had done. Alyssia didn't deserve to pay for Benny's sins. "Just promise me you'll try."

"I'll do what I can. You just worry about getting better." He leaned over and kissed her forehead once. "I have never been so scared in my life. Get better, Bryn. Fast."

Why did it feel like he was telling her something without words?

Brynna didn't understand.

She leaned back, too tired, too hurting, to try to figure it out.

There would be time to *think* later. Right now she just couldn't deal. Brynna closed her eyes one more time. She would just rest for a while longer. Try to forget…

Chapter 42

ALYSSIA CATHERINE RUSSELL, middle daughter of Bennett Russell, hadn't deserved to be dragged into this mess any more than Brynna or Gabby or Sara had. The girl's photo sickened Chance every time he looked at it. Big, pale-blue eyes, a slightly crooked smile. Freckles. She was six months older than Brynna, and the naiveté in her eyes was the same. The color reminded him of Gabby. The freckles and dark hair, his sister Sara.

Finding her was at least doing *something*, wasn't it?

Brynna and Gabby were still securely guarded at the Finley Creek General Hospital. Erickson and Foster, as well as two men from McKellen's unit, had volunteered their off time to guard the two women.

The TSP—and not just the Finley Creek post—were circling the wagons and protecting their own. Chance got it; people were pissed that two of their own had nearly been killed by a damned traitor in their midst. That the two involved were young *techs* just pissed off the detectives and officers and everyone else around.

Technicians with the TSP were civilians, not trained by the TSP Academy in Wichita Falls. They were the innocents of the organization, barely one step up from the clerks and administrative staff necessary to run the place.

It wasn't any wonder the TSP had been rumbling since the explosion happened.

He'd never forget the sight of what remained of the annex. Chance had gone back there with Elliot to be there when the crews had gotten inside the area where Brynna had almost died.

He'd *had* to go in. To see.

Elliot wouldn't let him; his brother had let him watch the video from the lone security camera that had remained functioning after the blast. It had been enough.

He'd never be able to get the sight of Gabby and Brynna both being thrown through the air after the room around them exploded. He'd watched as they'd fought off Russell with everything they had. Then he'd watched as Russell knocked Brynna to the floor and she didn't get up again.

And then he'd watched as sweet little Gabby had pumped every bullet in a .38 into Russell, keeping her body between *his* and Brynna's.

She'd saved Brynna's life, and her own, and no one who watched that video would ever forget what she had done.

Would forget what hell she and Brynna had gone through that morning.

Elliot had allowed Nora Russell to watch that video in part. Just long enough to see her husband plant and then detonate three bombs in the department he'd worked in for more than two decades. He'd cut it off before Russell's death, as a mercy to her.

She didn't need to watch someone she loved die like that. Not on video over and over again.

She'd fallen to her knees, and only Elliot's hands had supported her.

She'd clutched a long letter in her hands. She thrust it into Chance's, along with a photo. "I didn't think this was real. I didn't think it was real. My baby. My baby. Someone has my baby!"

Chance had read the letter quickly, the photo crumpled in his hand. And then he'd looked at the photo.

Saw the girl with long, brown hair with her hands tied behind her back, her shirt torn and her eyes terrified.

He'd looked at her mother and made a promise he doubted he'd be able to keep. "I'll find her. I'll bring her back."

He'd find her.

Even it if was just her body.

Her mother had lost enough.

Chapter 43

CHANCE SUSPECTED THE ONLY way he was going to find the body of Alyssia Russell was by luck or circumstance. Her remains were probably out there, rotting already. He wasn't so naive that he thought the girl was still alive.

She'd served her purpose as incentive; her father's cohorts had no need of her anymore.

Why the hell hadn't Russell named his accomplices in his Dear John confession to his wife?

It would have made things so much easier for everyone.

The *only* positive from anything that had happened was that they now had a definitive identification on *one* of the men in the video of what had happened to his family.

They just had to find the other four. With that first name, they had a start. With Handley Barratt's involvement, they had that first connection to explore. But it pissed him off to no end that yet another innocent, young woman had been dragged into this hell again.

Why? Gabby. Brynna. Even Brynna's sister Mel had almost been collateral damage. And now Bennett Russell's own daughter.

If he was investigating any other case, with no mention of the previous murders, he'd look at victimology for similarities and he'd be able to find them. White women, twenties, intelligent, low-risk lifestyles, all pretty women. All around five seven to five nine in height, thinner builds, and from middle-class backgrounds. *Low* risk.

They had a definite typology, didn't they?

Perhaps one of the sons-of-a-bitches had a thing for hurting young women? It was a line of inquiry he hadn't considered before.

Chance called Brynna's brother-in-law in St. Louis. The guy had easy access to all sorts of databases that could run previous cases, and he was more than willing to help Chance out without going through the TSP.

He got a list of names late the next afternoon, just after he'd stopped off at the Beck house for a shower and change of clothes. He'd spent most of the early hours at the hospital in the waiting room of Brynna's ward. He'd needed an update on how she was doing, how she had been during the night before he could even begin to think of hunting for Russell's daughter.

Kevin and his youngest daughter slept on the hard couches provided in the waiting room. Mel had sat by the sole window, staring out at the night sky. Jillian had once again been allowed to stay with Brynna, though it had taken some string pulling to accomplish it.

Occasionally Mel would slip out of the room and head down to the hall to where Gabby was. She'd sit with her long enough for Elliot to take a break or handle TSP updates.

His brother wasn't taking any more risks with Gabby, and Chance understood it. Supported it. If nothing else, his brother had figured out what he wanted from life, and he was going for it.

They'd told him they were getting married two hours after they'd learned Brynna's condition. Chance couldn't think of anything else that made more sense.

His brother was going to be *happy,* finally.

One good thing, at least.

Finally, Chance had had enough, and he'd scooped Brynna's sister up under her armpits and carried her to the waiting room. "Lay down, Mel. Rest. I'll keep the eagle eye for a while. You won't do your family a damned bit of good if you're exhausted. Bryn's going to be out for a while. And Gabby's already under. Sleep."

"I'm not sure I can. I can't get that stupid rubble out of my head." Her words were muttered, but he caught them. "How did we miss it?"

"I don't know."

"Benny was right there the *whole* time. And none of us saw."

"Because we trusted him. He grieved at the funerals. I know he did." And he'd hugged Chance over Sara's coffin and held him while Chance had cried for the sister he'd never see grow up. "I read the letter Russell wrote his wife."

"Elliot had Officer Journey copy the letter. She gave my dad a copy, on Elliot's orders. To see if it jogged his memory, but he's...*focused* on Bryn right now. I know from experience that he'll be that way until she's back with us."

"She's going to be ok." He wouldn't think of the video of her being thrown over the table Gabby had been working at. Wouldn't think of how her body had hit the wall.

"Yes. But what happens now, Chance? What do we do now?"

"We find Russell's daughter. Then we find every associate he's spoken with in the last two months. We go over every file he's touched in the past two decades. We hunt. Like we're good at."

"The zip drives Brynna had in her pocket. She cloned the TSP evidence databases right before. We have copies of everything that was scanned in four years ago. Chief Blankenbaker had the computer forensics and IT departments scanning in paper files four years ago. Brynna and Gabby were involved in that."

"So we have a place to start."

"I'm getting in, Chance. I'm going to go over everything that Benny touched. I'm going to find these guys *before* they hurt anyone else that I love."

"*Don't*. Don't let it drag *you* down with it. I've looked for ten years, and look what it's gotten me—people *I* care about, the only people I care about in the line of fire. It's not worth letting the hunt consume you." And he couldn't stand the thought of this woman, of anyone else *he* cared about, anyone *Brynna* cared about, being lost to these people again.

"I know the lines not to cross. But...I am also a trained investigator. And I was a good one until I was shot. And I know most of the initial players and *all* of the players on our team *now*. And like you, I'm no longer bound by the constraints of the Texas State Police."

"Then you report *to* me everything you find. I won't let Brynna lose *you*. She loves you too much."

"And I love her just as much. I *won't* lose her."

Chance looked into eyes so like Brynna's and saw just exactly who Melody Beck really was. He understood her, because the protector, the hunter, that was so strong in *him* lived equally as strongly in her.

Chapter 44

CHANCE SPENT THE LONG hours of the next day working at his brother's side, both on finding Bennett Russell's known connections and on ways to keep Brynna and Gabby from drawing those associates their way.

Benny had *not* been one of the three men to attack them in Oklahoma, but he had been one of the men on that video. The *fifth man.*

Somewhere was a record of his connection to those three men; Chance was going to find them. No matter what he had to do.

Brynna had had seven zip drives in her pockets that had survived Benny's attacks. Mel had grabbed a laptop from Dr. Coulter and opened several of the drives.

Brynna had copied the entire computer forensics department's files onto those drives after she'd clocked in that day.

As well as the files from the past forty-five years that had been scanned in to a database four years ago.

Her forethought had saved the Finley Creek TSP's bacon, and everyone knew it.

She'd copied *everything* in the CF department. Everything. No cases would be put on hold because of lost computer forensic evidence.

Some were celebrating her as a mini-hero for what she had done.

Chance was proud of her. He'd watched and rewatched how she and Gabby had fought to protect themselves. How they hadn't given up.

She was the strongest woman he had ever met, wasn't she?

After several hours of heated meetings with his brother, with the superintendent of the TSP, the governor, the mayor, and several others who thought they had a right to bitch Elliot out for Russell's actions, he headed back to the hospital.

She'd been quiet since she woke the day before; everyone was giving her time to process what had happened. Gabby was the exact opposite—chattering away about what she and Elliot had planned, talking with Brynna about their coding program, anything to keep herself distracted. Brynna would hum an answer now and then, which seemed to satisfy Gabby.

Chance stood in the door and studied them for a moment. Mel passed him on her way out. "They're yours for a while. I need to get home and start dinner before Syd and Jillian get home."

He nodded. "I'll be there in a bit."

"Jillian gets off in an hour. She'll need a ride."

"I'll get her."

"Good. Gab, Bryn, I'll be back before Gab is released. I'll stay the night, ok?"

Brynna nodded, her eyes on her sister. "I'm not exactly going anywhere."

"Not for a few more days anyway."

"Bring me something *good* to eat. They keep giving me chicken and rice. I hate rice."

"It's bland."

"It's allergen-free. They don't have much of a menu for me. Still, I'm alive, right?" Brynna winced as she shifted.

"You are." Thank God. Chance moved closer to the bed. "You can deal with rice for a few more days."

"Easy for you to say. You probably had a hamburger or something before coming in here."

He smiled. Brynna was feeling well enough to be cranky, wasn't she? Just like before. He didn't know why that reassured him, but it did. "Actually—I was in a meeting at lunch. It was catered. Elliot and I both got stuck with chicken and rice."

He wanted to touch her, confirm she was real and whole. But he didn't. Like it or not, *he* didn't have the right. Not like Elliot had with Gabby. The other man had stepped in right behind Chance, though they hadn't driven over together.

Elliot was already wrapped around Gabby, murmuring in her ear. Damn it. He envied the ease his brother had with his woman. But that way wasn't for him. Brynna was better off finding a whole man who didn't bring killers into her life.

Chapter 45

HE WAS SET UP EXACTLY where Golden Boy had ordered him to be. Damn, he hated taking orders at his age. He should be free to do whatever in the hell he wished with his life and his time. Instead he was Golden Boy's damned errand boy.

Still, he was where he could watch every move those damned redheaded daughters of Kevin Beck did. He had his favorites, of course.

If she wasn't crippled, he'd bet the oldest was quite a fighter. He knew she'd once been a cop. He liked her hair—and her ass. She had an ass perfect for grabbing, and her tits were just the right size for a man's hands.

If she wasn't so broken, he'd go for her. Just for a little bit of fun.

But he'd always enjoyed more of a challenge. A woman that couldn't run wasn't much fun.

The other girl was just a teenager, and he didn't think she'd fully developed yet. A tad bit too young for his preference, though if the opportunity ever presented itself he'd have a bit of fun with her, too.

No. He preferred women just a bit over twenty-one. Old enough to have been out there in the world a bit, but still young enough for him to watch the innocence drain from them as he robbed them of breath. As he used his knife to show them exactly *how* he wanted them to move beneath him.

His body tightened as he thought of Beck's daughters. The damned autistic one was just the right age, just the right build. Just the right combination of awareness and innocence in her big, brown eyes.

He'd have her beneath him. *Soon.*

But it was her smaller sister who really caught his attention. Her hair wasn't orange like her sister's. The nurse had dark-red hair that looked soft and silky. He loved to tangle his hands in hair like that.

She wasn't very tall. The other sisters were a few inches taller. He was a strong man; he could lift this one easily enough. *She* didn't look like much of a fighter, either.

But he bet she would squirm with a knife pressed to a naked breast, wouldn't she?

He cursed.

There would be time enough for Kevin Beck's other daughters. Time enough.

For now, there was one he *owed* a little attention.

A car pulled in at the Beck place, and a woman got out. The crippled one. He watched her for a moment, imagining everything he'd do to her.

His breathing picked up in anticipation.

Soon.

It would be soon.

Chapter 46

CHANCE KNEW SOMETHING was wrong the minute Jillian turned the knob to the back door of the Beck house. He grabbed Jillian and moved her off the back porch with half a second's pause. "Stay here. Better yet, get back in the car and stay there, engine running."

"What's wrong?"

"It wasn't locked." He pulled his weapon from the holster. Jillian gasped and covered her mouth. Wide eyes turned toward the door.

"Mel's inside; maybe she…"

"Mel knows to lock the door." He pointed toward the car. Jillian, unlike her sister would have been, was far more obedient. He pushed the door inward the moment he saw Jillian reach the car.

The kitchen told him everything he needed to know. The knife Mel had been using to cut up peppers lay in the center of the floor. The peppers were on the cutting board.

Syd's science project on one end of the dining room table had been flattened—he had a good idea by what. Mel might not be strong physically, but she wouldn't have gone down without a fight. A few strands of long red-gold hair were stuck in the still-drying papier-mâché, confirming his theory.

Mel's backpack that she took with her every time she left the house still rested in its normal spot by the back door.

He searched the house quickly, knowing what he was probably going to find. Knowing that the odds of finding her dead were pretty damned high.

Why the hell hadn't they put a guard on the rest of Brynna's family? Just to be sure they'd all be safe?

He searched the house quickly. She wasn't there.

Instead, he found a letter in the middle of the woman's bed. He ripped it open quickly.

Melody owes me some answers. You'll get her back when this is finished.

It wasn't signed.

He hurried back outside to the younger sister, going around the front of the house.

Nothing else was disturbed.

She met him in the drive. "Where's my sister?"

He held the letter up for her to see. "*Someone* took her. I'm calling it in to the TSP."

"I need to get back to Brynna." Wild panic in the brown eyes that looked at him. *All* the Beck daughters had those soul-stealing eyes, didn't they? The eyes that made a man want to save the world for them.

He'd failed at every turn, hadn't he?

He tried not to think of Mel, of what she was going through at that moment. Whether she was dead or alive.

Not yet.

He had to deal with her family first. He pulled his phone free and dialed Erickson's number. He explained the situation quickly, then dialed his brother. Erickson would get men on the hospital and every other Beck out there and quickly.

Chance kept one hand on Jillian's elbow, mostly to keep her from rushing into the house and seeing for herself that her sister wasn't in there. And to keep her from collapsing, if it came to that.

The woman was shaking in his grip, tears running down her pale cheeks. He pulled her close to his chest and held her while the sobs almost shook her in two. She was smaller than Brynna, skinnier, shorter, more delicate, if possible. So damned vulnerable, all of them.

Damn these Becks, they'd somehow managed to get inside his skin when no one else had in ten years.

He'd started to care for the lot of them—and he was doing a piss-poor job of protecting them, wasn't he?

Chapter 47

BRYNNA KNEW SOMETHING was wrong the moment Elliot stepped into the hospital room she was sharing with Gabby for the next few minutes.

Her friend was being released, with antibiotics to deal with the pneumonia Gabby had developed from breathing in insulation and dust while dragging Brynna through the Tunnel of Hell.

Elliot was hovering, and while it was probably driving Gabby crazy, Brynna thought it was sweet. He loved Gabby, and she loved him. It was obvious for anyone looking at them to see.

But when he came into her room while Lacy was checking the stitches holding Humpty Brynna—as her family had started calling her—together again, he came to *her* bed. "Bryn…"

Everyone went quiet. Brynna shifted in the bed with help from Lacy. "What's wrong? What's happened?"

"Chance just called. He gave Jillian a ride home after her shift ended."

"What's happened?" Brynna bit back the panic. Thoughts of her dad and sisters rushed through her head over and over. "Who? What's wrong? What's wrong?"

He held up a hand. Lacy wrapped her fingers around Brynna's. Brynna yanked away. She couldn't be touched, not yet. Not if she was going to hold herself together long enough to find out what had put that *look* in Elliot's eyes. "What? What?"

"They can't find Mel, Brynna. Her backpack is still at the house. The meal she was prepping in the kitchen is still there. There is a sign of a scuffle. But they can't find her. There was a note, though. Chance is pretty certain she's been abducted."

Brynna wrapped her arms around her stomach, ignoring the pulling of the stitches. *Mel was missing*. Mel. Someone had taken *Mel*. No, no, no, no, *no!*

She closed her eyes as the screams broke free. As she called her sister's name over and over and over and over.

There were hands on her. Nurses, doctors. Gabby and Lacy.

She looked into Lacy's eyes as she tried to focus. Then Gabby's. Gabby had *blue* eyes, really blue. Lacy's were green. Green like Chance's. Chance's. Chance. Where was Chance?

"We're going to have to sedate her. She's not going to come out of this rationally," a harsh voice said somewhere near her left ear.

She didn't recognize the voice. Didn't recognize the face. That made it all the worse.

Where was Chance? Was he looking for Mel? He'd find her, wouldn't he? Chance wouldn't give up. He wouldn't. He'd find her. He'd find her.

Gabby was next to her, saying her name over and over. Trying to help. Trying to calm her. Trying to get her to focus on Gabby.

Brynna tried to calm herself down. She knew she wasn't helping anyone like this. But...she just *couldn't* stop the screaming. The yelling.

The fear.

Hard hands, male hands, were forcing her back on the bed. She looked up into the harsh face, an older man, younger than her father, though. A doctor?

He was hurting her, holding her too tight. Why was he hurting her? She kept screaming, and kept screaming, clawing at his hands.

Until her eyes got heavy and her muscles limp. She collapsed on the bed as darkness stole her soul.

Chapter 48

ELLIOT HAD A HUNDRED THINGS running through his head as he watched Lacy tear into the hospital chief of staff—her boss. The man had been far too rough subduing Brynna, and everyone in the room knew it.

He'd pulled the man off himself when he realized that Lanning wasn't helping calm her down in the least, that he was hurting her.

Finally, Lacy had ordered one of the nurses to get a sedative, explaining Brynna's condition quickly.

Gabby was still on the bed; Brynna had collapsed on top of Gabby when the drug had hit her. Gabby didn't seem to mind, just kept patting Brynna's head and holding her. While Gabby cried. She looked up at him. "She's not had a fit this bad in years. This is the worst one I've ever seen."

"What in hell happened in here?" Dr. Lanning demanded after Lacy was finished with her tirade. Lacy and the nurse carefully shifted Brynna and freed Gabby. Lacy straightened the blanket over the unconscious woman quickly. "What set the girl off?"

Lacy and Gabby looked at Elliot. He nodded. "This goes no further than this room right here, do you understand?"

"Of course." Lanning was belligerent. Elliot studied the man quietly. Something about him was off, wasn't it? Bloodshot eyes, shaking hands.

"Her sister has been abducted. We just learned," Elliot explained. "We'll need to increase security on this floor. Especially this room. Jillian and Sydney will also require security details. Dr. McGareth, if you could arrange for me to speak with Jillian's supervisor—she's going to not be able to work for a while. Until we ensure the entire Beck family is safe."

"I'll get her supervisor shortly. I'll need to speak with Dr.

Jacobson about Brynna first. When she wakes...she's going to have to hear it all again. It might...might be best to keep her resting for a while. Until...until we know more about what's going on with Mel."

"Thank you."

Lacy was still glaring at Lanning. "I'll come sit with her after my shift is over. I'm sure Jillian will want to be here, too. Has anyone contacted Kevin?"

"Chance was tracking him down. Kevin was supposed to be with Syd at her school."

"What are we doing to find Mel?" Gabby asked.

"McKellen's on his way over to the house now. There was a note."

"What did it say?"

Elliot waited until the nurses and Lanning were out of room at his order. He allowed Lacy to stay. She'd been in and out of Gabby and Brynna's hospital room for the past three days and in and out of the Beck house since Brynna had been released from the hospital the first time. She knew almost as much as the rest of the Beck clan. In fact, they'd seemed to consider her and Jillian's other friend, Ari, as honorary members of the family, same as they welcomed Gabby. And Syd's friends. As they'd welcomed Elliot and Chance.

"'Melody owes me some answers. You'll get her back when this is finished.'"

"What is that supposed to mean? He calls her by name? If it's someone Benny was working with, why would he take her *now*? And why would he say we'd get her back?"

"I don't have a clue," Elliot said just as Gabby's new cell phone rang. Her old one hadn't survived the explosion.

She grabbed it quickly. "Hello? Mel! Mel, where are you?"

Elliot grabbed the phone from her quickly. "Mel, it's Elliot, where are you?"

"Elliot, this asshole—" Mel yelped and he heard someone else in the background. But it had definitely been Mel's voice.

A male voice came on the line. "Marshall, as you can hear, she's alive. She's not hurt, and she won't be. I'll see to that. In the meantime, find my father before those bastards hurt him. You'll get Melody back then."

Elliot's mind seized on the only guy whose father was still involved. "Barratt?"

"Like I said, my father safe, you get her back. We have a deal?"

"Give us something to go on. We don't even know where to start searching for him."

"Neither do I. That's the problem. I *can't* find him."

"One hair on her head out of place, Barratt, and you'll regret it. Am *I* clear?"

"Find my father. I'll worry about Melody. I'll *keep* her safe."

Barratt ended the call.

Elliot could barely process what he'd just heard. Was the guy seriously trying to extort the TSP? How did this figure into any of what had happened? "Gabby, do not leave *this* room. Do you understand?"

"Where are you going?"

"To find my brother and Kevin. We now have a place to start looking for her."

"She's alive," Gabby said around a sob. "She's alive."

"She is. Now we just have to get her back." He looked at the second blonde in the room. "When does your shift end?"

"An hour." The doctor was pale and wide-eyed, as well. They were all in shock, weren't they?

Elliot looked over at the bed, at the unconscious woman there. She looked so damned small and vulnerable, didn't she?

And his brother loved her, Elliot had no doubt of that.

But how were they supposed to keep them all safe? Elliot understood Chance's reluctance to get involved, especially with such a family as the Becks. They had already lost so many close to them.

If Mel didn't make it through this, what would it do to the people who loved her? What would it do to Brynna and Gabby and the rest?

What could Elliot do to help?

He didn't have a clue at the moment. Except…

Look for Mel. Find her. Take that next step, while keeping the two women here safe. Somehow.

"Can you stay with them? Until family arrives?"

"Of course." Lacy followed him out of the room. She patted him on the arm once they were in the hall. "You'll find her. I have no doubt about that."

"I'm not going to stop until I do."

Chapter 49

KEVIN BECK WAS ONE of the strongest people Chance had ever known. That was made abundantly clear as he watched the older man process the fact that yet another of his daughters was missing. The younger girl was shaking and pale. She went right into Jillian's arms. Jillian accepted her father's quick hug while rocking the youngest Beck. Then the Beck family turned to business.

The business of finding their missing sister.

Elliot pulled in moments later and called Kevin's name. Chance stepped away from Erickson and McKellen—that damned McKellen was everywhere—to meet his brother. There was urgency in his brother's steps. "Elliot, what do you know?"

"Mel. She called Gabby's phone. She's alive."

"Where is she?" Kevin asked.

"Houghton Barratt. He has her. Says he wants to make a deal. We find his father for him, then he'll return Mel to us. He's making no bones about having her."

"You spoke with her?"

"Just long enough for her to say my name and call someone an asshole. And she spoke with Gabby for a brief moment, too. She's alive. She's alive, Kevin."

"Thank God."

Erickson said what they were all thinking. "Then let's get her back."

Chapter 50

CHANCE MADE CALLS TO every contact he had while Elliot sent McKellen and two of McKellen's detectives to Houghton Barratt's estate on the edge of Barrattville. Barrattville was a small town that was part of the Finley Creek incorporation, though it had been settled a decade before Finley Creek. It mostly boasted a health clinic that was the oldest in the state, a post office, a school, and a collection of ranches that were at least one hundred and fifty years old.

Houghton Barratt's property was one of the oldest and definitely the most prosperous. It had two homes on it—the original Barratt homestead, which was impressive in itself, and the newer mansion built by Houghton Barratt fifteen years earlier.

When he'd been twenty.

Chance had googled everything he could find about the Barratt family during the endless hours he'd been waiting for Brynna to wake in the hospital.

"How's Brynna?" he asked his brother after Elliot was finished with McKellen's people.

Elliot hesitated. Kevin turned at the question.

"Elliot? How's Brynna?" Chance asked.

"She didn't take the news well. They had to sedate her before Mel called. She doesn't know Mel is alive. Yet."

"What aren't you telling us?" Kevin asked.

"Brynna was hysterical, Kevin. It took four people to hold her down long enough for her to be sedated. They were afraid she was going to hurt herself more." Elliot's mouth thinned. Chance recognized it as a sign his brother was more than just irritated—Elliot was pissed.

He'd be questioning his brother the first private moment they got. "She's ok now?"

"Sedated. Lacy and Gabby are staying with her now."

Chance looked over at Kevin. "I'm going over there. See her for myself."

"I...I..." The older man was torn. He glanced at his two daughters standing beside him. "I'm not sure *where* I am supposed to focus right now. I need to call Carrie, let her know what's happened. I need to be with Brynna to help keep her calm. I *need* to find Mel. And *they* need me, too." He waved a hand toward Jillian and Syd. "What am I supposed to do now?"

Jillian wiped her eyes and squared her shoulders. "I'll call Carrie, Dad. And I'll stay with Syd."

"*I'll* go to the hospital with Brynna," Chance said. It was where he wanted to be.

Now that they knew her sister was alive—at least for now—he needed to check on Brynna himself. Then he'd see about getting her sister back.

—

BRYNNA was still out when Chance walked past Det. Evers and into her hospital room. Dr. McGareth was out in the hall, arguing with two people, including Dr. Coulter, the hospital administrator. Gabby was by Brynna's bedside, playing a game on her cell phone. She looked up when he walked in. "Chance. Where's Elliot?"

"He's still at the Beck house with Kevin. He's waiting on word from McKellen. He sent him and some of Major Crimes people to Barratt's place in Barrattville. See what they can find there."

"You think she's there? Wouldn't that be too risky? I mean, you can get a warrant and walk right in, right?"

Chance shook his head. "A single phone call from a burner phone—even to the chief of the TSP—isn't enough to get a warrant that quick. We'll get one, but it'll take a while. But we can ask questions, if the people there are willing. But we'll get her back—don't doubt it."

"Doesn't he have a place in Mexico? Brynna and I googled his dad and found that they had properties in Mexico."

"I'll make a few phone calls. I have friends over the border." It made sense, didn't it? If *he* was kidnapping a woman to extort a police force into doing what he wanted, he for damned sure wouldn't keep her somewhere she could be found so easily.

But across the Mexican border was a whole different ball game, wasn't it? Getting through the red tape to get in there would take a few days at the least. If they were certain beyond a doubt that that was where she was. And that she didn't go willingly.

The small sign of a scuffle and the note and phone call weren't much. And Chance knew it. Maybe stateside, but enough to cut through international red tape, not likely.

First, though, he wanted to take a good look at Brynna for himself.

"How is she?"

Gabby's eyes filled again. "It was awful, Chance. She was screaming Mel's name, and then yours. It took me, Lacy, a nurse, and that stupid jerk Dr. Lanning to keep her from hurting herself."

"Stupid jerk?" He stepped over to the bed.

"He was threatening to tie her down, Chance. Right in her face. He was *two inches* from her face."

"Like hell he would." Hot anger rushed him, and he took a close look at her. "They drugged her?"

"Lacy did. It was her only choice. She was trying to calm Brynna *and* keep Lanning in control."

"What did he do?"

"He bruised her. He held her down and yelled in her face. Elliot pulled him away, and Lacy ordered a sedative for Brynna. When Kevin gets here, or Jillian, someone who can make medical decisions for her, they are going to discuss keeping her on a mild drug to keep her calm. She'll be awake, Lacy said, but…won't freak out again. Or won't be able to hurt herself if she does."

"And Lanning?"

"Lacy's speaking with the hospital administrator now. She's lodging a formal complaint. The nurse who was in here is collaborating. I already did. *This* was the last thing Brynna needed right now. She already hates hospitals as it is."

Chance shifted the nightgown Brynna wore. Livid, red marks were on her pale shoulders. Thumbprints? He lifted her a bit, just enough to see her back. The guy had gripped her, hard.

When she was already terrified and hysterical? Chance forced his fists to unclench.

"We can't deal with him now. We need to focus on finding Mel. What did she say when you spoke with her? How did she sound?"

"She sounded angry. She just said, 'Gab, it's Mel.' That was it. I wish she'd said more, but Elliot took the phone. That's all I know."

"It's not much. It's proof she's still alive. But it's a direction, at least. If we take the son on his word that he'll keep her alive while we search for his father..."

"He will, won't he? Why else would he let us know that he is the one who has her? If he hurts her, we'll know it. We'll arrest him and send him to jail."

"That's what we're counting on."

"Then why would he do this? He has to know."

"I don't know. Desperation, maybe. If he's not *involved* with his father and Russell, maybe. We'll get those answers, Gab. I promise."

Because like she said, Houghton Barratt had to know what would happen the minute he stepped back on US soil.

Nothing Barratt had done made any sense.

Chapter 51

CHANCE STAYED BY BRYNNA'S bed while she slept. He wasn't leaving her alone for even a moment, not after what had happened. They didn't have definitive proof yet that Houghton Barratt was the one who had Mel. It could have all been a set-up of some sort. Something to distract them from their true purpose. He didn't think so. They had had no way of knowing Elliot would take Gabby's phone. And Mel had recognized his brother's voice and called him by name. That alone told them she was alive at the time of the phone call.

It was reassuring, at least.

Dr. Coulter had stepped in the room a few moments ago, with Dr. McGareth on her heels. Both were friends of the Becks, and he knew they would protect Brynna's best interests while she was in their hospital.

Dr. Coulter checked the chart at the end of Brynna's bed. "We can gradually bring her out of it in a few hours. I want to do it slowly so we can tell her about her sister while she's still calm enough to get through the initial hurdle."

"I'll stay as long as necessary. Thanks to Lanning, I have a three-day vacation, after all," McGareth said bitterly.

"Circumstances aside, you broke protocol, Lace."

"And you'd have done the same if you had seen how afraid she was of him. How tightly he was holding her. *Do no harm*, remember?"

"You got *suspended*?" Gabby asked, her eyes wide. "Because of what he did?"

"Well, you can't tell the chief of staff he's a damned drunken ogre and *not* get some sort of reprimand," Dr. McGareth said, shrugging. "It's not the first suspension I've had. Nor do I think it'll be my last."

"Lanning's lucky I wasn't here." His respect for the blond doctor went up about ten notches. She had a fiery personality that he liked. That it was directed toward taking care of Brynna was all the better. Chance fought the urge to hunt the man down and ram his fist into his face. Show him what it was like to be helpless and defenseless. He tamped down on the urge. It would have to wait—keeping Brynna's *entire* family safe had to come first, didn't it?

He, Gabby, and Dr. McGareth spoke for a while longer about what the next steps would be in finding Mel. Elliot had to play by the constraints of the TSP, but Chance didn't.

Chance could hop a plane into Mexico and get her himself—*if* they knew where she was being kept. And how many guards Barratt had in place.

If that's what it took, then he'd do it. In a heartbeat.

It was becoming less and less about finding answers about the past and more about finding ways to keep Brynna and her family safe, to keeping Gabby safe, wasn't it?

He looked at Brynna sleeping in the bed and made her yet another promise.

He was getting her sister back for her, no matter what he had to do to do it.

Chapter 52

GABBY SPENT THE TIME Brynna was sleeping googling Houghton Barratt. Their earlier searches had focused on his father and whatever property the older Barratt might own.

Now she focused on his son.

She had to admit his son was one of the most beautiful men she had ever seen. He was tall—taller than Elliot and Chance by a good two or three inches, she thought—and built along the same lean lines Chance was. Elliot was bulkier, more muscled than Chance.

Houghton Barratt was tall and lean, with black hair trimmed short and dark eyes. His teeth were perfect white and straight.

There were certainly uglier men out there Mel could have been kidnapped by. A completely ridiculous thought, but it popped into Gabby's head anyway.

Was her friend scared? Mel had sounded more mad than scared, hadn't she? Was that a good thing or not?

Gabby reminded herself again that Mel was the strongest person she knew. Mel would be ok. Gabby knew it.

She had to be. She just had to be.

Gabby wrapped her hand around Brynna's. She needed the contact.

Lacy was still there. The other woman patted Gabby's shoulder. "She'll be ok. They all will. I just know it."

Gabby just hoped she was right.

Chapter 53

IT WAS THE MIDDLE OF THE night when Brynna next opened her eyes. Chance made a point of being there. He'd had Gabby and Elliot head over to the nearest computer store and pick him up a laptop. Gabby had quickly installed everything he'd need to work remotely. He wasn't leaving Brynna's side until he absolutely had to.

He had a friend who lived in northern Mexico. The guy was former military and damned good at ferreting out information. Torrez was going to call Chance as soon as he confirmed Mel was in Mexico. It was going to take him at least the next twenty-four hours to do that.

Brynna shifted on the bed, then blinked. Looked around with a hazy expression. He leaned over her. "Hey, babe. I'm here. You're safe."

"Chance." She closed her eyes again. "I *knew* you'd come. I needed you, and you came. Knew you would."

With those soul-racking words, she went back under.

Chance leaned back in his chair as the trust she had in him went straight through his gut. Made him wish he had all the answers or a magic wand to erase every moment of pain and fear away from her life.

How he wished he could do just that.

It was a long while before he was able to stretch out in the chair and sleep. He had a lot to think about.

Most of it centered on the woman in the bed. And what he wanted from her from the rest of his life.

When morning came, he still didn't have the answers.

Chapter 54

BRYNNA *COULDN'T* FOCUS her eyes on anything. No matter how hard she tried. Finally, she gave up and closed her eyes again. A warm hand wrapped around hers.

"They gave you something to calm you down, babe. It'll make you a bit cloudy for a while. How much of what happened do you remember?"

"There was a man there. And he was hurting me, yelling at me. I was…upset. Because Elliot…" She thought for a long moment. "Elliot said something had happened to Mel. Where's my sister, Chance?"

She forced her eyes open again and focused as best she could on his face. "Where is she? Is she dead?"

"No. Elliot and Gabby both spoke with her briefly. But she has been abducted. By Houghton Barratt."

"The son? But why? Why?"

"He wants to force us to find his father. He says we'll trade your sister for his old man."

"But we don't have him, do we? Will he hurt her?"

He hesitated. "I don't know. We don't plan to leave her with him long enough for that to happen. As soon as we find out where he's keeping her, I'm going to go get her."

"Promise?"

"With everything I got. I'll bring your sister back, babe. I swear. You just sleep. Rest while you can. Let *me* worry about Mel for you, ok?"

She closed her eyes and nodded. Whatever they'd given her, it was strong. Strong enough to override every thought she had in her head. "Bring her back, Chance. Just bring her back. Make all of this just go away, please."

"I'll do whatever I can." She felt him brush her forehead with his lips, and then she was under again.

Chapter 55

ELLIOT WAS AT THE BECK house when Chance arrived early the next morning. He'd waited until Erickson and Foster arrived to relieve him of guard duty for a few hours.

He looked at Kevin. "I got a call from…a friend…south of the border. They've confirmed Mel's passport was stamped at 6:43 last night. Houghton Barratt's was a minute later. Once they left there, though, we haven't confirmed anything."

"But she's south of the border and with him," Kevin said. "How the hell did he get her passport? We keep all passports in the safe in the study."

"He's duplicated hers. Which takes time. He's been planning on *her* specifically. It might be enough to get someone down there to get her. But that's provided we can cut through the red tape," Elliot said. "We're looking at days or even weeks if we go through the traditional route."

"I'm going. I promised Brynna I'd bring her sister back myself." Nothing was making sense. From the moment this had started, it had been about engineering opportunity to take out those who were *direct* threats to Russell and his associates.

Mel, not even a member of the TSP, wasn't much of a threat to anyone, was she?

Unless Barratt truly *was* using her as incentive to manipulate the TSP. A bold move, and one that would earn him a hefty prison term once they got him and charged him with kidnapping and extortion, as well as a host of other crimes. Unless he was just that desperate to find his father.

Chance could *almost* understand that.

"And how are you going to do that?" Elliot asked.

"We need a way to find out where exactly she is and how to get to her. Then I'm going to go get her. No agency can send a team to get her back, not under these circumstances. Not without with some serious backing. More than we have right now."

"We need to find another way," Elliot said.

"Give me fifteen minutes to shower. Then we'll figure out that other way."

Chapter 56

CHANCE FINISHED HIS SHOWER in record time, then made his way back into the kitchen. "So now what?"

"I've gathered everything we could find on Houghton Barratt." Gabby was in the kitchen now; Chance should have figured she'd be around the house somewhere. His brother wasn't going far without her these days.

She'd just been released from the hospital yesterday, though, and *should* have been resting. He stepped behind her and dropped a kiss on her blond head as a rush of affection he hadn't been expecting hit him. She was going to be his sister-in-law, after all. She'd never take *Sara's* place, but she was a living, breathing connection to that young girl. And she was a connection to his brother. *Family.* It mattered again, didn't it?

The ring she wore was his grandmother's. It gave him a start to see a woman wearing it again. She would have approved of Gabby. He had no doubt of that. "Good morning, Gab."

"Morning." She looked up at him with surprised blue eyes. "How is Brynna this morning?"

"She's fighting off the drugs. I told her what we knew, but I'm not so sure how much it registered. Lacy was there when I left, along with her friend Ari. Lacy's going to stay with her today as long as needed."

"That's good. Guess the suspension is working in our favor, isn't it?" Gabby's expression told him exactly how she thought of what had happened. But Lanning was a problem for another time.

"Apparently. So what have you learned about Barratt the younger?" His favorite little *blue-eyed* hacker had probably already been at work on that very subject.

"Not much. He runs half the companies under the Barratt-Handley umbrella. His father inherited the company forty-five years ago from his grandfathers, Harrison Barratt and Leon Handley. They have their fingers in a *lot* of pies. Houghton handles mostly technologies-based companies, it seems. He's supposed to be well above average intelligence—MIT educated, even—and owns several patents for his own inventions. This is not a stupid man, by any means. On the personal front, he's got a bit of a reputation as a playboy billionaire and a master strategist. But he hasn't been linked with any woman at all in at least the past eighteen months. He's supposed to be ruthless at business. But there's nothing about him on a deeply personal level. Not even names of his primary contacts. He guards himself well; I can give him that. I've gone through main channels so far. I'm going to do some black hat digging this afternoon. I *really* wish I had Bryn's help, though. She's better at the hunting in the dark corners than I am. Far more diabolical—and logical—than I am."

"She's going to come out of the sedative sometime soon. I plan to be there when she does."

"Then I'm going in with you," Gabby said. "Kevin and Syd and Jillian are staying here, with two details from the TSP to keep guard."

Elliot protested. "I'd prefer you stay here, Gab."

She shook her head. "This is my best friend that's missing, and my other best friend is so upset by the news they had to *drug* her to keep her calm. I can't be with Mel right now, but I *can* be with Brynna, Elliot. I *need* to be."

"I don't like it."

"They're not going to attack in the hospital. Not with the sheer number of guards on the place."

"Gab…"

"I'm going. Brynna needs me."

"I'll keep her with me," Chance said. "I'm leaving in fifteen. Get your stuff together, Gab. Hell, Elliot, she's probably safer at the hospital with me than here or at the TSP right now."

No one could argue that point with him.

"And at least then I'll be doing something that could help Mel."

Chapter 57

BRYNNA WAS AWAKE WHEN they made it back to the hospital. Lacy was trying to distract her with the TV. It wasn't working.

She looked right at him when he walked in. "Have you found her yet?"

"We know what country she's in. And a general area. I have people confirming her exact whereabouts now. Gabby's going to find out whatever else she can on Houghton Barratt from here."

"I'm going to help," Brynna said, her tone daring anyone to contradict.

"I have your laptop here." Gabby placed the backpack on the bed.

"How are you feeling first?" Chance took in the freshly washed and brushed hair and the clean hospital gown.

"Like someone drugged me." She shrugged, but there was a world of hurt in her eyes. Chance wanted to hold her, but he kept his hands to himself. "I understand why it was necessary. I...freaked. I'm sorry that you had to deal with that, Gab."

"*Don't* apologize, Bryn. How many times have you brought me back off the ledge of craziness? It's what we *do* for each other. It's kind of our *thing,* after all." Gabby grabbed the bag and pulled out Brynna's laptop. "Your dad is keeping Syd and Jillian at the house today. Elliot's got the house practically surrounded with TSP. All your neighbors are yapping about it."

"For how long?"

"Until everyone involved in what happened to my family and what has happened to yours is apprehended. We're not leaving your family unprotected again. Even if we have to hire private security. I have friends who are in that business. People I trust. People that owe me big."

She looked at him and nodded. "Help me up, please?"

Chance took the hand she reached out toward him. He stepped closer, then helped her sit.

She exhaled slowly. "Hurts more this time than it did the last time."

"Well, you were hurt a bit more this time than last," Gabby said, pulling a pillow out of the cabinet and putting it behind Brynna. "More glue holding Humpty Brynna together again this time, remember?"

"I *don't* like this. How long until I am out?" She looked at Lacy, who had been mostly silent since Chance and Gabby had arrived.

"I told you, barring complications, you'll be out of here within the next three days, Bryn. Any complications and we'll add a day each time. You don't want to rush it. I'd hate to see you back under the knife, getting sewn back together," Lacy said.

"Let's get Mel back so she can greet you at the door, ok?" Gabby said. "I've checked every database I can get into for stuff on Houghton Barratt. Guy has *no* dirt on him anywhere. Not so much as a speck."

"Until now. But I bet *Carrie* could find some."

"Use my phone. No one has replaced yours yet."

"It didn't survive, did it?"

"Nope. Neither of our bags did. Your phone ended up imbedded in Benny's office door, Bryn."

"Glad it was the phone and not one of us." A look passed between them, one Chance knew he would never forget. Something had changed between them in that explosion. Drawn the two of them even closer together, if possible. But their relationship had changed somehow, too. How they viewed one another. They were aware of each other's strengths, and weaknesses, more than they probably ever had been before.

They were going to have to find their way through it—*once* things got back to normal for them both. Or until they—as he'd heard Gabby put it—found their *new* normal.

He sat back while the two of them went to work, their fingers flying over their keyboards faster than the speed of light. They spoke in their own style of shorthand, asking questions and offering solutions before he could even ask for clarification.

He contented himself with speaking with his various contacts—he'd built up a variety of connections all across the western hemisphere over the last decade, and he was shameless about using them now.

If he thought it was the best course of action, he'd have a team assembled to get him inside Barratt's compound without the Damned Billionaire ever being aware they were there.

But there was no way to get Mel out of there except carrying her. The woman wouldn't be able to run if they had to. That would leave her as a sitting duck. It wasn't an option.

Unless someone physically carried her out of there. Which his people probably could do, if necessary. But that was a weakness he didn't want to plan for her.

He'd still rather find another way to do it.

Chapter 58

HE'D FELT A BIT USELESS as Gabby and Brynna had done things he hadn't thought possible with their laptops. They had just about everything one could hope to find about Houghton Barratt spread across their screens. They'd taken Brynna's hospital room and turned it into a remote computer forensics lab with a skill that had his respect for them going up even further than it already had been.

Which was saying a lot.

And they'd done it without acknowledging *he* was even in the room—well, Gabby had at least looked at him from time to time.

Brynna not so much.

"Look, Gabby. Look." Brynna's excitement had him turning toward her several hours after they'd gotten started. "Check this out."

"What is it?"

"The technology conference, TechCore 3000. It's being held at Barratt's hotel in Mexico City. Look who else is one of the main speakers. It's *Luc*. Luc. Luc."

"Who?" Chance leaned over her until he could see her screen. All he saw was a generic website with a bunch of floating head pictures, with small bios. Houghton Barratt's was one of the top ones. He read it quickly.

"Ari's brother. The man who's buying my computer program we're designing. He's going to be there, too." She beamed at Chance. "He could get someone to Mel's side. I don't doubt it. *Luc* can do anything. He even broke a human trafficking ring almost by himself."

"It's a stretch. I don't see Barratt taking her there with him." Most likely the man had her stashed away somewhere under heavy guard. *If* he'd kept her alive, that was. "He's probably got her locked away somewhere. It's what I would do."

"Maybe not," Gabby said. "But if he shows up—and he's still on their itinerary—maybe someone could get *him*."

"Tell him he has to give my sister back," Brynna said, finally looking at him. "Can we do that? Force him to trade Mel for his own freedom?"

Chance thought about it for a moment. "It wouldn't be *legal*. Not for anyone in law enforcement. But I'm not a cop anymore. I could probably do it."

"At least it would be *something*," Brynna said, deflating. "Mel has to be so scared right now. What if he *hurts* her? She can't fight back. Not anymore."

It was the defeated look in her eyes that made him seriously consider it. "What we need to do is find out where he has her, *first*. When is this conference?"

"It starts tomorrow afternoon and goes through the next three days."

"So we have some time to surveil him. Come up with a plan." He looked at Barratt's photo and that of the man they'd pointed at as Luc. *Davis Lucas* was what was listed on the webpage.

He'd heard of the guy. Some bigwig in St. Louis who preached green technologies and had several companies responsible for manufacturing law enforcement equipment.

And he was a connection of the Becks, one who could move freely in an area Houghton Barratt was expected to be. Men like that...men like that had entourages. Had security and employees that went with them everywhere. If someone wanted to get in…

It just might work. Provided this friend of Brynna's was agreeable and they could isolate where Mel was being held captive.

Chapter 59

BRYNNA'S FATHER MADE THE call from Brynna's hospital room twenty minutes after Chance's contact in Mexico confirmed that a woman matching Mel's description had been hurried into Houghton Barratt's Mexican home and hadn't been seen since.

He had another contact verify via one of the Barratt's servants that the woman was there in his home and was pissed as a rattlesnake at whatever Barratt had done to her.

The servant hadn't said what that was, just that it was significant.

And that there had been a lot of yelling. From the woman.

Well. He didn't know if that was reassuring or not.

Kevin put his oldest daughter and her husband on speakerphone, and they introduced Davis Lucas, for Chance's benefit.

The guy agreed to the plan as soon as he learned it was Mel that was missing. Apparently Mel and the guy's other sister were close.

Lucas said it himself—Mel was like extended family. He was happy to help however he could. And if their plan failed, he'd offered up a team of security "experts" willing to go back and carry her out physically.

Now all they had to do was wait until the next day to see if Barratt showed up at the conference.

If he did, he was the first step in retrieving the missing Beck daughter. Then they'd deal with Barratt, once they had Mel back where she belonged.

Chapter 60

CHANCE HAD TO GIVE IT to the guy—Lucas made things happen. Or rather, his *sisters* did. And Mel's. Lucas arrived with Brynna's oldest sister and another dark-haired woman later that evening. Elliot and Chance met them at the airport.

The guy had his own private jet. Chance couldn't fathom it.

The dark-haired woman shook his brother's hand. "Chief Marshall, fancy meeting you here." She smiled, and Chance blinked. She had one of those smiles that stayed with a man, didn't she?

She also wore a rock the size of Chance's fist on her left ring finger. From the way her stomach was gently rounded, it was clear this woman had been claimed by some lucky man somewhere.

"Agent Brockman, it's good to see you. I wish it was under better circumstances," Elliot said.

"I know. We'll get Mel back and get this figured out. So how can we help?"

"Simple," Chance said. This was Brynna's plan, and he was in charge of executing it. He took that duty seriously. "Barratt is supposed to speak at a technology conference in Mexico City tomorrow. Rumors have it he may be bringing a female companion." Unconfirmed, but it was a direction they could go in.

"And how can we help with that?" Carrie asked.

"I think I understand," Lucas said. "Barratt and I have run up against each other before over the last fifteen years. Damned smug bastard knocked me off a bridge once. *I'm* also scheduled to speak, but was thinking of backing out. The wife, you know, she doesn't like it when I'm gone more than a day or so."

"Brynna said you could probably get someone in." She'd had faith in the guy, hadn't she? And she had faith in *him*.

Chance didn't take that lightly, even if there weren't any *strings* between them. Brynna was counting on him to get her sister back. Hell, the entire Beck clan was.

"I have room for a guest. As a member of my personal security." Lucas eyed Chance and Elliot. "One of you feel like heading to Mexico?"

"I've already got my passport." Chance looked at his brother. "I told Brynna I'd bring her sister home no matter what."

"Then let's head back to your dad's and figure out a strategy," Agent Brockman said. "That doesn't get one of you in serious trouble. Or a Mexican prison. Luc, you have bail money?"

"Payton's already prepared. She'll get me out of trouble if needed." He grinned and Chance half thought the guy was looking forward to it. Thrill seeker, maybe?

"I don't care what we have to do. We just need to get Mel back." Why hadn't someone thought to keep security on the rest of Brynna's family? It had been a stupid mistake, and one he wasn't about to repeat. He turned to Brynna's sister. "You make sure to watch your back, too, while you're down here."

The eyes just like her sisters' widened. "Why?"

"For all we know, whoever is doing this could be after the rest of you Becks, too. Your father was TSP just as long as mine was. And now *two* of his daughters have gotten caught up in this. I don't want to see another."

"Oh, don't you worry. We'll keep Carrie safe," Lucas said. "If we don't, I'm afraid her husband will pull my guts out through my nose. He's cranky like that."

"Luc, behave," his sister said. "This is serious. We need to focus on getting Mel back."

"Oh, I am, Paige. I am. Nothing pisses me off more than to see women I like and respect targeted by men who ought to know better. To be honest, though, I never thought Barratt would ever do something like this. He may be an arrogant asshole, but he's never come across as a criminal. Or someone who would hurt an innocent woman. I just don't get it."

"I hope you're right, Luc. I really do," the sister said. "Mel has been hurt far too much lately. Through no fault of her own."

Her brother patted her on the shoulder at the pain on her

face. "I know. We'll get her back. One way or another."

—

DAVIS Lucas—"just call me Luc"—was extremely diabolical. But Chance liked him. His younger sister Ariella was one of the women who had been in and out of the Beck house at pretty much all hours of the night, and his other sister, the pregnant one with the killer smile, was some bigwig with a missing children's division of PAVAD. She was a tie to the Becks and, from what he overheard, was good friends with several of the sisters.

By the time they'd finished the sandwiches the younger two Beck sisters had whipped up, they had a workable plan.

It was clever in its simplicity.

He and Lucas would go to the conference and isolate Barratt. Find out where Mel was. Then they'd force Barratt to have Mel brought to *them.* Then it was simply a matter of flying the woman home where she belonged. If that didn't work, Luc's men were waiting to storm his house and get her back.

That was a more complicated plan than he wanted, but…Chance knew to work with what he had. Plan C involved a few of Chance's contacts doing the same thing.

Three plans. One was sure to work. If not, they'd come up with more and more plans until they had her back.

They were leaving in the morning and weren't coming back without Melody Beck.

No matter what they had to do.

Chapter 61

THE CONFERENCE WAS held at—ironically enough—the Barratt International Hotel—Mexico City. Of course the bastard's family owned the hotel. Why wouldn't they?

Luc strode right into the building like he was some type of god, bent on conquering the peons of this world. Chance stayed at his back a few paces, like a good bodyguard would. Behind the dark glasses he wore, he studied the crowd.

They'd need to deliver Lucas's speech, find Barratt, and get him alone.

Somehow. In a crowd of more than seven hundred people.

He kept his eye out for Barratt but didn't see him. Not yet.

It took them a few hours after Lucas's speech was delivered to find where Barratt—the star of the damned show, apparently—was holed up. What kind of man abducted a woman and then gave a speech about technology?

And then they waited.

The man himself walked in surrounded by bodyguards and what passed as the press. Trade journalists would no doubt be covering any new inventions or projects, for certain. There had been a dozen present at Lucas's speech, as well.

Chance nearly swallowed his tongue when he saw who walked at Barratt's side. It was simpler than he'd ever have expected.

Right there, in the midst of Barratt's entourage, was a stunning woman in a skimpy green dress, her strawberry-blond hair swept up in one of those sophisticated twists that left a woman's neck and shoulders sexily bare.

Barratt held her close on the side not using her crutch. Chance half suspected his grip wasn't just to keep her steady in the jostling crowd, but to keep her contained. Surely, she wasn't there by *choice*?

He discarded that thought. Mel wouldn't leave her family to

worry like that. Not with the way she was so rabidly protective of them. Not her.

"There," Chance's new best friend said. "Look right there. Who would have believed it? There's our girl. What do you say we get a little closer?"

"Oh yeah." He took his first real look at Barratt in person. The guy looked like a younger version of his father, and was just as tall as Lucas. Just as dark. More muscled. Probably had about forty pounds on Chance, at least. Just as arrogant as Lucas, for that matter.

He had to admit, Barratt and Mel made a damned beautiful pair.

"Those Beck sisters sure do clean up nicely. Wow. Not as well as my Payton, of course, but…"

Chance had to agree. He'd only seen Mel in casual clothes and she'd given the impression of practical, down-to-earth wholesomeness.

The woman next to Barratt was the picture of icy sophistication. Anyone looking at her wouldn't doubt for a moment that she belonged on the arm of a billionaire. Would want her.

It was a bit disconcerting.

And it brought up one question he didn't like to consider—*had* the woman gone with Barratt willingly? Abandoned her family for Handley Barratt's son?

He didn't *think* so. But there was something about the way the two of them were looking at each other. Something in the way Barratt held her close.

They'd been lovers—he'd bet every penny he had on it. And he had quite a few pennies saved up.

The two had a history together; it was just unclear how *recent* that history was.

Chance and Lucas made their way closer, careful to use the crowd as a cover. Chance knew he'd blend in to the background, though Lucas was only a few inches taller. It was the way the other man commanded attention—and the way Chance deliberately made himself less noticeable in a crowd.

But *someone* saw him. Someone extremely observant.

He was maybe fifteen feet from Brynna's sister when Mel looked up. Glanced between the two bodyguards who walked at Barratt's back.

She saw Lucas, and her eyes widened slightly. She covered her surprise by swaying slightly and grasping her crutch more tightly.

Barratt leaned down to her and said something, blocking Chance's line of sight. He shifted her closer, until she almost leaned against his chest. Barratt's hand trailed up her back, left partially bare by the lower cut of the dress.

They'd confirmed she was there, all right.

Now all they had to do was get her away from Barratt. Barratt, who was acting every inch the possessive lover.

—

THE opportunity came a little earlier than they thought. Lucas hailed Barratt just after Mel had stepped into the elevator. The bodyguards turned to look.

Lucas followed Barratt into the elevator with a hand on the other man's shoulder.

Chance slipped behind Barratt's bodyguards and slammed the button to close the door before the guards could slip in. He used his body to block their entrance into the cart. "Sorry, boys, the boss needs some time alone with Barratt. Trade secrets and all that shit."

He waved to the guards and shoved the bigger one back out of the elevator when the man tried to charge him. "Take the next one."

As soon as the doors closed on the guards, Chance turned to Barratt.

He had to give the guy points—the man had somehow herded Mel into the back corner of the elevator and was blocking her with his own body. To protect? Or to possess? "All right, Lucas, what are you up to now?"

Lucas ignored the other billionaire.

"Well, Melody, my dear. Seems you've gotten yourself into a tight spot there. Hope Barratt wears decent deodorant," Lucas said.

"Hey, boys. Figured someone would show up to get me sooner or later. Didn't expect you, Luc."

"Well, Mexico City was on my itinerary. And Payton wanted

me to ask you for that biscuit recipe you make for Brynna. She's in the mood for homemade biscuits. I *told* her the cook could make them, but she wants to do it herself."

She stepped out from behind Barratt.

"Chance, how is my sister?"

"She's a bit freaked out by what's happened. Misses you. Worried. They all are."

Barratt was obviously not happy with Mel moving out from behind him. He grabbed for her.

Chance did the only thing he could. He knocked his fist into Barratt's face.

Chapter 62

HE HAD TO ADMIT, RAMMING his fist into the face so like the elder Barratt's was immensely satisfying. If Mel hadn't stopped him, he probably would have hit him again.

But she did. "You keep that up and we'll never get out of this damned hotel, Chance."

"She has a point. Mel has always been brilliant," Lucas said. He reached down and hauled the other man to his feet. "Here's the plan, Mel. We *were* going to take Barratt and force him to hand you over, but since we have you—looking stunning, by the way; green is so your color—we can skip that step."

"Let's take him back with us. I have questions. And the guy did try to extort my brother. And the TSP." Chance thought quickly. "There will be a host of charges, including kidnapping and trafficking."

"It'll take him a decade or more to get out of jail. I have to admit that sounds wonderful to me."

"No."

Chance looked at the woman next to him. "What?"

"No charges. I won't make a statement. I'll talk to Elliot, too." She stared at Barratt. "But…we could use him to flush out his father. I have no doubt about that."

"You don't want him to go to jail?" Why? It shocked the hell out of him; he'd figured Mel would be the one squawking for the guy to be arrested from the very beginning. But she wasn't. She was just looking at Barratt with a confused expression in her brown eyes.

"No. I don't. He didn't have anything to do with what happened to your family. Or to Brynna. He was just trying to find his father. I don't want him to go to jail for caring about his family, Chance. No matter what stupid things he's done."

"Melody…," Barratt said, looking at her. "We need to talk.

You know that."

"Not now. I'm going home, Houghton. I…*need*…to. It's where I belong."

They'd been lovers. Chance had no doubt about it now. What that meant for the rest of the situation, he didn't have a clue.

—

LUCAS paid off a Customs official to ignore the fact that Barratt's hands were bound. It had been a simple matter of getting him out of the hotel to the limo Lucas had waiting. They'd forced Barratt to call his guards and send them back to his house to wait for him there.

Chance wasn't stupid. The guy was being far too cooperative. Barratt was up to something. But did it have to do with his father? Or with the woman riding in the limo next to him?

Chance refrained from asking her any questions in front of Barratt. He sensed there was a fragility about her that hadn't been there before. *Had* Barratt hurt her more than she'd let on? There didn't seem to be a bruise on her that he could see. Still, she looked bruised somehow. Broken.

Hurting. That's what it was.

He grabbed her a blanket from the back of Lucas's private jet. "Here. You look like you can use the rest."

He kept his words low, not wanting the other men to hear. Barratt did anyway. The guy stared at Mel with eyes that took in everything about her.

Mel shivered.

"Mel? Sit. Take a break. We'll be back in Finley Creek soon." Chance's phone buzzed as he followed her to the couch. He read the text quickly.

He cursed. Loudly. "That little idiot!"

"What is it?" Mel asked.

"It's from your father," Chance said. "Your sister has checked herself out of the hospital against medical advice. Says she's determined to be there when you get home."

"Brynna. Of course." Mel sighed, then laughed. "She needs a keeper. I swear she does. It takes all of us to keep her in check sometimes."

Her laugh turned into a light sob and tears started to fall.

Barratt's eyes widened, almost in fear. Chance *almost* felt sorry for the guy.

Not him. He was *almost* used to weepy-eyed Becks. Or he was getting there, at least.

He handed Mel a tissue. "Here. Wipe your eyes. Your mascara is going to run if you don't. Completely ruin the effect of that dress. Or what passes as a dress."

She laughed. "Never knew you cared."

"Shut up, Beck. Of course, I care. I'm here to rescue you, aren't I? For the second time, I might add."

"You're making a habit of rescuing Beck sisters, Chance."

"I know. Just can't seem to help myself. When we're back in Finley Creek, I'm so going to spank your sister's ass for this."

Mel held up a hand. "Too much information, there. I don't need to know about any *proclivities* the two of you have. But on a side note, I'll hide all the Cheerios for you. Just in case."

He glared. But at least the distraction had worked.

She no longer looked like she was going to break into a thousand pieces.

Chapter 63

BRYNNA YELLED HER SISTER'S name the instant Mel walked in the house. She struggled to stand, and moved too quickly. Her stitches protested, but she didn't care.

Mel looked just fine—she actually looked very nice.

The dress she wore probably cost more than Brynna made in three months at the TSP. Definitely more than Mel could afford now. It was a green shimmery material, and her hair was swept up off her neck. Mel actually wore more makeup than usual. She looked beautiful, sophisticated, and expensive.

She hardly looked like someone who'd spent three days with an abductor.

Mel hugged their father first. Then Jillian because she was closest to the door. Then it was Brynna's turn. And Gabby. Everyone wanted to touch her, to make sure she *was* real. That the nightmare was over.

Brynna cried. Jillian and Syd were crying, too. Gabby was a blubbering mess. Brynna grabbed tissues and shoved them into Gabby's hand. Even Ari and Paige and Carrie and Lacy were teary-eyed. Elliot looked like he was about to panic as he passed more tissues around.

And then Chance was coming in the door, and she forgot all about her sister.

At least for a minute. He was safe and right there in front of her. He wasn't off in a foreign country where anything could happen to him.

Luc and Chance pushed a tuxedo-clad man into the living room in front of them. Bound with duct tape and gagged.

"Chance? Why...why...why...why is Houghton Barratt in our living room like *that*?" Brynna said the question she knew was on everyone's mind. "And how did you get him here?"

"Same way he got Mel out of the US. Right through Customs. Figured *Mel* could decide what to do with him now.

He's her hostage now. Whatever she wants to do with him. Or…we figured we could trade Sonny here for info on Daddy dearest. Trade him *to* his father for his father's turning himself in. We got Sonny on several charges *if* Mel here wants to bring them. If she doesn't…"

"Why wouldn't she?" Brynna asked. "He took her from our home. I think he needs to rot in jail forever. He *deserves* it."

Her sentiments were echoed by Syd and a few others in the room.

"Sometimes things aren't so black and white, Bryn," Mel said quietly. Sadly.

Brynna looked at her sister, leaning heavily on the crutch that went with her everywhere. But…that wasn't Mel's crutch, was it? It was a new one, wasn't it?

Mel's had been white. This one was sleek black and different shaped. Had *he* bought it for her or something?

"What happened in Mexico, Melody?" their dad asked, his hand still on her shoulder, as Chance forced Houghton Barratt into a chair. Jillian calmly handed Chance a roll of duct tape from the kitchen, without being told to. Brynna recognized it as the rainbow-colored tape Syd had been using for her science project.

Chance and Luc made a big production of taping the man to a dining room chair. She was almost certain the two were *enjoying* it. They were certainly rough about it. Houghton Barratt didn't fight them either. Why wasn't the man fighting to get away?

Why was he just staring at everyone that way?

Brynna studied the man who had taken her sister. He definitely *was* a pretty man. Bigger than Chance and Elliot, and slightly heavier than Luc. Dark, too.

He *almost* looked like he could be related to Luc, with black hair and dark eyes and so tall.

Brynna turned toward her sister. Mel was most definitely *not* looking at Houghton Barratt. Something *more* was going on, wasn't it? Not for the first time she wished she understood people better. "Mel? Are you ok?"

"Of course, I am. I'm home, now, Bryn. So…who's going to tell me what I've missed?"

"First, why don't we ask Houghton here some questions?" Elliot asked. "We need to find out what he knows."

"It's not much," Chance said, finishing with the billionaire. The one taped to the chair. The *other* billionaire had moved to hug his youngest sister, where she stood next to Jillian. The one who reminded him of Sara sometimes. Sara had had dark hair and pale skin, too.

Damn these Becks and their friends. They were sneaking their way in to his mind, weren't they?

Ari and Lacy had been there, helping Jillian prepare dinner while they waited on information. One big normally happy family in the midst of a family crisis. One in which *he* had played a big part. Almost as if he belonged.

Why did that sound so tempting yet so terrifying, too?

"You know, I think Elliot and Carrie and I *should* protest this. It's not exactly how we're supposed to do things," Paige said. "Civil rights, and all."

"Close your eyes, sis," Luc said. "And your ears. We're calling this...an intervention, not an interrogation."

"Intervening with what?"

"Why, his stupidity, of course. It's up to us to make him see that by not cooperating he's making a stupid mistake."

"Seriously, though," Elliot said, looking at Carrie and Paige. "Maybe the two of you *should* find another room to hang out in for a while."

The two looked at each other for a moment, then Carrie shocked Brynna with her answer. "He *took* my younger sister. I want to know why. But...what happens has to *stay* in this room. We can't let anyone know what we're doing."

Carrie was right. They deserved to know why, didn't they? Brynna stood, then walked across the living room into the dining room and looked into Houghton Barratt's dark eyes. She stared down at him for a long moment. He stared at her. He didn't have mean eyes, at least. That was something.

Everyone went quiet, or so it seemed to her.

She looked around the room. Their home was open concept, and she could see from the front door clear to the back. It was large enough that, even with everyone in there, it didn't seem too crowded. She liked it that way.

This was her home. It was Jillian and Syd's and Mel's. And if it needed to be, it could be Carrie's, too.

It was their *home*. Their safe place.

This man had violated that. She wanted to know why.

She looked at Chance. "The tape on his mouth?"

He pulled it off the man's mouth. "Ask him what you want, babe. I can guarantee he's not going anywhere until he answers our questions."

"I don't want to talk to him. But I think the rest of you will," Brynna said slowly, as more emotion swelled inside her. More emotion than she honestly thought she could handle at that moment. She wrapped her arms around her stomach and shifted her weight from side to side. She focused on her breathing, on calming herself down before she flipped again.

"Bryn?" Mel said her name, then stepped closer carefully. Mel *always* moved so carefully now, didn't she? Bryn grabbed her sister's free hand, then looked at Gabby, who still clung to Mel's arm. "Let's go upstairs. You don't have to look at him any longer if you don't want to."

"No. It doesn't upset me to look at him. He's not his father." If it had been the older man there, she'd be in a full-out Gabby-worthy panic, wouldn't she?

But this man was *not* his father. She had to remember that.

"What are you thinking, Bryn?" someone asked. She thought it might have been Gabby.

Brynna looked up at Chance as the words started to flow. "How much longer can this go on? How much longer can we do this?" She turned to where she could see almost everyone. Everyone in the room who mattered to her—these people were her world. They were. "You are all my *world.* Every one of you, in some way. We're a…family. All of us. Maybe not by blood, but…maybe we haven't even known each other all that long, for some of us. But we still all care about each other. Would do *anything* to protect each other." She struggled to find the right way to express what she was feeling.

Chance held out a hand to her. She shook her head. She *couldn't* be touched by him right now. No matter what she felt for him. "This man…he was just another link in the chain of whatever *this* nightmare is. His father was right there when I was sliced open with a pocketknife. When I almost died, *the first time,* when Chance almost did. I could have died in that rental car with Chance there beside me. Because of something I still don't understand. Because of what happened ten years ago? When Chance and Elliot's family was ripped from them? From *us*? Mel and I were on way there that night, too. We were *minutes* away from being killed back then. We all know that. And Gabby. Benny *knew* she saw what happened. He watched all of us for years, didn't he? All those times we went to him, all of the times we trusted and depended on him? How much longer can we *do* this? I don't know. None of *us* do. And it didn't end there, did it? Someone shot at my sister, at my best friend. At Elliot and Chance. For reasons we still don't understand entirely. They were lucky not to be hit. Mel could have been shot in a hospital parking lot *again.* For what? And then what was it? Oh yeah…Benny blew the world up around Gabby and me. He'd been *watching* us for years. Knowing every move we made. How do we know his friends haven't been, as well? How do we know they're not out there following Syd or Jillian or even Carrie around? It could so easily have been one of *them* who took Mel when we weren't looking. Now Mel's been dragged into it by *him.* Benny's daughter Alyssia is *still* missing. She's probably dead. We all know that, yet we don't talk about that, do we? And it's all because of stuff that happened so long ago. What's next? When is it going to end?"

"Bryn…" Her father said her name and trailed off. Brynna *had* to say what she was feeling. Had to get it out there. Somehow.

She looked around at the people, hoping they understood. "*Who* is next? We got lucky. Lucky that *one* bomb behind *me* didn't go off and kill me and Gabby just like that. We got *lucky* that Elliot got Gabby out of the way of a bullet and lucky that Chance was there to get Mel back inside. Because *she* couldn't run to save herself. We got *lucky* to get Mel back this time. But when does our luck run out? What are we supposed to do now? Does *he*—" She waved a hand at the man who was still silent behind her. "Does this man have the answers we need?"

"Brynna, babe…"

She looked back up at Chance when he interrupted her. "Do what you have to do to find those answers, Chance. I've never believed in *luck.* In luck. In luck. I believe in *family.* And…I'm tired of *my family* being in danger for something we don't even understand. For now, I'm just…going to be happy that I have my sister back and she's alive. Be happy that Gabby and I made it through that hell that we will never forget. I'm going to try to forget that the son of one of the men responsible is right here in my dining room. I'm going to forget that his father was the one who told me to run. To leave you behind and save myself because *your* time was almost up. Because there was no hope for you, for the both of us. He wanted me to run. He did. Handley Barratt didn't want to hurt me. But I think he would have. I think he would have. But I can't forget. I still see and hear and smell and feel every single detail from the moment his father helped pull me from your car and into this hell. I'm not sure how long I can hold myself together anymore. Humpty Brynna. That's exactly who I am, isn't it?"

Her words were cut off when strong arms went around her. When Chance lifted her carefully off of her feet and just held her. When he gave her the comfort she needed. Brynna's arms slipped around his neck, and she held on as tightly as she could.

CHAPTER 64

FOR THE FIRST TIME SINCE he'd learned of what was happening, Houghton started to doubt that Brynna Beck was mistaken. For the first time he started to doubt his father's innocence. With a crowd of at least a dozen people staring at the woman now in Chance Marshall's arms, a crowd that actually believed his father was guilty of what they'd accused, it was hard for Houghton to say definitively that his father wasn't.

Melody stepped closer to her sister and put a hand on the younger woman's back. There was such pain on Melody's face. He wanted to make it all just go away, for her.

"Bryn, we'll get through this. I promise. We're Becks, after all. Nothing can stop us, right? Bullets and bombs certainly haven't. We'll get through. Chance, take her to her room. I think *this* is just too overwhelming for her now. We'll—*I'll* deal with Houghton. You take care of her."

Marshall carried the still crying woman out of the room, leaving Houghton facing the crowd. His executioners?

"Dad, we're going to have to go. Go. I need to get back to Maddie. Sebastian was called out again," one of the redheads said. He studied her for a moment—she looked like his Melody. "We're going to fly back with Luc tonight."

"I need to get back and get Payton. She's going to join me for the rest of the tech conference. Barratt, I'll make your apologies to the board. I'm sure they'll understand that you're indisposed right now." Lucas smirked as he said it. What *was* his connection to these people? How had Houghton's people missed it? If he'd known, he wouldn't have taken Melody to the conference where Lucas could get to her.

Lucas hugged a dark-haired woman who stood from where she'd been sitting cross-legged in front of one of the Beck sisters. Side by side, it was easy to see the two were related. As was the only other dark-headed woman in the room. The one next to the eldest Beck girl. How had he missed it? Lucas had family ties to the Becks, didn't he? Damn it.

Houghton wasn't used to making those kinds of sloppy mistakes. He'd walked Melody right into a trap. That they'd meant her no harm mattered little.

Within half an hour, a third of the room was empty, and several of the women—there were pretty women *everywhere* in the Beck house, it seemed—were setting the table. Around Houghton. As if he didn't even exist.

It irked; he wasn't too proud to admit it.

Mel disappeared down the hall and returned a few moments later in jeans and a thin sweatshirt. She'd pulled the pins from her hair and left it loose in a wild mess of tumbled curls over her shoulders. He found her just as alluring in jeans and sweatshirt as he had in that skimpy little green dress. He so wanted to touch again. But now wasn't exactly the best time to be lusting after Melody, was it?

"What are we going to do with *him*?" A slim woman with blue eyes and platinum-blond hair asked.

"It's up to Mel," the older man in the room said. He recognized him easily. What would Kevin Beck do when he learned exactly what had happened between Houghton and his daughter? "Honey?"

"Tape his damned legs to the chair and free one arm. He's sneaky, but we probably should feed him."

"You're so full of heart, Melody." It was the first he'd spoken since he'd been dragged into the warm home that Melody had grown up in.

"Shove it. I still haven't forgiven what you did."

"You will. Eventually. We have a lifetime to work on that, after all." He grinned at her.

Her eyes widened. "Houghton, shut up. *Not now.*"

Chapter 65

CHANCE RETURNED TO THE DINING room in time to catch the exchange between Barratt and Mel. Brynna had fallen sound asleep within minutes of him holding her; he'd covered her with her blankets and fought the urge to go break every bone in Houghton Barratt's body, just as a substitute for what he wanted to do to the man's father. Not honorable of him, but it was real emotion.

The room had gotten quiet when Barratt spoke.

He got what caught them up. There was a familiarity between Mel and the other man. One that spoke of long acquaintance.

"How long have you known Barratt, Mel?" Chance demanded the question that had been in his mind since Mexico.

Mel looked at him with guarded eyes. "What do you mean?"

"I mean…he's said a few things that have implied you've known him for a while. I want to know if it's true."

"Chance—" Elliot started. Chance held up a hand.

"No. The only way we're getting the answers we need is with information. If she has some we need to know…"

Mel's shoulders slumped, and a flash of pain hit light-brown eyes. Surprisingly *deep* pain. "I know him. We met eighteen months ago, but it hasn't been a lasting acquaintance. I didn't even tell Gabby or Brynna or Jillian about it. I didn't know enough to help with what happened to Brynna. I'm sorry. I probably should have mentioned it—*him*—right away."

"Yes, you should have."

Kevin stepped up to his daughter's shoulder, and Gabby was immediately at her other side, glaring at Chance. "Leave her alone, Chance. If she doesn't want to talk about it, she doesn't have to. Now isn't the time. If Mel thought *he* was important, she would have told us."

Chance took another close look at Mel. Pale, upset. And having just returned from being abducted. Now definitely wasn't the time. "I'm sure she would have."

He looked at Barratt. It shocked him to see the sudden rancor on the man's face. Elliot had freed one of the guy's hands, and Barratt had reached out. *Toward* Mel.

What had happened between the two eighteen months ago? Chance was starting to get an inkling.

"Dinner's ready," Jillian said, with a light touch on Chance's arm. "You plan to wake Brynna?"

And have her sit down at a table with *Barratt*? Not yet, not tonight. "No. She needs to rest more."

With an efficiency that spoke of many such dinners at the Beck house, Jillian and her friends had dinner prepped and on the table within a few moments. Mel took one side of Barratt. Chance took the seat across from him.

It didn't surprise him at all that Elliot took the other side of the interloper in their midst. Protecting the rest of the family from the possible threat.

It was just their way.

As was the blessing Kevin Beck asked over their meal. It had Mel reaching in front of Barratt and grasping Elliot's hand. Barratt gawked, like he hadn't ever sat down to such a family meal. Chance half knew how the man had felt.

He'd been uncomfortable the first time he'd sat down with the Becks, too. And *he* hadn't been duct taped to a dining room chair at the time.

When Kevin was finished, Chance looked up. Standing in the dining room behind Barratt was Brynna. She looked at him for a moment. "I'm going to be at the table for the first meal with Mel back where she belongs. With my family."

Chance stood and grabbed the extra chair from the corner. He put it right next to his—between him and her father. "Sit, babe."

She did.

Within moments, some of the tension leaked out of him. It was hard for it not to. Kevin had made it very clear that the dinner table would *not* be filled with discussion of the threats over their heads.

Chance understood that, now. They had to be reminded

that this wasn't their whole world. That *family* was.

Tonight it dealt with the possibility of Luc purchasing Brynna's program and how soon that would be. And what she was going to do with the money. Chance had a good idea what it was, but she wasn't talking about that. Keeping it as a closely held dream, wasn't she?

He'd taken a look at the house himself when arranging security with Erickson. It was very much like the one she lived in now, but slightly bigger.

She would be happy there; he didn't doubt it.

And eventually she'd find a man to share that house with her, to help her fill it with pretty redheaded children and make it into a real home for her. Much like this one.

He frowned at that.

He didn't want to think of another man sharing that dream with her.

Mel had filled a plate for Barratt, and he was struck by the incongruity of it. She was serving dinner to her abductor.

Apparently without a second thought.

Chance studied the two of them again. They weren't talking. She was barely looking at Barratt.

He was looking at her, though. He ate with his left hand, the one Elliot had freed from the tape. Mel was on his left side, but he didn't move to touch her. Yet he was close to her.

Almost hovering, if possible. Strange to see in a man taped to a chair, but it was there.

Protective? Possessive? Lust? Chance tried to identify what it was. He saw all three, and more.

His attention shifted slightly to his brother and Gabby. His brother held his body almost exactly the same way Barratt did. Attuned to Gabby's every movement. Every damned twitch she made, Elliot was aware of it. Chance would bet good money on that—because *Chance* was hyperaware of the carrot-topped woman on his own right.

Elliot leaned closer to Gabby, murmured something just between the two of them. Something intimate. Light from the fixture winked through the ring his brother had given her. The ring on her *left* hand.

Barratt leaned closer to Mel and said something with a smirk. But it was a *knowing* smirk, wasn't it? She finally looked up at him and shook her head. She reached with her left hand for the salt and handed it to him.

Barratt covered her hand with his own. Said something else. Startled eyes went straight to the set of rings on her finger that he was touching. Chance felt shock run through him.

The rock she wore put the one on Gabby's hand to shame.

Mel paled and Chance watched her try to surreptitiously pull the rings from her finger, but they wouldn't budge. She looked at the rest of the people at the table, then dropped her hand to her lap.

What was she hiding?

He looked at Barratt's hand, and there it was. Exactly what he suspected he'd find.

"Wedding rings." His voice was loud enough to cut over the top of the low conversation the rest of the table was having. Every head turned in his direction.

"What?" Elliot asked.

Chance stared first at Barratt and then Mel. She shook her head slightly, an almost pleading expression on her face. He ignored it. He'd already started it, might as well finish. "Wedding rings. They are *both* wearing them. Rings Mel didn't have a week ago. I didn't notice it earlier. Unless Barratt has a wife we don't know about? Or…he does. And she's right there."

She paled even more—which for a Beck was saying quite a lot—and turned toward her father. "Dad…it's…I…"

Her father reached beneath the table and pulled her hand up gently.

The evidence was right there for everyone to see. And a hell of a rock it was. It would probably pay for the house Brynna wanted, easily.

Barratt smiled a coldly taunting grin, right in Chance's face. The challenge was clear. He and Barratt were going to tangle and soon. "Did we forget to mention something? Melody and I were married two days ago. At my home in Mexico."

Mel jerked to her feet as fast as she was capable. She wobbled and both her father and Barratt reached to support her. Barratt was caught up short by the duct tape restraints. "Damn it, Houghton. Shut up! *Yes,* I'm married to him. Yes. I knew him eighteen months ago. And *yes,* we've slept together, ok? That's all I am saying about it *now!*"

"Mel…" Chance felt like a total ass seeing the pain and confusion on her face.

"Oh, just *shut up, Chance!*" She threw her bread roll at his head. He caught it before it could do any damage. Apparently, Brynna wasn't the only Beck who threw things when upset.

She stormed around the end of the table where her father sat and headed toward the hallway, toward the privacy of her bedroom.

No one tried to stop her. No one spoke. Her door slammed behind her.

Kevin's fist shot out and connected with Barratt's face, knocking the man's chair over.

Had Elliot not been in the way, Barratt would have hit the floor.

"*That* was for whatever you've done to my daughter."

Well, dinner was pretty much over after that, wasn't it?

Chapter 66

BRYNNA STARED AT HER FATHER. She had never seen him hit another human being in her entire life. And he'd done it so *calmly.*

Elliot caught the man's chair and steadied him. There was blood on his mouth. Houghton Barratt reached up and felt his teeth. He grabbed a napkin and held it to his lip, while glaring…*at* Chance. Not her dad.

Why was he mad at Chance?

Because Mel was?

Mel.

Mel, who never walked off like that. Who always stood and fought. Brynna hadn't missed the tears on her cheeks. She stood. Gabby did the same. Together they headed down the hall after her sister. Mel needed them, and that was where they were going to be.

She knocked on Mel's door, then pushed it open slowly. "Mel? Can we come in? It's just me and Gabby."

Her sister was on her bed, staring up at the ceiling. Her cheeks were wet.

She held the rings in her hand. She turned toward the door. "What was that noise?"

"Dad. He punched that man in the face and knocked him into Elliot."

"He did what? Is Houghton…?" Mel sat up. She cut herself off. "You know what, I don't want to know."

Brynna snagged the set of rings from her sister's hand. "These are real."

"Yes. I think they are."

"You're married to the billionaire." Gabby gawked. Gabby was good at gawking. "How did it happen?"

"How was it even possible? Isn't there a waiting period in Mexico?" Mel hadn't been missing long enough for a waiting period, had she?

"He had the paperwork all ready. Even managed to get the blood test done on samples they'd taken while I was in the hospital after we were shot at. I wondered why they were taking them, but the nurse just… Money gets you everything you want, after all. He planned it. Said he started when he realized who I was. He's been planning it since the day we did that news conference outside the hospital."

"Ok, you're going to have to start way at the beginning. Let's just assume he's innocent of his father's doings." Gabby curled up on the foot of Mel's bed. Brynna sank into the desk chair and rolled it closer to her sister.

"How did you meet him?"

Mel sighed. "There was a benefit. One Blankenbaker needed someone to attend with him. His wife had been ill, and she'd suggested I go with him. He wanted someone to charm the donors, actually. I was happy to do it to help the TSP. I met Houghton in the elevator there. I'd just closed a murder case, you two. And it had been a bad one. The victim looked so much like Syd it made me sick to even think about. She'd been a runaway like Carrie and I just…couldn't handle it. He was there, and he was charming, and he helped me forget. At least for a little while. It was the one and only time I've *ever* done anything like that. The next morning, I panicked and I ran. I didn't even give him my full name. He said he's been looking for me ever since. But I wasn't on the original guest list for the banquet, and he never knew who I came with."

"So he realized who you were once he saw you on the TV and what?" Gabby leaned forward. "Decided he couldn't live without you?"

"Please. Nothing like that. He showed up here and drugged me, Gab. Not exactly romantic." She sighed. "Houghton Barratt always gets what he wants, apparently. I'm his *in* to the search for his father. That's all he wants from me."

"He didn't have to marry you to get that, though." Gabby made a valid point, didn't she?

"Did he hurt you? Force you?" Brynna asked. "Is it a legal marriage?"

"It's legal. And the marriage license has my name on it, damn him. Legal signature. I didn't know *what* I was signing at the time. And the official didn't speak English, nor a dialect that

I am familiar with. I think Houghton arranged it that way on purpose. He's canny and crafty and so damned sneaky I can't get ahead of him for anything."

"It's not *legal* until you sleep with him, though, right?" Gabby asked.

"I think that requirement is a bit outdated, Gab. Marriage is a legal contract, and there's no way to prove if someone sleeps with someone or not. I think, if the documents are signed, she's married," Brynna said. "You *didn't* sleep with him again, did you?"

Gabby gasped. "You *did!*"

Mel didn't say a word.

Brynna couldn't imagine what her sister was thinking. "So why did he marry you?"

Mel's cheeks went fiery red. When had Brynna last seen her sister embarrassed like this? "I don't really know. But I can guarantee he has something else planned. He doesn't do anything without a plan."

"You're sure it's a legal marriage license?"

"I don't know. He has it in his home in Mexico."

"We can request a copy from the Mexican government, but that'll take time," Gabby said. "Elliot can do it. If you want."

"No. Whatever Houghton is planning, I want to play it out. I think…I need to. I need to do something to get him out of my head." Mel's mouth trembled. "It took me months to forget him last time. This…this is going to be so much worse. I think I need to finish this to the end first."

"Oh, Mel. I *knew* something had happened eighteen months ago to hurt you. Something with a man." Gabby threw her arms around Mel and hugged her. Brynna reached for her sister's hand. "You'll get through this. We all will."

"I hope so. It took me months to get him out of my head last time. I'm…not sure I can go through that again."

Brynna thought of Chance and knew just exactly how Mel felt. She surprised the both of them when she threw her arms around her sister and hugged her as carefully as she could.

They were more than just hurting physically, weren't they?

Chapter 67

LACY TOOK CHARGE OF CLEANING Barratt's injury. She declared it needed stitches, so Jillian fetched the necessary supplies from the first aid kit in the bathroom.

"It's not the first time we've set stitches in this dining room," she said, holding out the sterile package.

Chance helped clear the table. Mel's and Brynna's plates were mostly uneaten. He gave them to the youngest sister, and she covered them.

"They'll be hungry in a little bit," the kid said. She was seventeen, wasn't she? Chance hadn't interacted with her much at all. How was she holding up under all of this? She'd had two sisters missing in less than a month—it was bound to scar a kid. Hell, she was no older than Sara had been.

"They'll be ok, Syd." Her eyes were darker than Brynna's, but they still had the soul-stealing super power that her sisters' did. When she was a few years older, she was going to be a real heartbreaker, just like the rest of the Beck sisters. "They're tough."

"I hope so. Thank you for bringing Mel back. For taking care of Brynna, too. I don't know what we'd do if you hadn't." She surprised him by hugging him quickly. "We're all glad you're here now."

He hugged her back. "I'm glad to be here, too."

And he meant that.

There wasn't anything he wouldn't do to protect this family. He needed answers, and the first place he could get them was right there in the dining room.

He walked back over to the table. Lacy was finishing setting a stitch in the man's lip. Kevin had done a good job of making his point. Lacy stood and pulled off the disposable gloves. "Well, I have to say, here in Beckville things are always interesting."

"Thank you," Baratt said.

"Well, you're welcome. I can't say it's nice to meet you. Not under these circumstances. Ironically, you're not the first man I've stitched together who was restrained at the time." She looked at the Ari. "You ready to take off?"

"I think so. Jillian, call if you need us again."

Jillian hugged the both of them. "Thanks, Ari. For you and Lacy making dinner. For getting Luc to help. It's appreciated by all of us."

"Anytime. I knew having an older brother would come in handy someday."

Chance waited until the two were gone and Syd was in her room before he nodded at his brother.

Elliot and Kevin pulled out chairs at the dining room table. "Barratt, we have a few questions." Elliot took the easy, businesslike tone.

Kevin was still glowering. He'd gone down the hall a few minutes earlier to check on his daughter. His expression had been even darker when he'd returned.

"I'm sure you do. Shouldn't Melody be in here when you ask them?"

Chance couldn't figure out the guy's tactic. What in the hell had he been thinking? "Why did you take Mel that way?"

"Melody and I have things to deal with between us. They've been there a lot longer than a month." His eyes narrowed. "I'd have married her eighteen months ago if she hadn't gotten spooked and run away like she did. Little rabbit. It has nothing to do with my father. That's all any of you need to know about that subject. The rest is up to her to tell."

"So why did you abduct my daughter?"

"I didn't think she'd cooperate, with everything that's happened."

"So why was it so important?" Chance asked. "Why did you marry her?"

"Someone *shot* at *her!* You weren't doing a good enough of job of protecting her!" Barratt's expression hardened. "My father is missing. There are people trying to kill Melody's sister. Someone shot at *her*. I can and will do the job so much better. Even if I have to hire a private army of my own to do it. I will protect her."

"You abducted her to protect her?" Kevin asked, incredulously.

"Somehow that seems backwards."

"You think so? Let me just say this. *If* my father is involved in this, the last woman on earth he'd ever let get hurt would be my wife. He wouldn't do that to me. And people will think twice about bothering her now. Because she is *mine*. Like I said, I would have married her months ago. If she hadn't run away after the first night we spent together."

Chance had to hand it to the guy. He had balls. Chance still had difficulty meeting Kevin's eyes when he thought of the things *he'd* done to one of Kevin's daughters. To boldly look at the man and say it aloud, that was either damned manipulative or damned ballsy.

Chance wasn't sure which.

"Have you heard from your father?" Kevin asked.

"No. None of my contacts have, either. I'm not convinced he's involved in this. At least not in the way you've implied. But I can't find him to confirm that. It's not like him not to have made contact for this long. We're…close. I generally speak with him daily. It's been almost three weeks."

"How do you think he's involved?"

"I think he's stumbled into something. And is trying to fix it somehow. It's the only thing that makes sense. Or he knows something about the key players. He's out there trying to evade them."

"Seems like your time would have been better spent searching for *him* rather than abducting my daughter. If I find out you hurt her or forced her in any other way, I'll probably come close to beating you to death."

"I didn't hurt her," Barratt said flatly. "I never would. I never will. She's my wife. I don't take that fact lightly. I meant the vows I said."

Chance thought he understood the man a bit better in that instant. Whatever was going on with his father was one thing; whatever was going on with Mel was an entirely different *thing*. And things had just gotten a bit more complicated for all of them.

"Pull the tape off him," Chance said. "He's not going to go anywhere. Not as long we have *his wife*."

Elliot pulled his pocketknife free and sliced through the tape. Then pulled it off of the other man completely. Barratt stood.

Stepped closer to Mel's dad. "I'll give you that one hit because of what happened. But…I'm going to be the one taking care of her from now on. You'd best get used to that. You're not getting rid of me. And neither is she."

Barratt stalked down the hall, straight to Mel's room. Where Brynna and Gabby still were.

Chance and Elliot were steps after him.

—

MEL was still talking when the door swung open again. Brynna was expecting to see her father or Jillian or Syd.

Not Houghton Barratt, followed by Chance and Elliot. She stood carefully. Now that some of the excitement was over, she was starting to feel the pain again. That, and it was time for more of the pain pills she'd been prescribed. Brynna stood, then stepped in front of her sister. She glared at Houghton Barratt. "What's he doing in here? He should go away. He's upsetting her."

"No, Bryn. I'll deal with him. You and Gabby go. *Finish* eating or get dessert or something." Mel stared at the man. "Go on. He's not going to hurt me. If he even tries, I'll yell and Dad can shoot him, ok?"

"You sure, Mel?" Elliot asked. The two of them were getting closer, too. Brynna had noticed that before. Almost like Mel and Jarrod, sometimes. Easy, friendly. Chance and Mel were more likely to snip and snap at each other, though.

It really felt like Chance and Elliot belonged around there. She ignored the pain that thought brought. As soon as this was finished, Chance was heading for the hills.

It wouldn't do for her to forget that. In spite of how he'd comforted her before.

Chance was not permanent.

Any more than her newest brother-in-law was.

"Gabby, you guys leaving?" Mel asked.

"We're going to stay another night, I think," Gabby said. "Elliot and your father are going to dig around in some of his old case files tonight. Brynna and I have some coding to do."

"Ok. We'll talk again later." Mel stood. Houghton Barratt didn't move.

Gabby wrapped her fingers around Brynna's and pulled her past the tall man and out into the hall.

Chance surprised her when he pulled the door shut behind them, leaving Mel and Houghton Barratt in her bedroom... alone.

"Why did you leave him in there?" she demanded.

"They have some things to figure out," Chance said. "We should give them the privacy to do it."

Chapter 68

WHATEVER WAS GOING ON in the room right next to the study, Barratt was probably enjoying it. Chance wasn't stupid—he knew exactly what was happening between Barratt and Mel right at that moment. He also knew they probably thought the rest of the house was sound asleep.

He should be. But the pullout couch in Kevin's study was damned uncomfortable.

Gabby and Elliot were on the other side of him in the guest room that he'd been informed had once been Syd's room. She'd moved upstairs to allow Mel to move downstairs after she'd been injured. Before that, the back room had been Jillian's. Syd had implied the four Beck daughters had traded rooms off and on for years. Just another way they had a history, a life together.

He hadn't missed the telltale giggles from Gabby a few hours earlier, either. Chance sighed as his body tightened. Even if he had been lucky enough to share a room with Brynna tonight, she was in no condition to do what his body was demanding. But he could have touched her, kissed her. Held her.

A door somewhere nearby creaked open. Soft footsteps sounded on the hardwood. Chance stood.

He even recognized her footsteps, didn't he? She was moving slower, but he knew. Chance followed her into the kitchen.

She was pulling open the cabinet when he stepped in. "Hungry? There's some type of ice cream plus pie. I think Jillian made it all."

"We do homemade ice cream. Dairy-free. For me. Everybody says they like it better, but I know the truth. I've seen Mel with Dairy Queen."

"They love you."

"I know. Can't you sleep?"

"No. Too many sounds."

She frowned. "What kind?"

"Let's just say, whatever is going on between your sister and Barratt, they are definitely still in the newlywed stage."

"Huh?"

He smiled. Sometimes the woman just did not get euphemisms. "Bryn, Barratt and your sister got a little loud while they were fooling around. Having sex."

"Sex? Seriously?" Her lips quirked. "And you had to listen?"

"I didn't have to. I'm out here, aren't I? And it's not like it's the first time tonight I heard someone getting lucky." He looked at the ceiling. "*Gabby* likes to giggle, apparently. Your dad needs to better insulate the interior walls of this place."

Brynna lost the battle with a full-blown laugh. She wiped at her eyes. "Gabby Giggles. I am so calling her that tomorrow. It'll flip her out."

"No. Then she'll look at me, and we'll both know what she was doing with my brother. I don't think I can handle that." He stepped closer to what dessert he truly wanted. Tonight's pajamas were little short and tank-top wisps of nothingness. Satin nothingness, actually. With tiny frogs printed on them. Where did she find them? Why did he find her nightclothes so damned alluring all the time?

"Bryn…"

"What?" She held the ice cream in her left hand.

"This." Chance took the container from her hand and tossed it into the sink. Then he had his hands around her waist and he was lifting her, oh, so gently. He hadn't forgotten how close he'd come to losing her. He put her right back on the kitchen island where he'd kissed her before. "You tempt me. I wish…I wish I was in your bed tonight. Just holding you."

"You can't be."

"I know. We both know why it wouldn't work."

"No. Not that. Jillian's in my room. In the spare bed. In case I needed her." She leaned her head down until her forehead touched his. For someone who supposedly didn't like to touch people, she didn't seem to mind when *he* touched her, did she?

"Kiss me, babe."

"Why? We can't do *anything* right now. And it wouldn't mean anything. I don't think I can do the no-strings thing anymore, Chance. I…changed in that rubble. I think I've grown up some. The *next* man I'm with, I'm going to hope it's forever. I'm not going to do no strings, anymore. I hope you understand…"

He did.

The next man wouldn't be him. He lifted her off the counter carefully. "Eat your ice cream, babe. I'm going outside to take a look around."

"Ok. Be careful. Chance?"

"Yes?" He looked at her and *knew* in that instant. If his family hadn't been killed, if his world hadn't changed so horribly ten years ago, *this* was the kind of woman he would have wanted for his own. Sweet, open, loving, so damned complicated.

"I'm sorry. If I hurt you. I don't mean to. But…I think this is for the best, don't you?"

Brynna, his Brynna. He'd give anything to be able to keep her. "Yeah. You're probably right. You're better off with someone else. I think we both know that."

He forced himself to step away.

That man she was with forever, it would not be him. He just hoped the guy knew what a lucky bastard he would be to get her.

Chapter 69

LACY HATED DARK PARKING lots, hated stupid men who thought that because they were in charge of something, it gave them a right to push others around—especially younger, more vulnerable women like Annie Gaines, who had never spoken a harsh word to anyone in their lives. Why did bullies always somehow find those who couldn't fight back?

She's spent most of her childhood—from the age of eight—defending herself with her fists, and anyone else she'd been close to at the time. She'd never been fortunate enough to find a foster home where she stuck for more than a year or two, but there almost always seemed to be younger kids around.

Lacy had been orphaned when her mother—a single mother of three—had been killed in a car wreck, along with Lacy's twin sisters, who had been too young to be in school at the time. She'd gone from being one of the Barrattville McGareths to being a foster kid in the middle of Finley Creek.

It had taken her nineteen years to get back to Barrattville, and the home that had once been her mother's parents'. It had nearly bankrupted her to buy the old two-hundred-acre ranch. But it was hers.

The house was barely livable—she *probably* shouldn't be living there, not with the holes in the living room floor and the toilet that leaned oddly to the left—but it was hers. The first place that had ever been *hers.*

Once she was finished, she hoped it would be as warm and inviting as the Becks'.

Jillian's dad had brought Jillian out a few times. He'd even taken it on himself to grab a piece of plywood from the old barn and patch the worst of the holes in her living room floor. He'd accepted a hug and a peck on the cheek as payment.

Kevin and the rest of the Becks were the closest thing to a real family she had had in almost ten years. She didn't take them lightly.

Jillian and Ari had helped her redo the one room in the house that was functional—her bedroom. They'd sanded and painted and tiled until they were so sore they could barely sit up long enough to eat pizza.

She and Jillian had been friends since before Jillian was old enough to drink—Ari had joined them when she'd transferred to Finley Creek University almost eight months earlier. She and Jillian had met in St. Louis—their older sisters were close friends—and had reconnected when Ari ended up in the same class as Jillian.

They just all seemed to *fit* each other well. She hated to see what was happening to Jillian's family now. The jerk she'd just finished arguing with had only added to the Beck family's problems recently.

Lanning was an asshole, and she was happy she'd told him that again. If it meant a suspension when she returned to the ER the next day for her shift…well, then so be it. Lacy would manage. She'd managed a heck of a lot worse before.

Someone called her name, and she turned around, expecting it to be Lanning again. He'd been a real pain in her ass—and most of the nursing staff and a third of the female physicians—from the very beginning. Ever since she'd told him she didn't date coworkers. At all. Never.

Dr. Logan Lanning did not take rejection well.

But it wasn't Lanning. It was some guy at least in his fifties, and in need of a good workout regimen.

"Yes?" she said, her hand going straight into her pocket where her cell phone waited. She wasn't stupid. Strange men in a dark parking lot could mean big trouble for a woman. She knew that. "Can I help you?"

"Yes, you can." He grinned at her, and Lacy started backing away. This guy meant no good, and every instinct she had was telling her to *run*. Fast.

She ran.

A dark sedan pulled out in front of her, blocking her exit. She screamed.

He wasn't alone.

The man's hands tangled in her hair, and he yanked, pulling her off of her feet.

And then the true hell began.

She screamed as he drove his knees into her kidneys, as he backhanded her so hard she thought her cheek had fractured.

He kept hitting and punching and doing whatever he could to hurt her. She couldn't fight him off, no matter how hard she tried. And she tried.

When she knew there was no hope, she did her damnedest to make sure that whoever found her would find *him*. She dug her nails in to the flesh on his arm and clung. She'd get his DNA, even while she died trying.

He leaned close to her and said something. He said it again and made her repeat it. His words were ones she would never forget.

If she lived.

The sedan's window rolled down, and the man inside spoke to the one looming over her. "Get in, now! The message has been delivered."

Someone shouted. He jerked away. "Don't forget. We know everything about you…and about them, bitch."

Someone shouted again. Lacy pried open her least injured eye. Lanning. It was Lanning.

She didn't know whether to laugh or cry.

She tried to curl up in a ball; it took every bit of strength she had. Her attacker dove toward the car just as the window rolled down again. He climbed into the back as a hand extended.

Lacy watched in horror as a gun fired, right over her head.

Lanning screamed and went down. Lacy closed her eyes, knowing she was going to be next.

Instead, the car drove away.

She forced herself to her knees, forced herself to crawl to Lanning's side.

She covered the hole in his stomach with her hands and prayed someone would find them soon.

Chapter 70

THE BRUISES DIDN'T DETRACT from how pretty Dr. McGareth actually was. Had he fully looked at the green-eyed blonde before? He honestly didn't think he had.

He'd been so consumed with his girl-woman that he hadn't noticed any other woman but her. That should tell him something, shouldn't it?

The doc's eyes opened, and she looked around. He leaned over her. "Lacy? It's ok. You're at the hospital."

She smiled ruefully. "I just can't seem to escape this place, can I? I'm starting to wish for a career change about now."

"Can you tell us what happened?" Foster asked. He leaned over the bed, opposite Chance.

"There was a man..." A bitterness slipped into her eyes. One that spoke of old hurts. "Isn't there always? Slaps. Fists. A knee to the kidneys. Just when you think you're safe again..."

Chance looked at Foster as a suspicion slipped into his head. Someone else had hurt this woman in the past, hadn't they?

She seemed to realize what she was revealing. "Anyway. I was walking to my car. I'd just finished arguing with Dr. Lanning about what had happened before. I decided to take the high road and walked away."

She shifted in the bed and grabbed her stomach. Foster had shared the medical report with him on the sly. She'd taken a few knees to the gut. A tap to the kidneys.

Her attacker had wanted her to *hurt*.

"What happened next, Lace?" Foster asked softly.

"Lanning followed me. But he was too late. This big guy. Probably in his late fifties. Rough. He attacked me. And he said..."

She looked at Chance. "He said, 'We know everything about the Becks. Those bitches will never be safe. We know where they are and who their friends are. See that their daddy gets the message.'"

"Can you describe this guy to a forensic artist?"

"I can do better. I...scratched him. Several times. I wanted his damned DNA. I made Dr. Jacobson swab my nails, boys. I dug in until I drew blood. After that...Lanning was there. The man shot him. I crawled to Lanning, tried to stop the bleeding. Samples are probably contaminated, though. With Lanning's blood."

"He's going to live, Lacy. Lanning will recover," Foster said. "I'll talk to Jacobson, track down the samples. You just rest. When you get out of here, do you have someplace you can go for a while?"

She shook her head. "No. Just the Becks. They're all I've got. Them and Ari. Keep them safe. Promise me."

"We will."

"She'll come with me," a female voice said from behind them. "I'm going to St. Louis. Luc and Paige are insisting."

Chance looked at Ari, who stood in the doorway. She was pale and frightened as she stepped up to her friend's bedside.

Hell, he understood it. He *never* would have expected those sons-of-bitches to go after Jillian's friend. But...Dr. McGareth had been on the fringes of the Beck family from the very beginning, hadn't she? She'd even sewn up Elliot after he'd been nicked when they'd been shot at in the hospital parking lot. And they had the Beck family on total lockdown right now.

Bastard couldn't get to one of the Becks, so he'd gone after who he could.

"When are you getting out of here?" Chance asked Lacy. "How soon?"

"This afternoon, I think. Nothing he did caused major damage. Just hurts like hell. Help me sit up. I can't lay around here like this all day. I'll go mad." She reached for Chance's hand.

He helped her sit up. Hell, she was in the same damned room Brynna had been in—both times. Might as well rename it the Beck room.

She wasn't a Beck, but she was damned close. "I'll get the son-of-a-bitch, Lacy. When I do, you can have a turn knocking his balls into his throat."

"I'll take you up on that."

Chapter 71

DANIEL MCKELLEN WAS A couple of years or so older than Chance, and a couple of inches shorter. He was hard, tough, and damned good at his job.

People listened to the other man. Chance had to respect that. But the guy didn't need to be panting over someone like Brynna. Didn't he understand that?

This was the first time Chance had ever had to talk to the guy professionally. What he wanted to do was demand the guy leave Brynna alone. Stay far away from her.

He knew he was being completely unreasonable. If she wanted McKellen, he had no doubt the other guy would be able to take care of her. Protect her. Hell, probably better than Chance could. Guy had an entire department of fiercely loyal detectives he could command to keep one redheaded girl-woman and her family safe if needed.

He was almost as good as Elliot.

"I've put a rush on the DNA sample," Elliot said from behind his desk. McKellen and Chance were in the chairs opposite the desk that Chance's father had once occupied. The office was starting to feel like Elliot, wasn't it?

His brother hadn't been chief long, but he saw touches that reminded him of his brother. There were framed commendations on the wall. A few photos. He wasn't surprised to see one of Gabby on the edge of his brother's desk.

Once his brother made a life-altering decision, the guy went all in. There was an even smaller photo of the entire Beck family on a shelf behind Elliot's chair. Gabby was at the center of it. It was a fairly recent photo—and had a few of the fringe members like Lacy and Ari and Foster included. Elliot was embracing his new position with the Becks fully, wasn't he? He'd envied his brother before, but never more than now. Elliot was far braver than Chance ever would be.

"She's also given a sketch artist enough details." Elliot passed a photocopied sketch to Chance.

He swore. "That's the bastard who cut Brynna, both times."

"How is she this morning?" McKellen asked softly. Asked Chance.

There was significance in that, and all three men knew it. McKellen was stepping aside, giving Chance a clear path to the woman they both wanted.

All he had to do was step up and take it.

"She's upset over Dr. McGareth. And worried. About every friend she has, especially Gabby. And worried about her sisters." Chance thought of how quiet and subdued she had been that morning before he'd left. "I don't know how much longer she can handle this."

"She's stronger than people realize," McKellen said. There was a look in his eyes that Chance recognized. McKellen wasn't just attracted to Brynna, was he?

It went deeper than that.

He understood the hurt the guy had to be feeling right then. No one involved in this ordeal had missed that Chance and Brynna had been intimate. That there were feelings between them. McKellen, included.

Too many people were getting hurt because of this.

"She is." Chance looked at his brother. "I want to focus on finding *this* guy. I promised Brynna I would. But I also promised her I would find Russell's missing daughter, somehow. I can't do both."

"I'll do it. I'll find Russell's daughter. We need to be honest here; we're probably looking for her remains. I doubt they've kept her alive this long," McKellen said.

"We estimate she's been missing seven to eight days. She *may* be alive, but the odds aren't high," Elliot said.

"She didn't deserve this. No matter what her father did."

"No, she didn't," McKellen said. "I'll get Foster on it. He's the best I have. I'll work with him myself. If I have permission from this office."

"You have it. Don't even have to ask," Elliot said. "Just find that girl."

—

CHANCE left Elliot's office and drove back to the Beck house. He had to go through two secure checkpoints to get back on their street.

His brother's doing, he knew. Elliot and Gabby had agreed that it was too difficult—and cost too many resources—for the TSP to secure two separate locations. They'd agreed to stay at the Becks for the duration.

He found Gabby and Brynna in the midst of their family. They were watching the action between Mel and the billionaire who'd followed her home.

"What's going on?" Chance asked Gabby as he took the bar stool next to her.

"He is angry that Lacy was attacked and by the message sent. He wants Mel—all of us—to move in with him. He says we can't trust the TSP at all." Brynna was the one who answered. She sat on the stool next to Gabby's. Chance leaned forward to take a look at her. "He says he has armed guards and will hire more if necessary."

"Hell, how do we know we can trust him?" Chance looked at the other man. Barratt looked more screwed up than he had last time. Guy's hair was a mess and his cheeks flushed. His shirt sleeves were unbuttoned and rolled halfway up. His tie hung loose.

"Damn it, Melody! Why do you have to be so damned stubborn?" Barratt yelled. "Can't you see that I want you *safe?*"

"Can't you see that I make my own decisions?" she yelled right back at him.

Chance studied the two of them—they were yelling at each other, all right. But they were also both *touching* each other. He had his hands on her waist. Hers were pushed against his chest.

They looked like they belonged together, didn't they?

He could have told Barratt to save his breath. Mel Beck was just as stubborn as her sister. He hadn't been able to stop Brynna from doing what she wanted yet. Why should Barratt and Mel be any different?

Kevin was carefully watching the discussion, his distrust for his new son-in-law plain on his face. But Chance knew the older man would only interfere if he thought it was necessary. Kevin apparently believed in letting his daughters live their own lives. Chance respected that.

Still. He couldn't blame the guy for trying. Barratt cared for Mel, and he wanted her safe. What could be so wrong in that?

Except that one of the men she needed protected from was Barratt's own father.

How much of what Junior was saying was real, and how much of it was just an act to throw them all off his father's trail?

They continued to yell at each other for a long while. Finally, Kevin stepped between them. "Enough, Barratt. Mel, go call your sister. See if you girls can stay in St. Louis for a while."

"All of us," Mel said pointedly.

"Luc said we can all stay with him." A voice came from the living room.

Chance hadn't even realized Ari and Lacy were there yet.

"My wife stay with *Davis Lucas*? No way," Barratt said. "She stays with me."

"*She* makes her own decisions." Mel shoved him lightly. Barratt still had a hold of her waist. All she managed to do was unbalance herself.

Her father reached for her, but Barratt's hands stopped him.

He lifted his wife straight off her feet until they were eye to eye. "I just want you safe, Melody. You know that."

Chance heard Gabby's *ahh* next to him. He snorted. Barratt was playing all of them, wasn't he?

"Houghton, I'll go to St. Louis with the rest of my family. But I'm not coming to your house. Not now."

"Not ever, you mean? You can't hide from me forever, little one. You know that." Barratt leaned closer and said something Chance didn't catch. But she nodded, then dropped her head to the tall man's chest.

Everyone looked away to give them a moment of privacy, except Brynna, who Chance couldn't help but watch.

She stared at her sister, puzzled. When she looked up, her eyes met Chance's.

That's when it sank in. The Becks were going to St. Louis.

Brynna was leaving.

And Chance was staying behind. Without her.

Chapter 72

CHANCE AND ELLIOT WENT back to the home they'd grown up in after they'd watched Gabby and Brynna and the rest of the Becks, plus Ari and Lacy, board the private jet that belonged to Lucas Industries.

Lucas had sent it to fetch his younger sister and whomever else wanted to spend some time in St. Louis.

He'd wanted to hold Brynna one more time before she left, but he'd forced himself to be content with just telling her goodbye and to stay safe up there.

She'd adjusted her sunglasses and nodded at him. "You, too. I know you're going to hunt for that man. Don't do anything reckless. And...keep Elliot safe for Gabby. And can you check on Houghton for Mel sometimes? I think she really does love him."

"He loves *her*." And Barratt was prowling around the tarmac behind them all. He'd carried Mel up the steps into the belly of the plane over her objections. After kissing the hell out of her.

The guy was seriously unhappy about his wife leaving Texas.

Chance never thought he'd empathize with Houghton Barratt, but he did.

He didn't want Brynna to leave, either.

That was why he forced himself to step away from her before he grabbed her and kissed the hell out of *her*.

Gabby was going, too. And Elliot looked just as sick about it as Barratt did Mel.

They were pitiful. Pathetic. Weren't they? All three of them.

As he watched Brynna climb into the plane after Gabby and before her father, an image flashed into his mind.

His father's eyes when Chance's mother had been killed right before him.

The devastation and loss, the torture the man had felt. It was enough to have Chance's resolve strengthening. Better now, than later, right?

He turned to his brother and Barratt. "They'll be safer in St. Louis. Lucas has the guards and resources to see to it. Here, they were just in more danger."

"Yes," Elliot said. "But watching her walk away...I didn't think it would hurt quite this much."

"I know." Barratt said it at the exact same time as Chance.

Chance felt his heart lurch out of his chest when the plane disappeared into the clouds a few minutes later.

He felt like he'd lost Brynna forever.

It was just a glimpse of what his future looked like, wasn't it?

He'd better get used to it.

Chapter 73

SHE WATCHED HIM FROM the window. Brynna knew it was pitiful, wasn't it?

Or at least she thought it was, until she looked at her older sister, who sat across from her, her forehead pressed against her own window. Until Gabby leaned around Brynna to take a peek herself.

"We. Are. Pathetic," Mel said, almost under her breath. "Look at us? A month ago, we were doing just fine, and now…"

"Well, we've all been through a lot in the last month." Gabby waved once. "A *lot* has changed. We've changed. Haven't we?"

"You know they probably can't see you, right?" Brynna asked, adjusting her earbuds. Mel had bought her a new player while she'd been in the hospital—the second time.

"I know. But I can still see Elliot." Gabby's sigh was long. "I didn't want to leave him."

"I know." And Brynna did. She hadn't wanted to leave Chance, either.

But then again, she had. She needed the space of several states between them in order to figure out what her future held. And what she wanted from her life.

Her father sank down in the seat next to Mel. "I know this seems like the end of the world, girls. But it isn't. And leaving Finley Creek is the best thing, right now. Being safe has to trump everything."

Brynna nodded. She knew the logic. She *always* knew the logical answer, didn't she? But it didn't erase the hurt. Or the belief that when it was finally safe for her to return to Finley Creek, Chance Marshall would be long gone. Out of her life forever.

Off chasing his next set of bad guys, leaving her behind with nothing but her computers…

Nothing but her computers *and* her family.

Her family—her one true constant. She looked at the people on the plane with her. Her family. At least she had them.

St. Louis would keep *them* safe. So that was exactly where she needed, wanted, to be.

She'd just have to forget that she'd left a part of herself behind in Finley Creek.

Chapter 74

CHANCE MISSED HER FROM the moment he opened his eyes in the morning until the time he closed them at night. He wasn't too proud to admit it—at least to himself.

His brother didn't help matters. Every time they spoke, Elliot made a point of telling him how Brynna was holding up. That it wasn't going well for her up in St. Louis brought a physical ache to his gut.

He felt like he'd cut out his lungs and tossed them aside like they had never mattered.

Strings? Hell, yeah, there were strings. And they tied him up all neat and tidy and tighter than he ever would have imagined.

The DNA samples from Lacy's fingernails had come back to two people, Dr. Logan Lanning…and a convicted offender named Charles Raymund.

Elliot had ordered Major Crimes to head up the search. Chance had wanted in on that, but his brother had told him that if he screwed it up somehow, Raymund could walk.

He hadn't liked it, but there were still other men out there responsible. And he'd *find* them. In the meantime, Elliot had Erickson and Journey searching out whatever they could find in Raymund's past to connect him to Chance's father—or anyone involved that they had identified. Somehow. It was just a matter of time.

Daniel McKellen and some of his people in Major Crimes found Alyssia Russell. Chance had been with Elliot when his brother got *that* call.

Against all odds, the girl had been found alive, fifty miles west of little Garrity, Texas. Elliot was familiar with the area, and he'd told Chance Alyssia was lucky she hadn't fallen in a damned ravine and been lost forever.

As it was, she had been in a coma when she'd been found

by one of the men who had previously worked for Elliot when he'd been head of the Garrity post.

She hadn't woken in that time, and it was going on almost a month since she'd been found.

There would be no help from her in identifying the men responsible. Chance was just grateful the girl had been found alive.

The doctors were cautiously optimistic that she would wake as soon as her body healed. Her family had *hope,* at least.

Chapter 75

GOLDEN BOY SENT HIM to St.-*fucking*-Louis after Beck's damned daughters. It was damned cold in Missouri this time of year.

It took him weeks to find where the girls were staying, and it had been Golden Boy who told him how to do it.

That still rankled. No one had ever gotten away from him like that before.

He had never had a girl escape him, not in the thirty-six years he'd been hunting them. Never.

That Beck's daughter had managed it still pissed him off. The girl was racking up marks against her daily. Marks he would be taking back from her damned flesh.

And he wanted to watch her pay. He'd even thought of videotaping what he would do to her so that he could rewatch. But he'd never taped a woman during the act before. Maybe he would tape her and then tape one of her sisters when he had *her* beneath him.

Kevin Beck *owed* him his daughters for the trouble they had put him through recently.

Beck's oldest daughter was right there in front of him, carrying groceries into an artsy-looking apartment building that was far out of *his* price range. Golden Boy had given him the address.

He'd been watching it for days. Waiting.

Finally, though, there they were.

The crippled one, the autistic one, and that damned blonde who'd caused them so much trouble. Too bad the orange-haired one and that blonde hadn't died in the explosion like they were supposed to.

They had their bags with them. Like they were going to stay a while.

He knew exactly where they were now. All he had to do

was wait for Golden Boy's signal.

Then he'd have that orange-haired little bitch all to himself. After that, he'd plan which one of Beck's daughters to go after *next.*

It was almost time.

Chapter 76

THERE WAS NOTHING BRYNNA despised more than being sick to her stomach. Twice in four hours, she'd found herself bent over the toilet in Carrie's spare bathroom, losing what little food she'd managed to hold down.

Not exactly an auspicious beginning to her day.

"Are you ok?" Carrie stepped into the bathroom the second time and handed Brynna a wet washcloth. "You look green. I never really understood that expression until I was pregnant."

"I'm not pregnant."

"No." Carrie stared at her for a moment. "I didn't think you were. Unless you are. You're not? You're sure? But...you are sick to your stomach, aren't you? Do you have a fever?"

"No." She felt perfectly fine, other than the inability to keep her stomach in control. "I think...I think it's stress. Jillian gets cramps when she's stressed. Guess I am now, too."

"Probably. You'll get through this, Bryn. I promise. I've seen lots of this kind of stuff. People get through, and then they're ok in the end. Look what happened to me. To Dan."

Brynna nodded. Minton Rush, her father's old partner, had tried to kill Carrie before they had met. Carrie's friend, Dan Reynolds, had stepped in front of Brynna's dad when Minton tried to shoot him.

Dan had recovered fully and remarried. He now had seven kids. The middle one, his daughter Gracie, was a good friend of Syd's. They hung out together whenever Syd was in St. Louis and spoke online all the time. Syd was with the Reynolds' family now.

"Yes. Thank you. For letting us stay here." Well, for letting *her* and Mel and Gabby stay there. Jillian was still out at Luc's with Ari and Lacy. He had a mansion built out of shipping containers that Brynna found fascinating. "Me and Mel and Gabby."

"You're my little sisters. Well, you and Mel are. And I like Gabby. You can stay with me forever. I...I never thought I'd ever have anyone other than Paige. Now I have Sebastian and Maddie, and Paige's family—and you, Mel, Syd, Jillian, and a real father. I want you all with me as much as possible." Carrie's eyes suddenly filled and she grabbed some toilet tissue and wiped at them. "I'm sorry. I'm feeling a little extra weepy again. I was the same way when I was pregnant with Maddie."

Pregnant. There was that word again. "Pregnant."

"Yep. We were going to wait a while, but..." Carrie smiled again. "I'm going to have another baby in April, Bryn. I told Dad last night. Now I'm telling *you*."

Brynna felt her own eyes fill. "Wow. That's...that's wonderful, Carrie. Just wonderful."

That was the moment Brynna started to feel like maybe Carrie was right. Maybe they would find *normal* again.

—

THEY went over to the Lucas compound—as Sebastian called it—for dinner with the rest of the Finley Creek refugees, as Luc had taken to calling *them*. Paige's husband was there, and he had his sister Al and *her* husband with him. Al's husband was Sebastian's brother. Their other brother was there with *his* wife and children, too.

It was very complicated. But Brynna enjoyed it. Mostly. It reminded her of a crowded Beck family dinner when all of her cousins and her two uncles would show up. She had two female cousins a little younger than Mel, and eight male cousins who were all older.

Whenever they would all get together it would be chaos. Although *Carrie* was the only Beck to have a child, yet.

Everyone was all excited by Carrie's big news.

It was loud and chaotic and more than Brynna could handle right then.

She waited until dinner was over then crept out of the main family room and found a quiet corner in the library. There was an old rocking chair there that she'd sat in before. It overlooked the back of the property. She could see a part of the St. Louis arch in the distance, and it was a painful reminder that she *was not* at home.

She knew what the problem was. What she was missing.

Carrie had Sebastian. Paige had her husband Mick. Al had Seth. Couples.

They laughed together, touched each other. Even kissed each other sometimes when they had quiet moments when they thought no one was looking.

Gabby spent most of her free time on the phone with Elliot. Even Mel had spoken with Houghton once or twice.

She'd never been jealous of her best friend and sister before and she wasn't about to start now.

But Gabby *had* Elliot. Somehow, Elliot had overcome his past—the same exact past as Chance, damn it—and made room in his life for Gabby.

But other than the Cheerios incident, complete with that scorching kiss, he had said and done *nothing* to her.

As far as he was concerned, whatever had been between them was over. Brynna was ok with that. She'd told herself that over and over again. She did not *need* Chance Marshall.

But she sure did miss him. Why else did she suddenly feel like crying?

It was one thing when they were in the same state and she had the possibility of seeing him. Of snipping at him.

Of being stupid and pitiful and pathetic. That's what she was being.

He did not want strings with *her.*

And that was all there was to it.

She had to just find a way to deal with the fact that all she wanted in the world was the kind of strings her sister Carrie had.

"Bryn?"

She recognized her slightly younger sister's voice and turned. Jillian stood just in the door of the library. "Hey."

"I wondered where you'd gotten to."

"It was just…loud in there. And the smell of the food was getting to me. I've had an upset stomach all day."

"Carrie mentioned it." Jillian took the chair opposite Brynna's. "Are you ok? I know something is bothering you."

"I want to go *home.* I like it here, but I want home."

"Let's be honest. You want *him.*"

She thought about lying, but Brynna made a point of trying to tell the truth to her family. As much as humanly possible anyway. "We agreed that whatever happened between us in that stupid cellar was just sex. Something to pass the time. To celebrate that we were still alive. I *never* wanted something more than that, Jillian. And he doesn't either. Doesn't either. But…but…but…"

"But it hurts that you're not with him?"

"When I was in that stupid explosion, all I could think about was seeing him again. Seeing him. Well…and telling you all that I love you. Because I love you all very, very much. But *he* was in my head, too. And now? It's been weeks, and I can't get him *out!*"

—

JILLIAN coaxed her back to the rest of the party. There were kids and babies everywhere.

Brynna scooped up her niece and snuggled her close. There was no kid on earth more special to her than the little dark-haired girl whose eyes were the exact same shape and shade as her own.

Talk turned to the FBI as it inevitably did with her sister and her friends. Brynna was used to it. A lot of her and Mel's and Gabby's conversations centered on the TSP.

Brynna still needed to decide if she was ever going to return to the TSP.

Gabby wasn't. She'd decided it would be best for Elliot's career if she didn't return. And her friend had been honest. The TSP was just a place to hide from life. Gabby wasn't going to do that anymore. She was going to work with Brynna on the coding and work on getting Anne Marshall's cookbooks republished. Everything had fallen in place for Gabby, and Brynna was thrilled for her friend.

But she still had to decide what she wanted to do with her life.

Someone leaned over her chair, and Brynna shifted her niece to the left so she could see him better. He was tall—at least as tall as Houghton Barratt—and dark-eyed. He looked like his sisters, Ari and Paige, though they were considerably paler. "Have a few minutes to talk computers?"

"Of course." She passed Maddie to Syd, then stood. She followed Luc into his home office.

She liked this man, a lot. And his wife was one of the nicest people Brynna had ever met. The conversation went about the way she suspected it would. But the figure he named was twenty-five percent higher than she'd even begun to hope for.

And he had the paperwork all nice and prepared, courtesy of his assistant. It was just a matter of agreeing to his terms and signing on the dotted line.

He arranged the payment and contracts and suggested she forward everything to an attorney of her choosing. She'd have to meet with him one more time within the next six weeks, and then it was over.

Her first goal was met.

And she'd have the money to buy the house she'd always wanted within two months.

It was finished.

So why did she feel so empty?

Chapter 77

AFTER THE FIFTH DAY OF LOSING every bit of food she tried, Brynna gave in to Mel's badgering. She let Carrie make her a doctor's appointment with her family physician the next day.

Mel took care of everything, including borrowing a car to drive her. Gabby stayed with Jillian and the others—she and Carrie were working on some of Carrie's own software to increase audio manipulation ability. Gabby was stronger with audio than Brynna, and they both knew it.

And Brynna was too tired to even think about working, on anything.

The doctor's office was the same as any other Brynna had ever been in, except there was a nice fish tank in one corner. They took seats near the tank, and she kept herself calm by counting the number of fish. Eight.

It didn't take long. Still, the movement of the fish was enough to help her forget for a little bit that she was once again at the doctor's office.

"Bryn? You ok?" Mel asked. She had a magazine in her hand and was flipping through the articles. Brynna read the headlines quickly. It was pregnancy related, wasn't it?

"Yes. Why here? Is this a gynecologist's office?" The one thing worse than a doctor was a gynecologist. Brynna tried to hide the revulsion.

"I think so. But it's who Carrie uses for general practice. I think there's multiple partners in here." Mel smiled. "You'll be ok. Look the walls are blue. Not yellow."

Brynna maturely kept her eyes from crossing and her tongue from sticking out at her older sister. Mel hadn't had to bring her today. She could have found her own way.

But she hadn't had to. Her sister had been there when she needed her—like always.

Sudden tears hit her eyes. "I love you, Mel. Thank you for bringing me today."

Mel's eyes widened, and she leaned closer. "Uh…you ok?"

"Fine. Fine. Just love you."

"I love you, too." Mel looked up when Brynna's name was called. "You want me to go in with you?"

Brynna considered it; she did. But…she was a full-grown woman. Time she acted like it. "No. I'm ok. I'm ok. I'll do this by myself."

—

THIRTY minutes later, she wished she had told her sister to come with her. Having Mel there would make *this* seem less confusing.

"Pregnant."

"Yes. At least six weeks, from what your hormone levels are. Everything looks healthy, although from what you've told me you've been through recently, we'll need to keep a close eye on everything for quite a while. You're underweight, and I suspect vitamin deficient. Do you have someone at home who can help you through this?"

Brynna just stared at the doctor for a long time. "Yes. My sister is almost a nurse practitioner. Almost. She has another semester or so. She works as a registered nurse."

"You live together?"

"Yes. All my sisters but one. We live together. In Texas. We are staying here for a little while. Until they catch the men trying to kill us."

The doctor's eyes widened and she leaned forward. "Are you in some sort of trouble, Brynna? Do you need me to call someone for you? The Missouri State Police?"

"No. It's not like that. My…the men who hurt me before. They haven't *all* been caught yet. But…but…but…the father of my baby…" She swallowed. "The father of my baby and the baby's uncle are with the Texas State Police. They are searching now. While my family stays safe *here*."

The doctor didn't understand, and Brynna was far too upset to make her. There was a baby. She and Chance had made a baby. "How is this possible? It was only eight times. And we used condoms every time. Every time. Every time. We were careful. I have goals for my life. I'm not old enough for children yet. I…I…I…"

The doctor leaned forward. "I can give you information about all of your options. Termination is still possible. And there is adoption. Or assistance programs if you decide to keep the baby. My receptionist can give you all of that."

"No! I am keeping my baby." Brynna looked at the doctor like the woman was crazy. "My baby. Mine and Chance's."

She was keeping her baby. Of that, she was absolutely certain.

"Is there someone with you today? Someone who can see you get back to where you're staying safely?"

"Yes. Mel. My older sister. She always drives me places. She's in the waiting room."

"Good. Do you have any other questions today?"

No. Any questions she had, she'd have Jillian or Lacy to answer them, wouldn't she? *They* would understand what she meant far easier than this doctor that was looking at her like that. Like she was crazy or incapable of doing this or something. "No. I'm ok. I need to go though. I have a lot of thinking to do now."

She needed to get out of there. Needed Mel. Needed to be alone where she could sit down and *think*, decide exactly what it was that she needed to do.

She and Chance had made a *baby*. The biggest *string* of all.

How was she going to tell him?

Chapter 78

MEL KNEW WHATEVER BRYNNA had learned had rattled her sister to the core. Brynna hadn't said a word when she'd stepped back into the waiting room. Her sister was pale and…looked broken and confused. Hurting. She walked at Brynna's side, not speaking. Mel took a quick look at the pamphlets Brynna clutched like a lifeline.

The glossy papers were crumpled, but one headline jumped out at her. *Nutrition during Pregnancy.*

Holy shit. Mel's eyes widened, and she nearly fell over. *No. No way. The fates wouldn't be that cruel to Brynna. Not now.* A baby would be the last thing Brynna needed right now, wouldn't it?

Their borrowed SUV was half a block away. Should she ask? Before they reached the car, a man crossed the sidewalk right in front of them.

His foot caught on Mel's crutch, sending her stumbling slightly. His hand wrapped around her free arm.

"Sorry. Didn't mean to trip you up."

"It's ok. Happens to me all the time. Should see me when I roller-skate…," Mel said, almost automatically. She barely looked at him, so focused on her little sister as she was.

He turned, slightly blocking Mel's path to the driver's side. She murmured a low "Excuse me," but he didn't move right away. Not until she looked right into his face.

"I'm sorry." He stepped aside, and Mel slipped around him carefully.

Brynna still hadn't said a word.

Chapter 79

IT WAS FAR TOO EASY TO do. He'd walked right up to the bitches, and the crippled one had looked right at him. Hadn't recognized him at all. Her orange-haired sister hadn't even bothered looking at him. If she had, would she have even known who he was?

What was her deal? He stared at her as she stood by her sister's car. He recognized the expression on her face—it was one he loved making his girls have. Shock. Confusion. Pain. It was all right there for him to see. Interesting. What was wrong with the bitch?

They'd come out of a doctor's office, and he looked over his shoulder at the sign. Obstetrics and gynecology. Was the girl *pregnant*?

If she was, it had to be Marshall's baby, didn't it?

Marshall, who hadn't been near her in weeks. Had the bastard screwed her and abandoned her, then? Oh, he'd thought better of the Marshall brothers, hadn't he?

Weren't they supposed to be good and honorable and all that other shit, like the news reports had said whenever the Marshall murders were brought up? Both had chosen law enforcement, were supposed to be damned heroes, weren't they?

Not the type to knock up his girlfriend and take off. He laughed.

When the sister pulled the car out into the traffic, he followed.

He wasn't supposed to hurt the damned bitches now. But that didn't mean he couldn't have a bit of fun, did it?

Hitting the gas, he sped up until his front bumper was close enough to do what he wanted to do.

Chapter 80

BRYNNA COVERED HER stomach with both hands as the half-ton truck bumped into the back bumper of the SUV Mel had borrowed from Luc for the duration of their stay in the city.

"Bryn, I want you to tighten your seatbelt. And reach back, grab that sweatshirt. Put it over your stomach, under the lap belt, ok? Right over where you were just hurt. And I want you to hold on."

Brynna hurriedly complied.

The truck came closer. Brynna murmured a small prayer.

Mel muttered a curse instead. She jerked the wheel, sending the SUV onto the shoulder. The truck missed their rear bumper by millimeters. Mel didn't hesitate—she threw the SUV into reverse and turned it back onto the highway. She gunned it in the opposite direction. Brynna looked over her shoulder.

She could see the truck flying up on their tail again. "Mel! He's coming back."

"And he's got a bigger engine. Well, we're Becks—that means we are smarter, doesn't it? Grab my phone. Call 911."

Brynna reached for the phone. She dropped it when they were bumped again. "The phone!"

"No! Don't reach for it. Tighten your belt over your baby, Bryn. Do it now. I'll get us all out of this." She sped up. Brynna closed her eyes, her hands tight over her stomach.

The baby. *Her* baby. She didn't want anything to happen to her baby. "Mel, I'm scared."

"Me, too."

The truck was getting closer. Closer.

"Someone's coming up behind us."

Brynna looked over her shoulder. A black sports car was speeding up the highway. Where were all the other cars? It was the middle of the afternoon. There should have been other cars, right?

But then again, the attack had lasted only seconds. Maybe two minutes, at most, right?

It just seemed like forever.

Mel waited until the sports car had almost caught up to them, then she jerked the SUV toward the side of the road again.

The truck caught them and sent them spinning into the guardrail.

Brynna screamed.

The sports car squealed to a halt beside them. Two men got out—with guns they aimed toward the now fleeing truck.

A second SUV was there within moments.

Two men ran toward their SUV. Brynna tried not to freak—it was too much like the first time with Chance.

"Mrs. Barratt, Mrs. Barratt. Are you or your sister hurt?" one of the men called.

Mel had a gun in her hand. Brynna pulled in her breath. Why did that surprise her?

"Who are you?" Mel asked the men as they got closer.

"Charlie Ortega, ma'am. Mr. Barratt assigned the four of us to protect you. We were cut off at the last traffic light. Are either of you hurt?"

"My sister needs to go to the ER. Do you have ID?"

"Of course."

Mel took it and studied it. It had the Barratt-Handley logo on the corner of the ID. "You were there in Mexico when I was, weren't you?"

"Yes, ma'am. I've been working for your husband for eight years now. I...uh...bought your wedding dress. And your new crutch."

When Mel was satisfied, she put her gun away. "I'm going to take my sister to the ER now."

"Ma'am, if you would allow Brighton to handle your vehicle? I would feel more secure if you'd ride with Jimmy in the Denali."

Mel looked at the second man. "You were in Mexico, too, weren't you? The driver?"

"Yes, ma'am. I drive Mr. Barratt everywhere."

"So why are you here and not with Houghton?"

The man seemed surprised. "Because Mr. Barratt wants

only the best watching over you."

Mel's shoulders slumped. "We'd be glad to accept a ride. I'm…I'm not really in the mood to drive for the moment. And I want Brynna to get looked at."

One of the men helped Mel from the car. Brynna had to climb over the gear shift and console to follow her sister out. Her door was bent too badly and was jammed against the guardrail.

Just how close it had been sank in, and she fought off a full-blown Gabby-worthy panic attack.

It had been too close.

Her hand covered her baby.

For all of them.

Chapter 81

BRYNNA WAS SHAKING when Houghton's bodyguards dropped her and Mel off at the front door to Luc's mansion. They'd spent the last two hours at the ER, waiting for her to get examined. The doctors hadn't told her much. They'd told her everything seemed fine.

They'd done her first ultrasound. She'd seen the heartbeat. Seen the proof that the baby was real had overshadowed everything else—and *almost* erased the awkwardness over the vaginal ultrasound.

She'd carefully tucked the small photos into the backpack that went with her sister everywhere. She'd also, for the first time in her adult life, sworn her big sister to complete secrecy.

She'd told Mel the truth—Chance should learn of the baby before anyone else. It was only the right thing to do, after all.

Mel had agreed.

She'd held Brynna's hand through everything. And had been there when they'd found the tiny little black blip on the ultrasound machine.

It was her baby. Hers and Chance's. And it was real. Mel had seen it, too.

And then got all gushy-eyed. All happy for Brynna. Worried, but happy. Excited. Just like Brynna was starting to be.

It was *real*. Real.

And someone had almost killed them all that afternoon.

What was she going to do about it?

She and Mel had also discussed how they were going to tell their family about what had happened.

They both knew the truth—somehow someone had followed them from Finley Creek to St. Louis. And knew enough about them to find them at Carrie's. To follow them to the doctor's office.

But who? Brynna had tried and tried, but no one stood out.

Not even the man Mel said had almost tripped her on the sidewalk.

Brynna had still been confused by the doctor's words. She hadn't even *seen* a man near her sister, had she?

But Mel said he'd looked right at her.

Had it been him? What were they going to do now?

Chapter 82

BRYNNA HAD KICKED OFF her blankets, like she always did at night. The sight of something so normal had Mel breathing again. Had her moving past *some* of the shock she'd just experienced. Mel moved as fast as she could through the apartment she, Brynna, and Gabby had borrowed from Carrie. She checked on them, starting with her sister.

Gabby was snuggled under at least two blankets, her head barely visible on the pillow.

They were safe. The fear that Handley Barratt had harmed them terrified her—but they both still slept.

It hadn't been a dream. She *had* woken up to see her father-in-law looming over her bed.

She stepped back out into the living room. The apartment was the largest in Carrie's building—her sister owned nine units plus the huge loft that she and her family lived in—and had three bedrooms. Mel sank to the chair. Thank God. She'd been so afraid when she woke and Handley Barratt and two of his bodyguards were leaning over her. She'd honestly thought the older man was there to kill her and then take out Brynna and Gabby.

Why? Was it just because of what his son had done? Was he trying to confuse everything they knew by throwing false information their way through her? It made a cagey kind of sense.

She pulled her phone free and dialed her brother-in-law quickly. Sebastian would double the guards on them and she knew it. He'd be far more effective at keeping Brynna and Gabby safe than she would.Handley Barratt had gotten into her bedroom. She'd never felt more vulnerable in her life.It was his father that had terrified her so badly, so why was she wanting Houghton so badly?

She called *her* father instead.

Chapter 83

IT WAS THREE A.M. WHEN someone pounded on the door to the apartment she and Gabby and Mel were sharing on the floor directly below Carrie and Sebastian's loft. Mel answered it quickly. Brynna half thought her sister had been awake.

It took her a moment to focus on the gun in her sister's hand. And the one in Sebastian's.

Her brother-in-law stepped into the apartment. "Mel?"

"Handley Barratt and two of his bodyguards were in my room less than three minutes ago," Mel said. "He wanted to *talk*."

Sebastian swore. "Damn it, Mel."

"Tell me about it. I opened my eyes, and they were there."

Sebastian looked at Brynna and Gabby. "Did you two see anything? Hear anything?"

Gabby shook her head, obviously freaked. Brynna waited for her friend to have a total meltdown. But she didn't. Gabby held herself together somehow.

She was doing a better job than Brynna was, that was for sure. "What did he want?"

"To talk. He mentioned being there the night Brynna was born." Mel's voice broke. Brynna's attention sharpened on her sister.

Mel was shaking, wasn't she? Scared. Why did it always surprise her when something scared Mel? "Why?"

"He said…he said he paid someone off the night Brynna was born. There had been a murder, and he was there to talk to the victim, but he was too late. Dad…Dad was there, but had to leave. Handley said…the Marshall murders weren't his doing and that he only suspects who orchestrated it. And he says he was there the night Carrie's mother and stepfather were murdered, Seb. He said he was the man who took her to Oklahoma. Unless it's all a lie." Mel sank onto the couch. "I don't know what to think of *any* of it. If what he said is the truth, this goes back a lot further than ten years, doesn't it? At least twenty-four, maybe more."

"Maybe it does. But what does it all mean?" Brynna asked. "And what are we supposed to do?"

"I don't know. But if this goes back to the night Brynna was born, to a murder scene your father was at *and* to the night Carrie's mother was murdered, it doesn't explain anything at all. It just makes things all the more complicated. I wondered if he was just trying to confuse us by adding misinformation to what we already know. He's probably crafty enough to do that."

"Strings. It all comes down to *strings*," Brynna said. "Strings that tie this and that together. But they all start at the center, don't they? But how do we find the center? How do we find it? Before…before…before…before…"

Sebastian put both hands on her shoulders and turned her to face him. Like she'd seen him do to Carrie a few times. "Focus on me, Bryn. Just focus on me, babe. Deep breath. You are *all* safe now. I can promise you that."

Brynna nodded and focused on her breathing. Focused on getting herself back under control. It was all she could do.

Sebastian turned to Mel and Gabby. "Why don't the three of you grab your things for in the morning? Come upstairs with me. You can take the guest room and the couch in my office and in the living room."

"We don't want Carrie and Maddie and the new baby at risk," Brynna said automatically.

"They won't be. I'm calling in some favors. I'm getting a team of agents to sit on the street for the rest of the night. And Seth is going to crash down here. Al's out of town and her mother has the baby." He patted her shoulder, then reached over to help Mel stand. She didn't have her crutch. Without it she was more than a bit unstable. "You'll be safe. We can decide what to do in the morning."

Chapter 84

EVERYONE KNEW WHAT IT meant. They weren't safe in St. Louis any longer. Brynna stayed quiet while Mel described what had happened. She was still too raw to be able to contribute much, and her sister seemed to understand that.

And she was half afraid she'd let it slip about the baby. She wouldn't do that to Chance. No matter what else was between them, he deserved to know about his child before anyone else. It was only right.

No matter how much she wanted to tell her father and the rest of her family.

"We can't stay here," she finally said once the initial excitement was over. "We can't. He, they, somebody…they know we are here. The longer we are here, the more we risk making Carrie and Maddie targets. And anyone else we care about."

"I can keep you all safe, Brynna," Luc said.

"*We* can keep all of you safe," Mel said. "By going home. At least Brynna and I can."

"And me. You go nowhere without me. We're a triple set, remember?" Gabby said at Brynna's left. Her friend had immediately taken the seat next to her. She thought Gabby *felt* her upset and was doing her best to comfort.

Brynna bit back a small smile. *Gabby* was going to be her baby's aunt, wasn't she? That mattered.

"What are you saying?"

"We're saying that if *we* go back home to Finley Creek, maybe these guys will follow us and leave Carrie and Jillian and Syd and Ari and Lacy alone," Brynna put it into direct words. "But I think Mel should stay here, too."

"Not likely. Where *you* go now, I go," Mel said. "Besides, Handley came to *me*. Not you. He's involved me in this, just as much as anyone. I don't know if he'll try to get to me again, and

I want Jillian and Syd far away from me if he does."

"I don't like this," their father said. "I don't like splitting you girls up. It makes us too vulnerable. Too hard to defend."

"You don't need to defend us, Dad. You need to keep Jillian and Syd and Carrie and Maddie *safe*. And Lacy and Ari," Brynna said. "We won't be unprotected. You know that. Elliot will see to it that we are kept safe. I trust him. Mel does, too."

"Damn it, I do, too. But no matter how much I trust him, I am still your father. I can't sit back and watch you just walk right into danger."

Mel held up a hand, and the room quieted. "Maybe not. But in Finley Creek we have an entire TSP post at Elliot's beck and call. We won't take unnecessary risks, Dad. But Brynna is right. With the three of us here, we're endangering everyone. It's better for us to be a contained target with just three people than more than three times that—including Maddie—like we are here in St. Louis. We're going back. It's the only option I can see that we have." She held out a folded piece of paper. "*This* is the man who nearly knocked me down outside the doctor's office. I'd lay good money he's the one who almost ran us off the road. Take a good look. The DNA sample Lacy got came back. To that man. A Charles Raymund, registered sex offender."

Their dad took the fax that had come to Carrie's home office earlier. He stared at it for a long time. "This is him?"

"Yes. It's him," Brynna said. "He's the man in the woods. The one that wanted to force me."

Lacy looked at the paper. "Yes. That's the guy who shot Lanning."

"Charles Raymund," her father said the name quietly. "Why does that sound so familiar? I don't recognize his face."

"That's one of the things we'll go back to Finley Creek to find out," Mel said, firmly.

Brynna got it—Mel had made up her mind. She was going back to Finley Creek.

And Brynna and Gabby were as equally determined to go with her.

Chapter 85

BRYNNA LOVED LOOKING AT Finley Creek from an airplane. It was even better on a private plane because she didn't have to worry about other passengers.

Well, except for Mel and Gabby, but they weren't paying attention to the windows at the moment.

Gabby was excited to be going back. Brynna knew her friend had been hurting without Elliot; even though they'd video chatted and spoken on the phone as much as they could—and Elliot had flown up to visit her twice—it wasn't the same.

Brynna knew that for herself. She hadn't stuck around when Elliot had visited; he looked too much like his brother. Reminded her of who she had tried to forget.

Her hand covered her stomach. She wouldn't be forgetting him anytime soon, would she?

"Bryn?" Mel asked. "You ok?"

Her sister looked at the hand she still had on her stomach. Brynna nodded. "Just thinking. Wishing… wishing this was all over and everything was normal again. It's going to be Christmas soon."

For the first time in her life, she had spent Thanksgiving in a place other than her own home. It had been nice to be with friends like they were, but it wasn't the same. And she'd been aware of that.

Elliot had flown up to join them, bring Jarrod with him instead of Chance.

Brynna had tried not to miss him. She really had. Even before she'd learned of the baby. But since she knew now…all she could think about was *him*. And what she was going to tell him.

"I know. But a lot can change in the two weeks or so between now and Christmas. We'll get these guys, and we'll get normal back," Mel said. "We'll *all* be ok."

Brynna nodded. She would. Eventually.

"We're descending," Gabby said, looking at the two of them. She knew something else was going on, didn't she?

Brynna hated not telling her friend what was going on. She never kept secrets from Gabby. Ever.

But this time…she had to tell Chance first.

The plane landed, and they were helped off by some of Luc's men. He'd sent bodyguards and the pilot and copilot, plus a private steward who had seen to their every need on the short trip. She wasn't used to someone catering to her every whim; that was for sure.

It took some maneuvering to help Mel down the small flight of stairs. When they were finally off of the plane they were greeted by a tall man in a dark suit.

Mel stopped walking. Brynna almost knocked into her. "Houghton."

"Melody. I heard you were coming home." Houghton Barratt turned toward Brynna and Gabby. "A little birdie told me what happened last night. I'm sorry."

Someone called Gabby's name, and they all turned. Elliot hurried across the tarmac of the small private airstrip. Gabby squealed and jumped into his arms. Brynna turned away to give them privacy.

Houghton Barratt was leaning over Mel, his hands on her waist. Brynna tried not to eavesdrop on what they were saying—Gabby and Elliot were kissing, not talking—but it was impossible.

He was apologizing for his father and was running his hands all over her sister. Was he trying to make sure his own father hadn't hurt her? He had his hands in her hair now. "I have missed you."

"Houghton, why are you here?" Her sister had missed him, too. Why didn't she *tell him* that?

"Because you're coming home with me. To my Barrattville place."

"No."

"So you are going to take your sister back to where? Your father's house? How are you going to secure it? The TSP? Well, that's not good enough for me, little one. It's not. Anything can happen. At least at my place I have guards that I trust. Armed guards, and I can hire more. Hell, even that fool Lucas has offered six of his own men to help. Would that make you feel more comfortable?"

"I—"

"Melody, I'm just going to have to kidnap you again. And your sister. I'm not going to let anyone hurt either of you." He leaned down and kissed her sister quickly and then pulled back. "Come with me."

Mel looked over at Brynna and stared at her for a moment. "Bryn?"

They had planned to go home with Gabby. But…Brynna wasn't certain that was what she wanted. She looked at Elliot and Gabby who were just now taking a breath. They deserved their privacy, didn't they?

Well, for that matter, so did Mel and Houghton. Houghton's house was a whole lot bigger—she'd googled and looked at photos. She'd even taken a virtual tour through an architectural website. There would be plenty of space for her and Mel. "I think we can go with Houghton."

Armed guards didn't sound so bad, either.

And maybe…maybe it would give her sister time to figure out what she wanted.

Mel hadn't stopped touching Houghton, any more than Gabby had stopped touching Elliot. Did her sister realize that?

Houghton surprised her when he leaned down and kissed *her* on her forehead. "Thank you, little sister. Consider my little cottage your own, ok?"

Chapter 86

ELLIOT HAD SEEN THE limo waiting in the airport parking lot when he'd driven up, and he'd suspected who he would find inside waiting. It didn't surprise him to see Houghton Barratt wrapped around Mel. He had yet to figure out what had happened between the two of them in the past, though he suspected whatever it was had been pretty intense.

The guy couldn't keep his hands off of her whenever she was in range. Elliot understood that himself—he had Gabby back, and he couldn't wait to get her somewhere alone.

It took him another fifteen minutes to get Gabby's bags from the plane and shake the Becks and Barratt. He felt momentarily guilty seeing Brynna. She still looked so...fragile, didn't she?

Tired and pale—paler than normal, anyway. He was only marginally reassured with the knowledge that she'd be under heavy guard with Barratt, and that her sister was watching her like a hawk.

It wasn't Elliot's place to interfere between Brynna and his stupid brother, though he knew Chance was beyond miserable.

His brother had missed that girl, probably more than Chance would ever admit. He'd bet good money that Chance had grieved her.

Which was just stupid on his brother's part. Brynna was right there, beautiful and his brother's through and through. All Chance had to do was step up and tell her that he wanted her. That he needed her.

Words Elliot was more than willing to tell the woman *he* loved.

He just had to have faith that Chance and Brynna would figure things out between them eventually. That was all that he could do.

His brother wasn't *completely* stupid, after all.

Still, having the three women back in Finley Creek changed things as far as their investigation was going. For one thing, he'd promised the superintendent and a few others of the TSP that there would be an official hearing to determine what happened in the explosion. He'd been able to put off the governor and superintendent by calling in favors—Marcus owed him quite a few—by telling him that Brynna was recuperating in St. Louis, but with her back…he *might* be able to delay the inquiry until after the New Year.

Hearings were difficult, he didn't want to put Brynna through that. Not with her looking as fragile as she just had.

Elliot waited until Gabby was in the SUV, then pulled his phone free and dialed his brother.

Chance deserved to know that Brynna had just been commandeered by the son of one of the men who had almost killed her.

Somehow he didn't think Chance was going to be too happy about that.

Chapter 87

CHANCE HUNG UP AFTER speaking with his brother. Brynna was back. Elliot had thought he'd want to know. And he did. He wanted to see her, touch her, smell her, taste her—everything he could do with her. But that wouldn't be fair to her.

He thought about her for a moment. What did he want from *her*?

What *did* he want in general? He wasn't certain he knew the answer to that question. He was thirty-four. He had decades left, God willing. Was this how he wanted to spend it? On the fringes of Elliot's life, not a real part of it?

Brynna was back, and that meant *Gabby* was back now. His brother could stop moping around, missing her.

Elliot and Gabby were going to make a life together; any idiot could see that. His brother would be happy. Fulfilled.

Chance would have his job, such that it was. What else?

Would he be forced to see Brynna occasionally, whenever he'd see Elliot? What if Elliot and Gabby married and had children? *Brynna* would be there at the kids' birthday parties, at barbeques, and every other damned thing families did.

Would he be forced to see her with the man she finally did marry? Would he see her have that man's children? What if the guy ended up being a real asshole who hurt her somehow?

Would he be able to stand seeing Brynna hurting, seeing her and not touching her, not having her for himself?

What was he supposed to think?

She'd arrived back in Finley Creek, and he hadn't even been told she was coming home. No one had bothered to tell him ahead of time. No one had considered that he had the right to know. And he didn't. He'd given up that right, hadn't he? *He* had given up the right.

Hell, Houghton Barratt had been there to make sure she

was safe. Not him.

Houghton Barratt, a man who thought nothing of abducting a woman and forcing her to marry him.

That didn't sit too well with Chance. Not at all. And Barratt's attention would naturally be on *his* wife. Who could blame him?

Elliot had Gabby and the life they were building out at the old homestead. Mel had whatever it was she was doing with Barratt. Where would that leave Brynna?

She thrived on routine, and he'd heard from Elliot that she had been struggling in St. Louis with the changes and traumas she'd been through. It was why they'd left Lucas' place and moved in with her sister, in the first place. Brynna was used to staying with the oldest Beck daughter, so they'd thought it would help her adjust to the lengthy stay in St. Louis. From what Gabby had told Elliot, it hadn't.

Brynna was struggling.

That tore at him, and had for the past week, since Elliot had first told him. How many times had he fought going to St. Louis on some pretext, just to see her? Just to check?

And now she was with Houghton Barratt, the day after the man's father had broken in to the apartment Brynna had been sleeping in.

How was she handling that? Had it terrified her? He knew it had, knew she had nightmares that Handley Barratt featured in strongly. To have him show up where she was sleeping had to have terrified her.

He wanted to see her, check on her, make sure she was ok. To hold her and tell her he'd never let anything hurt her again. But he would never be able to *keep* that promise, would he? He'd always end up hurting her somehow. She deserved far better than him.

And that was exactly why he was getting out of Finley Creek. His contacts had reported a man matching Handley Barratt's description entering Mexico less than two hours ago.

He wasn't coming back to Finley Creek until he had that man where he could never get near Brynna again.

Chapter 88

BRYNNA STARED AT THE realtor's website for what must have been fifteen minutes or more. The house represented a dream to her. Perhaps it was a foolish one—but she'd managed to scrape together most of the purchase price. It wasn't chump change for anyone. The house had mattered to her.

It had been a real, tangible piece of hope.

But so had the money. It had been a *real* sign of what she had done.

More than that, the money was going to help her with this. The next part of her life.

She could have applied the money toward the house, but that would have still left her with an astronomical house payment and no real savings anymore.

She didn't have a job. At least not one she wanted to do anymore. There was no way she'd ever be able to walk back into the TSP and not remember what had happened.

More importantly, she didn't want to. The TSP had never been her dream. It had been a way to get experience that she needed. And she had gotten that—far more than she'd ever have wanted. She touched a hand to the still healing scars just below her ribs.

Just how lucky she had been was something Brynna would never forget. Dr. Anderson had told her bluntly when Mel had taken her to him for a follow-up the day after they'd come home that she was damned lucky she had survived. That the baby, that tiny miraculous part of her and Chance, had made it this far was definitely against the odds.

Brynna preferred to think of it as meant to be.

Apparently, the house she'd wanted since she was a teenager wasn't.

She was allowed to feel disappointed by that.

And almost two million dollars would go a long way toward

helping her stay home to take care of her baby, wouldn't it? She'd already googled the approximate cost of a pregnancy and delivery at the Finley Creek hospital. She already had a wonderful home with her dad and her sisters. They would be shocked by her news—most of them, anyway, Mel was already knitting bunches of little hats and blankets for both her and Carrie—but her baby would be welcomed and loved. Her baby would grow up in a wonderful place. Just like she had.

If that was ok with Chance, that was.

He was the only real problem, wasn't he? They hadn't planned on anything like this. There had been no commitment, and Brynna was fine with that. Even though the thought of not being with him felt like her heart was being wrenched from her body whenever she let the thought linger in her head.

Brynna was an adult. She wasn't going to die from a broken heart. She wasn't.

How could she? She felt like she'd given the emotional heart to that man who obviously didn't want it. It had been long enough for her to figure that out. She had to get a hold of herself *now* though. She had to. Her baby depended on it.

He had been traipsing around Mexico for eighteen days. He'd missed Christmas with his brother and Gabby. He'd missed New Year's.

And she had to *wait* for him to show up again before she could tell him and then the rest of her family. If he was missing too much longer, she'd have to tell the rest of her family anyway. The nausea was getting worse, and they'd probably start to notice when her belly got round. Where was he?

Her father and Jillian and Syd had flown down with Carrie and Sebastian and the baby for Christmas. Her father and Jillian had stayed. They were all still under heavy guard at Houghton's, much to Mel's consternation.

Somehow she was managing to avoid Houghton, even in the house they all shared. Of course, it was a huge house. Plenty of places for Mel to hide when she wanted.

Brynna thought Houghton was having fun tracking her down every night before bed.

Jillian had had to go back to work, or she was going to lose her job. Brynna understood it. Their *lives* couldn't be put on hold while the TSP searched for Charles Raymund.

Life had to go on. And that meant she needed to speak with Chance. Somehow.

The only way she was going to be able to contact him was through his brother, wasn't it? Unless she found some other way to track a man who prided himself on being untraceable.

What did she really know about him? Three days together under extreme circumstances meant absolutely nothing, didn't it? They'd talked. They'd laughed together. They'd even argued several times—Chance was very stubborn, and they'd had sex. Eight times. She'd never had sex that much in her life.

There were a lot of things she'd never quite understood before recent events, were there?

"I promise, kid, that I won't screw this up for us. Ok?" She'd started talking to the baby when she was alone. She'd read that babies recognized their mother's voices early.

Sometimes she thought it had to be a girl. Other times a little boy just like his father had been.

How was she going to do it? Tell everyone?

Oh, by the way, Daddy, you're going to be a grandfather for the third time. Just a few short months after Carrie's baby is born. Remember those days I was lost in the woods with Chance Marshall…well…

Somehow Brynna suspected that probably wasn't the best way to tell him.

She really should tell Chance first.

That was the right thing to do.

As much as this baby was hanging out in her body, it was just as much Chance's baby as hers.

She took one last look at the house that had been her dream for nearly a decade and turned away. She reached out with one hand and closed her laptop. It was time to end the old dreams, wasn't it?

Brynna was growing different dreams now.

—

SHE tried not to let the hurt show to those around her, but it was obvious Mel knew. Her sister was angry on her behalf, but she wasn't saying anything bad about Chance. Which Brynna appreciated. She wasn't sure whether he'd left to escape her or because he was tracking Houghton's father.

It had been easier for her and Mel and Houghton to just not talk about Handley when they were all together. Brynna spent most of her time hiding out in the suite he'd given her. It had light-blue walls and a view of the back gardens. It was absolutely beautiful, and he was doing his best to make her completely comfortable while she was there. She was pretty certain Mel was going to stay with Houghton when it was all over with. And that was how it should be.

Her sister and Houghton were weird, though. Mel did her best to avoid him during the day, but as soon as he looked at her at night, Mel practically melted. Houghton had taken to stalking her around his house and kissing her whenever Mel would least expect it. Brynna was keeping score. So far Mel had eluded him thirty-two times. Houghton had caught her sister forty-seven.

It was her only source of entertainment as the days passed until her family arrived for Christmas. There was no sign—or word—from Chance in all of that time.

Gabby visited sometimes; Elliot would drop her off on his way in to the TSP. They'd work on the next big project—they were going to do something not law enforcement related this time. Brynna was thinking a video game—Mel had agreed to help them with the storyline. It was going to be the first project Mel had ever worked on with them.

When not working on that, Brynna was holing up in her suite going over the TSP files she'd duplicated before Benny had died.

Charles Raymund and Handley Barratt and Benny were in there somewhere. There was a connection, and she was going to find it.

Finally, two days after the New Year, she did.

It wasn't a thick file. It was less than five pages, just a witness statement and two police reports. A report of an aggressive man at a bar and a twenty-two-year-old woman. The report had been made six months before Brynna had been born.

Her father had been the assisting officer. His partner, Minton, had been the lead on the case. And the perpetrator had been Charles Raymund.

That was it.

She printed three copies; she'd give one to Elliot that evening at the dinner they were having at his home, one to Mel—who she suspected was doing her own digging, by using Houghton's access to his father's files—and fax one to her father.

Maybe they could make something out of it.

She pushed the laptop she was working at away. She was done. So done giving these monsters her life and energy. She wanted her new normal and it was time she went after it.

Brynna was tired of letting life happen to her. Wasn't that what Mel meant whenever she'd told Brynna to go after what she wanted?

Well, now she wanted safety and security and a good *life* for her baby. She wanted her baby to have his or her father, but if that wasn't going to happen, then the baby would have *her* father.

And the baby would no doubt have Elliot, no matter how awkward Brynna would find the entire situation. The baby would have Gabby and Mel and Carrie and Jillian and Syd, too.

They would have a *life* again. Her and the baby.

Even if they had to *stay* right there under armed guards for the next few years, no matter where or what situation she found herself in, her baby would have a *normal*. She'd learn to bake cookies—Mel would no doubt be willing to teach her. She'd learn to change diapers and give her baby a bath and feed the baby and everything *else* a mother was supposed to do.

She'd be a good mother. She'd do everything she had to in order to make that a reality.

She had almost two million dollars sitting in the Finley Creek Valley Bank. That would go a long way to making that normal for her baby, wouldn't it?

She'd talk to Elliot later that evening. She had no doubt that *he* knew exactly where his brother was. She'd find him.

Tell him. If he wanted to be involved, then fine. They'd plan together how they wanted to do it.

If he didn't want that big of a *string*, then she and the baby would be just fine.

They would be just fine.

She turned away from her laptop and toward the little present Mel had slipped into her room while she'd been sleeping.

The blanket was lilac and teal and light green and, oh, so very tiny. Mel was really good at knitting and crocheting; she'd practiced even more when Carrie had been pregnant with Maddie. It was just another sign that her baby would be just fine. Her baby would have a *normal.*

Chapter 89

GABBY WAS GUSHING TO MEL about wedding dresses and bridesmaids' dresses and flowers and making a total goob out of herself. Brynna listened with half an ear—just to make certain Gabby didn't put her in a bright yellow dress or something—but her thoughts were more on what she needed to say to Elliot.

He looked like his brother. The eyes were different. Elliot wasn't quite as lean as Chance. Chance was harder, faster. If Elliot was a strong leopard, Chance would be a huge black panther. Both were equally as deadly and from the same family, but panthers were just more dangerous because you couldn't see them coming. That was Chance.

Elliot was in the kitchen of the house that had once been his parents. It was weird to Brynna to be there again. It hadn't changed much since she was a child, though the living room and family room had all been hurriedly redecorated before Gabby moved in for the first time.

Who could blame her? Brynna had watched the video of the Marshall family murders enough times to be able to return the living room to the exact decorations it had had back then. What hell it must be for Gabby.

But she and Elliot were determined to fill the house with love again. Erase as many of the bad memories as they could.

They had left Chance's room alone, though. Sara and Slade's were being redecorated next month. While Gabby and Elliot were away on their honeymoon.

The kitchen had been recently repainted, and Brynna was careful to check for fumes before she went in. She couldn't tell Elliot that she couldn't be in his kitchen.

Well, she could always say that she was sensitive to the smells, right?

Sometimes sensory issues had their uses. No matter how dishonest she'd think that was.

Elliot looked up when she entered. "Hey, Bryn. What can I get for you? We have soda, beer, water, milk, lemonade…in the fridge. Just help yourself."

Brynna grabbed the water. "Thank you. I have a question."

"What is it?"

She pulled in a deep breath. Now or never. "I need to speak with your brother about something. Do you know how I can reach him?"

"I have a number. But he'll be here tomorrow for the TSP inquiry. If you want to speak with him face-to-face. Or is it something I can help with?"

"No. It's personal. I'll wait until tomorrow. I hate talking on the phone." And telling someone they were going to be a father wasn't something a decent woman did over the phone. Unless she had no other options.

That wasn't the case here. She could wait one more day.

"Ok. Brynna, it's over, you know?"

Her and Chance. Yeah, she had a good inkling it was. But the consequences were definitely still there. "I know."

"We're still looking for Handley Barratt, but the man who attacked you and my brother, we know who he is. And where he is."

"We don't have Raymund." They had *tips* that Raymund was in Mexico. Just like Handley Barratt.

"The Mexican authorities are pretty certain we do."

"We'll need to put it all together. Find all the connections. I've only been able to go so far."

"I know. But you don't have to push yourself."

"I'm not. And I'm not afraid." Not of Handley Barratt anyway. Mel had said the man had promised her the night he'd scared Mel in St. Louis that he would never hurt their family again. Brynna believed him. *He* hadn't wanted to hurt her out in Oklahoma.

"We can't live afraid, Elliot. I know that. After my mother died, I was afraid of everything. Of losing my dad and Mel especially. Jillian and Syd, too. But it was different with them since they were younger. Mel being a TSP detective didn't help. It took a while to stop being afraid all of the time."

"I know. I've been there myself. I'm not sure my brother has ever left that stage."

"Your brother doesn't let himself get close to anyone so that he doesn't have to fear losing them again." She wasn't great at reading emotions, but surprise was a pretty easy one to get. Elliot wasn't hiding it very well at all. "I've thought about him a lot. Tried to figure out why he does the things he does. We spent a lot of time together."

He leveled a look at her. "I know. I don't want to know any details, but I'm glad the two of you were together and kept each other safe. I'll always be grateful you saved my brother's life. And that he was there to save yours."

"But the rest of it is personal." Brynna pulled in a deep breath, and then put into words what she'd been thinking for a while. "I'm not going back to the TSP."

He nodded. "I understand. Same for Gabby."

She understood. She'd always suspected Gabby used the TSP as a hiding place because she'd been afraid the killers would be coming after her.

That one of those killers had been right there in the same room with them every single day made Brynna shudder. And feel like vomiting again.

Not that she hadn't spent fifteen minutes in the bathroom after waking doing exactly that. And then another twenty *after* breakfast.

"Things change. I have money. I don't have to do anything for a while. A long while, actually. Possibly years. I'm free to do nothing but work on my software designs." And have a baby.

But she wasn't telling the baby's uncle that quite so soon.

"Congratulations. That's quite a big accomplishment."

"Yes, it is. And it makes things easier, I guess. Thank you. I'll talk to your brother tomorrow."

Chapter 90

CHANCE HAD HIS BAG over his shoulder and knew the first thing he needed was a shower. He'd wash up and change into decent clothes, then head over to the TSP. He hated official inquiries, but the TSP bigwigs had finally gotten their asses in gear.

It was just the first step in a long process. Someone would have to answer for what Bennett Russell had done, especially to Brynna and Gabby.

Gabby.

Elliot had spent the last few weeks wrapped around his woman every night. He'd seen her across the breakfast table, ate dinner with her every night. Laughed with her over the little things.

Held her when the nightmares came.

Whereas Chance had bounced around a bunch of Mexican hotels, searching for that bastard Handley Barratt. Barratt had the answers he wanted.

Still wanted.

But Chance had woken up again in some hotel he couldn't even remember the name of, shouting Brynna's name and reaching for…*her*. The only thing he'd come away with was the realization that he could have been spending those nights with her. It had taken him *weeks* to realize that he could have had the only woman in the world who made him feel again right next to him. *He* could have been holding her the way Elliot had been holding her best friend.

He was just too damned cowardly to give them both that.

Let others find Handley Barratt. Chance had given enough of his life to finding the men who'd killed his family. He'd identified two of them, wasn't that enough?

Wasn't that enough to turn over to others now? Wasn't it time he lived the rest of his life?

Wasn't it time he had something—someone—for himself? There had been a redhead on the plane who'd looked so much like Brynna that at first he'd been certain it was her from behind. That it wasn't had hurt.

More than he'd ever thought possible.

Elliot had made a point of telling him every time they spoke about how she was doing. *Healing.* Had told him of how the Becks had gathered for Christmas, and he and Gabby had joined them. His brother had even sent him a photo of Brynna cuddling her sister's baby and smiling softly at the little girl.

He'd ached from that, but he'd told himself that she was doing ok. She'd looked happy. The baby looked like a dark-haired version of Brynna, and had gripped a lock of carrot hair in one tiny fist. His brother was a real asshole for sending him that pic, reminding Chance of what he could have had. If he wasn't so stupid.

Chance had studied that photo so many times since Christmas. He saw it in his dreams at night. He'd kept himself in another damned country to keep from going to her.

It was when he'd found himself staking out Houghton Barratt's Mexican estate on the slim possibility she'd come down to Mexico with her sister did he realize how utterly stupid and wasteful with his life he was being.

He'd stopped off at the bank and retrieved his maternal grandmother's wedding rings. What he intended to do with them had his gut tightening. Elliot had inherited his paternal grandmother's. That's what Gabby would be wearing after her wedding next month.

They'd buried their mother and father with the wedding rings they'd given each other. It had seemed like the right thing to do.

Elliot had found a photo in a box of others at the house. He'd sent Chance a copy of that one, too.

Kevin Beck's family and his. Right there, three feet from where Chance had been standing next to Elliot, was a tiny redheaded girl. He'd barely remembered that day. He was close to graduating high school; she was about seven or eight. Beautiful.

Proof they'd been connected for years. Or so he'd like to think.

Elliot had given him two more that he'd printed out; they

were still in his wallet. A quick snapshot of his mother in the kitchen—with that same little redhead wearing a too-big apron and a serious expression. And another of a little girl with a bowl on her head, batter dripping down her cheeks along with the tears. *He* was just visible in the background.

Chance remembered that day. He looked down at his hand. He still had the faint scar where Jillian had bitten him for what he'd done to Brynna.

He was turning into a maudlin idiot where Brynna was concerned.

The papers he'd signed that morning rested in his bag. He'd give them to her when he gave her the first of the rings. Chance hoped she'd just let him become a part of her dreams, too.

Chapter 91

BRYNNA HATED OFFICIAL hearings. She'd testified at one in the past, when a member of the Computer Forensics team had been brought up on review charges stemming from an evidence tampering case. Her colleague had been cleared, but the whole process was something Brynna hated.

To compound it, Chance was supposed to be there soon.

She wasn't ready to face him.

Not on top of everything else.

"Are you ok?" Elliot leaned down and asked. Chance's brother seemed to have taken it on himself to hover over Brynna whenever they were together. She appreciated it. She truly did.

But she just wanted to forget what had happened. All of it.

Forget the past. Move on to the future. Her hand covered her stomach. Where their baby rested.

She'd lain awake for hours last night, terrified that everything Benny had done and all the drugs the hospital had pumped into her had adversely affected the baby somehow. She needed to speak with her doctor again. They'd told her there would be concerns throughout the pregnancy, but that she most likely would have a perfectly healthy baby. But…she still needed answers. Otherwise, the questions were going to drive her crazy. Once she told Chance, she'd talk to Lacy. That's what she would do. Lacy would tell her straight.

"Bryn?" Gabby said her name again, and Brynna realized she hadn't answered Elliot's question. "You ok?"

"I…I don't want to go in there again." The TSP building stood at the center of the block, tall and imposing. She used to love going inside, heading to the back annex where she and Gabby would hide for hours on end. Now all she remembered was red. The red of Benny's blood, of hers. She didn't want to go in there ever again. "Gabby, I don't want to go in there again, again."

Elliot was there, strong and close and so much like Chance. He put his big body between Brynna's and the building. He stepped close enough that he blocked out the sight. "Then we won't. We'll use the courthouse for this. Or somewhere else. I'll make the calls. You and Gabby can wait right here."

Brynna nodded, feeling like a great big idiot. Benny was dead. He couldn't hurt her anymore. Raymund and Handley Barratt were both in Mexico. The third guy was probably dead somewhere—Brynna's cracking his head open had been pretty definite, in Chance's opinion. They were gone.

It didn't make sense that they'd ever come back. It was done.

"Thank you." She fought back tears. *Gabby* was the one who cried over everything, not her. "I just…can't go in there."

"I understand." He patted her shoulder lightly.

"I don't want to go in there either, Bryn." Gabby stood at her shoulder. "I think the courthouse would be much better. Or…a conference room somewhere. Anywhere else."

Elliot waved to someone entering the building. Brynna looked up, right into Daniel McKellen's warm brown eyes. "McKellen, can you stay with Gabby and Brynna for a few moments? They don't want to go inside the building, and I agree it's a good idea to move the hearing."

"Of course." McKellen smiled down at her. He had checked on her almost daily since she'd returned from St. Louis. He was a good friend, but they both knew there would never be anything more than that between them. She almost wished there was. It would have been so much easier, wouldn't it? "Anything you need."

Why couldn't she have loved someone like *him*? "I just…want normal back and soon, Daniel. That's all."

"Then let's get it for you. Gabby, how are you today?"

He chatted with them until Elliot returned fifteen minutes later. The longer he spoke, the more it became clear that while he was a wonderful man, her heart would always belong to Chance. Why did that depress her so much?

"The committee has agreed to meet down the street at the hotel."

"The Barratt?" Gabby asked.

Elliot winced. "I know. Not my first choice, either."

"But we just can't escape Houghton Barratt, can we?" Mel certainly couldn't. Her sister refused to even speak about the man she'd married. What was happening between them was anyone's guess, as far as Brynna could tell.

Mel wasn't happy. That was about all she knew.

Elliot and Daniel kept her and Gabby between them on the short walk to the Barratt-Finley Creek Hotel, four blocks down from the TSP.

"How long is this going to last?" Brynna asked.

"I don't know. Several hours, at least. I know there will be quite a few questions for the both of you. Both of you need to understand something. *You* control today. If you need a break or if anything upsets you, tell me. I'll get you a break right there. I'm not going to let anyone push you today."

Brynna nodded. It was nice to have the chief of the post so protective, at least, wasn't it? "We can do this, and then when it's over we can forget Benny, right?"

"Absolutely, Bryn. Then you can help me pick out bridesmaids' dresses. I was thinking banana yellow." Gabby grinned softly.

"That's wonderful. I'd even wear yellow for you, Gabs."

"I know. And that's why I'm thinking green. You and Mel would both look awesome in green."

There was some relief, at least.

Chapter 92

CHANCE GOT THE TEXT FROM his brother about the change of location just as he was pulling into the TSP parking lot.

What had once been the annex was roped off with crime scene tape. They were keeping it as is until all the forensics was gathered, all the reports written, and all the information gathered that they could get. Weeks of exposure to the weather wasn't helping erase the desolation of the rubble.

Chance despised the very sight of it. The betrayal that burned-out shell represented sickened him. The knowledge that Brynna had almost died there nearly brought him to his knees whenever he saw it.

He'd woken in a cold sweat more nights than not since it had happened. His subconscious had yanked him back to his family's funerals, only instead of them it had been Brynna in a coffin.

Brynna he had almost lost forever.

He couldn't deal with that. He knew what kind of coward that he was. She was right there where he could get to her, and he was too damned afraid to go to her.

She was with his brother now. He was going to get her. Everything else could wait.

Chance parked and started down the sidewalk toward the Barratt hotel. It was a luxury place right in the middle of Finley Creek. That damned Barratt was everywhere, wasn't he?

He'd spent most of the day before in Mexico tracking down a dead-end lead on Handley Barratt. Common knowledge said the man had a mistress a year younger than his only son south of the border.

Chance was a man, and he knew how it worked—follow the path a man's pants led him in, and you'd eventually find that man.

But it wasn't working out that way. Barratt the elder wasn't anywhere to be found. Cagey.

Chance was tired of chasing shadows. Tired of wasting so much damned time. He saw the group outside the Barratt when he walked up.

Carrot hair was hard to miss.

As was that damned McKellen, hovering at Brynna's shoulder. She was smiling up at the other man, a look of open gratitude on her pretty face. He knew what McKellen thought when he looked at her. Hell, Chance had the same damned thoughts, both awake and asleep.

Brynna was…Brynna was…

Damn it, she was his *everything.*

And he wasn't going to let her go to someone like Daniel McKellen. Chance might not be the best man out there for her, but he'd make sure she was safe and taken care of…and loved.

He couldn't deny that he'd loved her probably from the first moment she'd looked at him and asked why *couldn't* they have sex. The first moment she'd looked up at him with those eyes and cracked every barrier he'd erected around his heart.

The sun seemed drawn to carrot hair, just like he was. Chance stopped walking and stared.

He *loved* her. Loved her just as deeply as Elliot loved Gabby. Just as deeply as his father had loved his mother.

Putting distance between them to keep himself from getting hurt was never going to change that fact. All that did was keep them apart when they could be together.

He could have a thousand miles between them, and he'd still love her.

But what in the hell did he want to do about that?

It would be better for her if he just left her alone. Let her find another man, have her pretty house and her pretty babies and her pretty life with someone else.

That's what he should do, wasn't it?

But damn it, he wanted that pretty house and those pretty babies and that pretty female all for himself. Selfish of him?

Probably.

He patted his pocket—the papers and the ring box were right where he'd put them earlier.

But he'd spent the last ten years of his life grieving for his family. The one that he had lost. Maybe it was time he worked on building another family? One with Brynna and Elliot and Gabby and the rest of the Becks?

With Brynna.

Brynna in his bed every night, Brynna carrying his child, Brynna rocking his child at night. Brynna eating purple pasta sauce and telling him all about lightning or snakes or whatever subject she got into her complicated little head.

Carrot hair spread over his pillow at night. Light-brown eyes looking at him, making him feel like he was a slug whenever he did something completely stupid.

Her soft hands on his skin, his lips on hers. Her in his bed every night, looking up at him like he was the only man in her world.

That sounded like exactly what he wanted.

But did she? Or had his stupidity made her change her mind? Maybe *she* wanted Daniel McKellen instead?

Why else would the guy be right there with her and Gabby and Elliot—right where *he* should be?

Chance increased his pace. He wanted to have an opportunity to talk to her before they had to go in and explain to the TSP bigwigs how one of their own had gone off the deep end and tried to kill the two women in the world who mattered to Chance the most.

Chapter 93

SHE KNEW HE WAS THERE BEFORE she saw him. It was weird. It was like she had a radar or homing beacon where Chance Marshall was concerned.

For the first time since she'd met him, he was dressed in a suit and tie. Chance filled out his suit very nicely. He put Elliot and Daniel to shame, didn't he?

Elliot called his brother's name, but Brynna barely heard him. Chance was looking at her. And she was looking at him.

It seemed like it had been years since she had seen him last, instead of the forty-five days that she knew it had been. Where had he been?

It took every bit of self-control she had to keep from demanding the answer to that very question. It wasn't her right to know where he spent his time, was it? Instead, she kept her expression as neutral as she could. Which was harder than she thought it was ever going to be.

He moved right up next to her, sidestepping in front of Daniel. Chance stared down at her. Brynna looked up at him. It was just the two of them for a long moment. "Bryn."

"Chance." Did he hear how her voice wobbled? She fought the tears. He would not see her cry. He wouldn't.

"Ok," Elliot said from behind his brother. "Gabby and I are going inside. I trust you can get Brynna to the conference room on the third floor? It's the Turner room."

"Of course. I think we'll manage." Chance's fingers wrapped around her elbow. Brynna jerked her arm away before she thought about how it would look. If she let him touch her, she'd never make it through the day.

She knew that.

Daniel went inside after touching her on the elbow once. Brynna nodded, barely looking at him.

"You're angry."

She thought for a moment. Was she?

Maybe. Maybe not. Enough time had passed that she wasn't mad at him that much, any longer. More hurt. His fears had impacted everything, hadn't they? She was more confused than anything. More afraid. What was he going to do when she told him? "I'm not angry. But there's something I do need to talk to you about. Tell you. It's really important."

Would she ever be able to figure this man out? Would she even get the opportunity?

Brynna wouldn't be shocked if he ran right into traffic after she told him. If he tried to escape as fast as he could. Escape what she wouldn't change. Maybe he'd just go back to Mexico and no one would ever hear from him again.

Wouldn't it be best to just get it over with? Every minute he was there in front of her was one more minute in which she hurt for what she couldn't have. And she had to focus on what came next, not what had come before. It was vital, now more than ever. Because someone else was counting on her now. She touched her stomach lightly. "Chance, I have something I need to say to you."

"In a minute. I need to say something first. Make you understand that I know I shouldn't have left you. Especially for as long as I did."

"You did what you said you would. What we agreed to. I didn't *ask* for more than what we agreed to. I didn't." She'd hurt, a gut-wrenching aching hurt, when she'd left him for St. Louis. But she'd done it. It was the only real choice she'd had then.

Chance had his demons, and he was going to chase them. No matter what. And she may have fallen in love with him just that fast, even if she hadn't believed it possible before—however, that didn't mean he had fallen for her.

Or that she ever would have expected him to. He'd said so. No matter what had happened between them since that cellar.

"Maybe you didn't ask for it. But you should have expected more from me, baby. Instead...you just accept. I never should have left you. If I hadn't been such an idiot, I damned well would have been in that annex with you and Gabby."

"And possibly killed by the explosion. Gabby and I got lucky that day. The two spots we were in were the only ones that were even reasonably protected by the explosion. That's what the forensics teams told us. There's nothing that says you would have survived. How do you think I would have felt then? I'm happy, *thrilled,* that no one else was down there with us. We got lucky. How lucky would we have been if someone we loved had been down there with us and *died?* You or your brother or Jarrod? That would have been devastating, Chance. Don't you see that? Gabby and I protected each other and we survived. And we're moving past it. I think today is proof of that. It's the future. Not the past. I need that right now, especially right now…Chance…"

One look at his green eyes and she understood. Chance would *never* move past that. He honestly thought he would have been able to protect her, didn't he? No matter what she said, he'd always think he failed her. But why? They'd made no claims on each other, except for sex.

Except for the baby.

The *baby.* Her hand dropped to her stomach and stayed. "Chance…there's something I need to tell you. I *need* to. And I need you to *listen.* Before you say anything. I need you to just listen. Listen. Listen."

Chapter 94

HE HALF THOUGHT SHE WAS going to tell him to take off. To leave her alone forever. It wouldn't surprise him if she did. He deserved it. Still, she looked so pale, so worried. Her hand covered her stomach, and her eyes were damp. Worried. Hesitant. "Babe, do you need to sit down? Are you hurting?" It had been weeks since the explosion; Elliot had said she was healed.

"No. I need to be standing for this."

His stomach clenched. "Bryn, is there something going on?"

She closed her eyes, and her free hand wrapped over the other. Chance couldn't help himself. He stepped closer.

Brynna held up her hand to stop him. "Wait. Before you say anything. I think it's probably going to be best to just say this fast. Before I lose my nerve and completely flip out. I'm *pregnant*. Pregnant. There's going to be a baby. *Our* baby. And I need to know what you think you want to do now."

Every word he'd been about to say flew away, leaving him staring down at her, speechless. *This* was not what he expected; not at all. "Pregnant. As in...when we..."

"Yes. But we used condoms. Used condoms. I know we did. So I looked up the failure rate. It can be between twelve to eighteen percent, depending on the material the condom was made out of. If they aren't latex, it's higher. They weren't latex. And if they were old...they could have been degraded. We have no way of knowing how long—"

Chance covered her lips with one finger. He didn't need a Wikipedia entry on condoms. Only one thing really mattered. Pregnant.

Brynna was pregnant and spouting off the failure rates of condoms. Logical. Always logical, his Brynna. *His* Brynna, *his* baby. His for the taking. All he had to do was step up to the plate and be a *man* about it and take what Fate was offering to him. Pretty woman and a pretty baby. All he needed was the pretty house, didn't he? The papers in his pocket took care of that. "I need to think."

She paled even more. Her mouth trembled. "I'm sorry. I know this is a surprise to you."

And to her. She had plans, goals for her life. How would a baby factor in with all of that? This changed everything for her, too, didn't it? Was she happy about it? "You are keeping the baby."

She looked at him like he was an idiot, and her hands tightened on her stomach. Protectively. Where their child rested. Nothing else mattered to him but her and the baby they'd created. "Of course."

"How long have you known?"

"Three weeks. A phone call didn't seem right. I tried. But…I couldn't find you."

The expression in her eyes tore at him. So confused, so scared, so vulnerable.

So Brynna.

"So you've spent that time not knowing what I'd do or where I was and afraid?" While he was off doing stupid shit. Another black mark on his soul.

Her chin went up. "I'm not afraid. Well, not really. I know the baby will be taken care of. No matter what. He or she will have people who love him or her. He's a Beck, after all. And *I* can afford to take care of a baby. I *sold* some of my software. I made enough to not have to go back to the TSP. Ever. I don't want to, anyway."

"We need to sit down and talk. Really talk about this. About everything."

She nodded. "You're right. But not today. Today has to be for finishing up with Benny. Finishing up the past."

Not what he wanted, at all. He wanted to focus on *her*, on their family. Brynna and pretty babies—Chance fought the urge to smile and shout to the rooftops. Corny of him, he knew. But…Brynna Beck was having *his* baby. That meant something, didn't it? "We'd better get in there, then. But, Bryn…this doesn't change how I feel in the least. I'm here for you. I came back for *you*. Not to testify, or go after Benny's friends, or Handley Barratt. I came back because…I need you.

Not just because of this kid we made, but…I don't want my life the way it is anymore. It's missing something. It's been missing *you*. Don't forget that. I don't want you to have time for other thoughts, other worries. I'm here for you. I came back *for you*." He took her hand in his and kissed her palm. He covered her other hand. "Remember that."

He pulled her against his chest and just held her. Just for a moment, right in the middle of one of the busiest sidewalks in Finley Creek.

Chapter 95

BRYNNA DIDN'T KNOW WHAT to believe. He'd avoided her for so long, and now that she'd told him about the baby he was ready for strings? "It doesn't make sense."

"What doesn't?"

"You don't want strings or commitment. You told me that. Now you've changed your mind?" Only one thing made sense. Logical. "Because of the baby."

"No! Not because of the baby." He pulled back and looked down at her. Brynna tried to read his eyes, but...well, she'd never been good at figuring people out. "Because of us. I'm tired of being alone, and I...love you."

"You love me. After only eighty-three days. It doesn't make sense." But it worked for Gabby and Elliot, didn't it? They had been together just as long as she had known Chance, plus one or two days. And she didn't doubt that her friend loved Elliot. "Love doesn't work that way."

"Who says love has to work the same way for everyone, babe? I know what I feel. Hell, it's why I took off to Mexico."

"You went to another country to escape me?" Hurt twisted in her chest, but Brynna refused to let him see that.

"To escape the fear. I thought...distance would change how I felt. But it just made me *need* you more. I don't want to be away from you again. I'm not very good at this, babe. I need your help. I just...need you." His hands tightened on her arms. "Just give me a chance. We'll figure this out together."

Brynna found herself nodding. She wanted a *chance,* all right. She wanted *him.* For the first time since she'd realized how she felt about this man, she started to feel a bit of hope.

Maybe *he* did feel the way she did?

"Chance..." She couldn't do this, not here on the street in front of the hotel that her new brother-in-law owned. "We need to deal with this hearing. Then we'll talk."

"Let's get inside, then. But first…" Chance leaned down and kissed her. Just the way she had wanted him to. Brynna clung to him, taking in the feel of his strength as he held her. He pulled something from his pocket. "I want you to keep this. Look at it *after* the hearing. Then you and I will talk about what it means."

She took the papers.

"Put them in your bag, babe. Look at them later, ok?" She did. He bent down and kissed her right on the forehead, then held her against him for a long, long time.

Why was it that one man could make her world *feel* right with just one touch? Would she ever be able to figure that out?

He pulled away, and Brynna let him lead her inside the hotel, completely rattled. What was she supposed to think now?

She'd honestly thought he'd run the instant she told him of the baby.

Chance didn't *want* a family. He had made that very clear. So what had changed his mind? Just responsibility?

What was on those papers? Her fingers itched to pull them out, but he had asked her not to. That mattered. *Trust* mattered. Now more than ever.

He held her hand in his and she let him.

No guy other than her father had ever held her hand. Only Chance.

Brynna couldn't help think about that first time he'd held her hand. In the middle of Oklahoma, when it had just been them, the storm, and the men who wanted to kill them.

A lot had changed since then, hadn't it?

Brynna didn't say anything as they stepped into the hotel.

Chapter 96

BRYNNA HATED TESTIFYING. Hated it. They kept *staring* right at her, asking her those questions and barely giving her time to think. To remember. She finally held up her hand. "Stop! Stop, stop, stop!"

Everyone went silent. Chance stood from where he sat next to her and put his hands on her shoulders. Brynna closed her eyes and took a deep breath. Focused on *him*. Her hand dropped to her stomach. She could do this. This was the end of *her* TSP story, wasn't it? She could get through this, and then she and Chance were going to talk about what was important. Important.

"What do you need, Bryn?" Elliot asked. Gabby was on the other side of her with Elliot on the outer edge. It honestly felt like it was the four of them against the rest of the room.

"I need people to let me think. Let me think. Think." She opened her eyes and looked across the table. The guy sitting there was one she recognized—Marcus Deane, governor of Texas. Chance's cousin. They had the same green eyes, didn't they?

That helped her, a little. She took in a deep breath. "I have to start at the beginning. I can't answer questions thrown at me like this. Like this."

"Start at the beginning, Bryn. Don't let this upset you," Chance said. "They'll get their answers when they get them."

She nodded. "Gabby and I and my sister Carrie built this program. I started it three years ago, a year after I began working for Benny. When I was ready for the work with the audio portion, I asked Gabby and Carrie to help. To help. Gabby is better with audio. Audio. I don't hear variations like Gabby does. We had just finished the main product when I signed out a copy of the video from the murder of the Marshall family. I told Gabby what I was doing. I knew the video was older, and I wanted to see what our software was capable of. Benny was listening. Benny." She hesitated for a moment and looked toward her friend. "And I have been working on the Marshall case privately for two years. Since I learned that Gabby had received emails from the killers. When I was in St. Louis, I had access to my sister's servers."

She paused and took a drink of the water Chance held out to her. "Carrie is with the FBI's PAVAD directorate. She's head of computer analysis with the Complex Crimes Unit. The CCU. I used *my* program and her server to run the video. I discovered that someone had erased a fifth man from the video. I wanted to get that information back to the TSP as quickly as possible, and I wanted to be able to show the new chief of Finley Creek. Elliot. So I found Chance, who was also in St. Louis. He agreed to drive me home."

He snorted. "Agreed, babe?"

She smiled up at him. "Maybe not. Chance drove me home, but we didn't make it. Didn't make it. Two men—Handley Barratt and Charles Raymund—ran us off the road." She shivered as she remembered those early morning hours. "They pulled me out of the car. Over the glass. They wanted me. They wanted my laptop. Me. Me. Me."

Chance's hand wrapped around hers. Gabby touched her shoulder, lightly. She wasn't alone. She could do this.

She continued until she reached the end of what had happened in the lab that day. Until she looked at the governor—it was easier to look at the man who resembled Chance and Elliot than any of the other people staring at her—and told them about losing consciousness inside a tunnel of rubble. Of knowing they were going to die.

She couldn't go on. She looked at Chance. "I need…I need to go outside for a minute. I need to breathe. Please. Please."

He jumped to his feet immediately. "Let's go."

Her stomach rolled and her hand covered her baby. "I need…a few minutes alone. Stomach is…upset."

She'd seen one, just at the end of the hall. Less than fifteen feet away. She could hide out in there. Just for a few minutes. Before she went into what all had happened to her, to them, next.

"I'll wait right here," Chance said.

"Do you need me to go with you?" Gabby asked.

She shook her head. "I just need to be alone for a minute. To think."

"Of course."

Brynna turned and left the conference room.

She just needed to breathe.

Chapter 97

HE FOLLOWED THEM FROM THE TSP building down the block to the *Barratt* hotel, making sure to keep a good distance between them. The chief of the TSP kept a close watch on the two women, and he recognized the Major Crimes asshole, as well.

He couldn't get to them now.

But he had some clear orders now. Take them out. Any means necessary. Chuck wasn't going to stop until he had them.

He just didn't know how he was going to do that, yet.

The *Barratt* wasn't a secure location, and he had no trouble finding his way to the large conference room the TSP bigwigs were holed up in. There was a man on the door, a solitary man sitting in a chair just outside the door.

Chuck studied him for a moment—guy was armed. It would have to be a quick attack, then.

Before he could do anything, the conference room door opened. There *she* was. The orange-haired one.

The cop stood up and hovered over her, turning his back to the hallway behind him.

"Brynna? Are you ok?" the Major Crimes guy asked.

"Restroom. I need the restroom. Need. Need to breathe."

Chuck heard the panic, and he smiled. It was going to be far too easy, wasn't it? Hardly a challenge at all.

He pulled his gun from his pocket holster and cracked it on the guy's skull as hard as he could. Cop went down almost without a sound.

Big light-brown eyes looked up at him. She screamed before he could cover her mouth. Screamed Marshall's name.

Chuck grabbed her by the arm and dragged her down the hall behind him. He'd have only seconds to get her out of the building and away from that damned Marshall forever.

Chapter 98

HE JERKED FROM HIS CHAIR THE instant he heard the scream. Heard his name.

Chance rushed through the door, his brother on his heels. He saw the man on the floor the instant he stepped outside the conference room.

"Go! They can deal with McKellen!" Elliot yelled. Chance barely heard him as he leaped over McKellen's body.

Where was Brynna?

Chance was already running down the hall. If someone had taken her in the two seconds she'd been out of his sight, then they were going to try to get her out of the hotel without her making a fuss.

Brynna would make a fuss. He had no doubt about that.

He headed for the stairwell. If he was nabbing a woman out of a hotel, he wouldn't wait around for an elevator.

He got lucky.

Chance caught a glimpse of carrot hair four flights of steps beneath him. *"Brynna!"*

"Chance! Help me!"

"I'm coming!"

The first bullet ricocheted off the handrail two inches from his stomach. Chance kept going.

Elliot was right behind him.

Chapter 99

BRYNNA KNOCKED THE HAND holding the gun with her free hand. He wasn't going to hurt Chance. He wasn't. Not if she could stop him.

He backhanded her with his gun hand. Brynna would have fallen to the floor if he hadn't been holding her with his other hand. "Stupid bitch. *Nothing* but trouble."

She tried to claw at his face. He raised his hand to hit her again, but changed his mind. Raymund yanked her back to her feet.

He dragged her through the doors and into the lobby. "Make a sound and I shoot you now. And that sister you have in the lobby. The *crippled* one. Think she'll be able to run away from me?" He laughed. That was what terrified her the most. She hadn't known Mel was downstairs. Was he lying? What if he wasn't? Mel wouldn't be able to escape a gun. "Come on. Move. Before I decide to knock off the boyfriend once and for all. Damned Marshalls. I told Golden Boy we needed to take them out years ago."

He dragged her behind him until they reached the main portion of the lobby.

Chance was right behind them.

Raymund picked up speed.

Chance yelled.

People turned and stared. Screamed.

Mel. Mel and Jillian and Lacy were *right* there in the lobby, sixty feet away. Their dad was there next to them. Her *family*. Mel struggled to her feet, yelling Brynna's name.

"No, Mel! Stay away! He said he'll shoot you!" Brynna yelled it as loud as she could, praying her dad at least would understand. Would keep Mel safe.

Raymund cursed and swung her around. People screamed everywhere.

Everything froze. Brynna's eyes met Mel's. Her sister was trying to move closer.

To save and protect. Like Mel *always* did.

Chance was behind her. Raymund yanked her to the side, where he could see both her sister and Chance.

"Over there, Marshall. Where I can see you. Or I give your girlfriend another hole in her head."

"You have to know that we'll stop you."

Raymund laughed, his mouth right by her ear. Brynna tried not to puke. Her free hand went over her stomach. Her baby. She looked at Chance.

"Chance…"

"It's ok, Bryn. We'll *all* be ok."

Raymund snorted. "Think so, Marshall? Think this shit is over? I have been after this bitch from the moment she kicked me in the balls. Have a score to settle."

"She was protecting herself, Raymund. How can you be angry with someone doing that?" Chance asked. He wasn't moving, but he had his gun raised.

There were people around. But they were moving. Brynna looked around quickly.

Mel was standing still. Their father was holding her back, his body in front of hers. Protecting her. Their dad would take care of Mel, wouldn't he?

But who would take care of Chance? If she died today, what would it do to *him*?

"I love you." Brynna looked right at him. She'd never told him, had she? Why hadn't she told him that this morning? "I love you. It doesn't matter how long we've known each other. *I love you.*"

He looked at her quickly. "I know. I love you, too, babe. Once this is over, I'm going to show you just exactly how much, ok?"

Raymund grabbed her hair. Brynna cried out when he pulled her head back. "Isn't that sweet? *She's* not getting out of here alive, Marshall. Say goodbye now."

"*You're* not getting out of here alive. I can promise you that." Chance's words turned cold. "I'm going to take that knife you used on her and use it to filet every inch of your body. While you scream. You *touched* her. And for that you will pay."

"Think so? I can *crush* her with my bare hands. She's

nothing. Wouldn't take much to break her neck, one handed. All I have to do is *this*."

Raymund's hand squeezed her neck, cutting off her air.

Brynna lost the battle with the panic gnawing on her mind.

She went limp and fell against the man holding her as blackness overwhelmed her.

Chapter 100

HOUGHTON WAS TOO DAMNED far away to grab his wife and get her safe. But he was going to damn well try. He moved around the lobby, his focus intent not on the man holding Brynna, but on Melody.

Her father was there, bodily between her and the action. Where Houghton should be.

"Nobody move!" the guy yelled. Houghton looked at him. "Anyone moves and I take out every damned woman I see!"

He arched the gun in front of him for a second, lingering with it pointed toward the Becks. Toward Melody.

Houghton froze, as did everyone else in the lobby. Kevin stepped in front of Melody more fully, earning Houghton's undying loyalty in that moment. Dr. McGareth and Jillian were on the floor behind one of the large couches, two of Houghton's security team covering them bodily. They were as safe as they could be at the moment.

But Brynna…the girl had fallen to the ground, right between Marshall and the bastard. Was she conscious?

Marshall jumped over Brynna and put his body between hers and the gun.

Brynna shifted, rolling to her back. She wasn't fully conscious, was she? Had she fainted?

What Mel had told him that morning when they'd argued about her coming to the hearing ran through his mind. Her sister was pregnant. Pregnant women fainted a lot, didn't they?

Houghton didn't have a clue. He didn't know anything about pregnant women. But what did it matter?

She was too damned close to what was happening. If she rolled once more, the bastard could reach down and grab her.

Use her again. Houghton changed paths. He went toward his sister-in-law instead.

Chapter 101

CHANCE GRUNTED AS RAYMUND slammed his fist into his face.

He had to get to that gun, before Raymund pulled the trigger. Brynna's fainting had precipitated a direct attack. Chance knew the odds he faced. Someone was about to get hurt.

He'd make sure it was him rather than Brynna.

Raymund held the upper hand, and they both knew it.

There were far too many innocent people around. That put the ball in the psychopath's court.

Brynna was on the floor behind him, too damned close to Raymund for Chance's peace of mind. Chance had holstered his own weapon the instant Brynna had fallen to the floor.

He'd known what the odds were and what he'd have to do.

One man against a killer with a gun.

But he wasn't *one* man, was he?

No.

He had Kevin Beck, and he had Elliot. No doubt the two were also armed.

They could take the shot. All he had to do was get Brynna out of the way. And anyone else the bastard could hurt.

He risked a look over his shoulder.

Brynna wasn't where he expected her to be. His surprise cost him. Raymund aimed a blow that would have broken his neck if Chance hadn't rolled at the last minute.

He caught a glimpse of carrot hair and a big man in a dark suit.

Raymund snarled.

He had about fifty pounds of solid muscle on Chance. Was filled with rage and desperation. And hatred.

Raymund rolled, bringing the gun up.

Chance made a desperate grab for it, knowing he wouldn't

be able to get to it in time.
Raymund fired. Fire bloomed along Chance's arm.
People screamed. *Brynna* screamed.
"Chance! Down now!" Elliot yelled.
Chance listened to his brother. He hit the floor, fast.

Chapter 102

CHUCK KNEW HE WASN'T GOING to come out of this, and as the bullet tore through him, rage followed in its path. Those damned Becks; they'd been ruining things for him for thirty-six years.

He'd hated that damned Kevin Beck since the night the sanctimonious bastard had arrested him after his first girl.

It was all Beck's fault, all of it. The bastard had been fucking up everything for decades. Why should his daughters be any different?

Chuck saw Beck, knew he was one of the ones with a damned gun. Hell, it was probably Beck who'd shot him.

He considered, in that quarter-second when he still had a chance, taking out Beck once and for all. Making things easier for Golden Boy and the others. But fuck them! They'd led him to *this*, and he knew it. Didn't see them getting their hands dirty, following the Becks around. Beating the shit out of that blond friend of theirs. Chuck had seen her in the lobby next to the nurse, too.

Damn, if he'd only had another day with them, he'd get one of those girls for his own.

He'd never have a girl of his own again. Never.

The rage consumed him. He'd never have a girl of his own; but that didn't mean he couldn't take out one of theirs with him.

He looked for her, that damned little orange-haired bitch. He found her.

The Damned Billionaire's boy was pulling her away.

Well. That cinched it. There would be a double sort of revenge, wouldn't it?

Billionaire loved that son of his more than anything.

Chuck pulled up the gun and fired.

Barratt and the orange-haired girl went down.

Another weapon fired somewhere, and flame burned through his shoulder.

Chuck hit the ground for the last time as they wrestled his gun away. As hard hands turned him over and cuffed him.

They had him. It was over.

For the first time in a long time, Chuck had lost.

He looked at the orange-haired girl.

She was yelling, but didn't appear hurt too badly.

She was going to be fine; she'd won. For the first time, one of his girls had managed to get away from him before the end.

It was over for him, and he knew it.

Chapter 103

THE BLAST OF MULTIPLE WEAPONS being fired echoed through the lobby.

Raymund went down, his gun three feet away. Chance kicked out his foot, sending the weapon even farther away.

Toward Kevin.

The older man kept his own weapon trained on Raymund, who was screaming and writhing on the marble-tiled floor. Mel bent down and grabbed the gun, securing it quickly.

Chance heard sirens outside.

He looked at his brother—Elliot had his weapon trained on Raymund, as well.

He and Kevin would handle Raymund. Chance was done.

His family needed him.

Chance looked for carrot hair.

All he saw was red.

"Brynna!"

—

SHE knew she'd been shot. Brynna knew it, but apparently everything she'd gone through in the last few weeks had inured her to being more accepting of physical injury.

It was the man over her who concerned her most.

When she'd opened her eyes, she'd looked right into dark-brown ones. Houghton had lifted her to her feet and tried to pull her away from Charles Raymund.

Charles Raymund and Chance.

She'd just looked over her shoulder when Elliot had yelled. When guns had gone off.

Houghton had wrapped his body around hers and taken them both to the floor. He'd covered her head with his arm.

She'd never forget how he'd jerked against her. How his blood had felt burning as it flowed over her arm and chest.

At first she'd thought the blood was all his. But the bullet had brushed against her arm after it had left *his* body.

She had her hands on her brother-in-law's shoulder, applying pressure to the injury. He needed a doctor, didn't he?

"Mel! Get over here now!" Brynna yelled. "Lacy! We need a doctor *now!* Now! Now!"

"Hey, little sister. I'm ok. Were you hit?" Houghton smiled at her, but he was so pale.

"I think it grazed me. But you're really bleeding." Brynna kept her hands in place when people suddenly surrounded them.

"Let me through!" she heard Mel's voice. Heard the fear. Then Mel was there, Lacy beside her.

"Bryn, keep your hands right there, ok?" Lacy said. "Elliot's ordering an ambulance."

"Bryn, how bad are you hurt?" Mel asked, as she knelt down beside them. Her words were for Brynna, but she was looking at Houghton.

"It just grazed me. It's *his* blood. Houghton's."

Mel looked at the blood and paled. "Houghton..."

"Yeah, I'm here. Remember me? Your husband? Don't worry, little one. I'm not going to die and make you the richest woman in Texas for a while yet." He grinned again then grimaced. "You'll have years with me before that happens."

Mel wrapped her hand around his. "You idiot."

"Hey, I resemble that remark. Is the other guy dead?"

"Not dead. But he looks worse off than you do," Lacy said. "Can't say I care. That's the guy who worked me over. In fact, I think I'd rather just let him bleed out over there. Unless the ambulance gets here first. Ok, Bryn, you pull your hands back and let me take a look at Super Boy here."

Brynna leaned back. Mel slipped behind Houghton and he rested his head on her sister's shoulder. "I'll live, right, Doc?"

"Hell, I think you may just need stitches. Went right through here and came out the back. Hit the fatty area. It might sting for a few days. Cover it if you take a shower. Now, that will be sixty thousand dollars to the receptionist on your way out. And I'll get you a sucker and sticker for being such a good boy."

Houghton looked up at Mel. "I think I like her. Can we adopt her?"

"Ha ha. Lacy, is he seriously going to be ok?" Mel asked.

"He'll be just fine. We'll just keep pressure here until the ambulance arrives. And on his back." She handed Mel something. Brynna took a close look at it. The table runner? Jillian passed another one to Lacy, who held it on Houghton's shoulder.

Then Jillian turned toward Brynna. "Where are you hurt?"

"Just here." She pulled up what was left of her shirtsleeve. "It's not much."

"You're still going back to the hospital," Mel said.

"She is." A voice came from behind them all.

Brynna turned, and there *he* was. She stumbled to her feet. "Chance!"

She had been afraid to look at him before. Afraid he would be gone, just disappear. Like he hadn't really been there. And she'd been so focused on Houghton, on making sure he wasn't going to die, to even think in the few moments since Houghton had been shot.

Chance wrapped his arms around her. "Bryn. How's Barratt?"

"He'll live," Lacy said. "Will have an interesting scar to show the ladies, if Mel lets him."

The paramedics were there. They tended to Houghton, after listening to Lacy give them orders. Then they came to her. It took them all of five minutes to clean the wound and put on a bandage.

She didn't even require stitches.

"Most likely you were hit by a piece of tile that ricocheted," Chance said. He hadn't let go of her, not for a moment.

"I'm ok. Where he hit me hurts worse." She touched her cheek. It was definitely going to bruise, wasn't it? She looked over at where Houghton was. They had him on a gurney, even though he was protesting.

When Houghton Barratt protested, people listened, though. The paramedics paused for a moment. He hooked the arm on the side that wasn't injured around her sister's waist and lifted Mel, right onto his lap. "My wife goes with me."

"Houghton!" Mel gasped and tried to keep herself from

falling off the gurney.

"Go with him, Mel," Kevin said, helping Mel down. "We'll see you at home."

"Brynna needs to be looked at," Mel said firmly. She looked at Chance. "Soon."

He nodded. "She will be. I'll drive her to one myself."

"Good."

With that, Mel followed the paramedics outside.

Chapter 104

CHANCE TURNED BRYNNA AROUND and studied her. Her cheek was swelling. "He hit you hard."

"Yes. But nothing is broken. I'm ok."

He slipped his hand down to her stomach. "We need to get you and the baby checked out as soon as possible."

"Baby!" The word came from several different directions. Chance looked at Brynna's father and winced.

He was thirty-four years old. A woman's father shouldn't be able to make him feel like a seventeen-year-old caught in the girl's bedroom.

Brynna's hand covered his. She raised that stubborn little chin of hers and looked her father straight on. "I'm pregnant. I'm having a baby. At the end of June."

"We're having a baby," Chance said, firmly. "Together."

"Well," Elliot said, putting his hand on Chance's shoulder. At least he had his brother if Kevin tried to kick his ass. "Congratulations."

Their family formed a small circle around them—Kevin was at Brynna's shoulder, Jillian on his other side. Lacy had stepped up to them, and stood at Jillian's side. Elliot and Gabby were at Chance's left. A unit. A family. "Thank you. Now…"

"Ok, wait a minute…Bryn's pregnant. At least nine weeks? That asshole over there knocked her around?" Lacy asked. Chance nodded. "Then she needs to go to the hospital and have a full exam. Including ultrasound. After what's happened to her recently, she needs to be looked at. Just as a precaution."

"Then that's exactly where we are going." He wrapped her hand in his.

"Bryn…we'll talk when you get home, ok?" Her father stepped aside as he looked at Chance.

Chance wasn't stupid; he knew what the other man was doing. Kevin was accepting Chance's role in Brynna's future, wasn't he? "I'll see she's taken care of, Kevin."

"I know you will, son." Kevin held out his hand. Chance shook it. "Bring her home when you've finished at the hospital, ok?"

"Of course."

Home. Sounded pretty good to him.

Chance looked over at Raymund, who was being wheeled out on a gurney. He stopped the paramedics. "*Not* Finley Creek General, you understand? Some of his victims will be there."

"Sir?"

Elliot flashed his badge. "Take him to Finley *County*. The prison ward there."

"He's going to live?" Lacy asked. "Pity. I'll make a few phone calls, Bryn. I have a friend who's a wonderful obstetrician, Dr. Kaur. I may be able to get her to meet you there. She'll be able to answer any questions."

With that, he looked down at Brynna. "Ready?"

She nodded at him and smiled. Her hand covered his. "Ready."

Chapter 105

THEY WERE OK. HIS FAMILY WAS going to be just fine. Chance drove her back to the Beck house. And that's when he remembered.

He had Brynna's bag.

She started up the sidewalk to her family's home.

"Bryn? Not there. Come with me."

"What?"

He rounded the car, one hand already in the side of her laptop bag. He pulled the papers free. "Come with me. Here."

"Chance?"

"Just walk with me."

He led her across the yard.

Chance looked at the house again. It was a soft earth-green color with natural stone accents. There were six bedrooms and three baths.

It was big enough for *his* family, wasn't it?

Maybe his family wasn't big enough to fill it—yet. He was more than willing to work on that.

"Bryn…look at the papers."

—

SHE took the papers from him. "Chance, why are we here?"

"Look at the papers, babe."

Brynna did. "This is…"

She looked at the realtor's sign. "It's sold."

"No. It's *bought*. It's mine, now. I was hoping you'd live here with me."

"You want me to live with you?" She totally didn't understand. "Here. And you bought this house…" She looked at the date. "This morning?"

"I spoke with the realtor from my hotel in Mexico. Had that idiot Barratt act as proxy for the negotiating, then I signed this morning before driving to the TSP."

Before she'd told him of the baby. "Why?"

"Because I was thinking of my own dreams. What I would have wanted if I hadn't spent the last ten years hunting for the men who killed my family. And…my dreams looked just like yours—as long as you were in them with me. Although I know you're not thirty or so, I was thinking maybe you'd want to speed up the timeline of those dreams. And…have them with me."

"I don't understand. You need to be very specific, Chance." She knew what he was saying. How could she not? "What do you want from me?"

He stuck his hand in his pocket and pulled something small free.

"I want forever, Brynna. I want you to marry me and have my children—more than just the one we have already made—and I want you to build a life with me. Like my parents had together for thirty years. Like your parents had. Like Elliot and Gabby *will* have. Marry me, Brynna, please? Make those dreams *with* me."

Brynna threw herself at his chest and wrapped her arms around his neck. "I think that sounds absolutely exactly like what I want."

He scooped her up and carried her up the steps. "I picked up the keys early. Want to take a look inside?"

"I can't think of anything I'd rather do more."

Epilogue

KEVIN STOOD AT THE WINDOW of his front living room, watching the house next door. He smiled, a weight lifting off his chest as Chance scooped Brynna up and carried her inside the house he knew his daughter had always dreamed of having.

He hadn't missed the *Sold* sign in the front yard—or the fact that Chance had the keys. The boy had planned this, hadn't he? It took more than a few hours to buy a house of that magnitude.

Kevin had known the man would figure out what he wanted sooner or later, and he was glad to see that Chance knew what it was *Brynna* wanted. What his daughter needed.

Chance wasn't exactly the kind of man Kevin had always pictured for Brynna, but he was the right one. It was obvious Chance was the kind of man who saw his daughter for the beautiful, strong, capable young woman that she was. Chance *loved* her. That was all he could ask for, right?

"Dad? Are they back?" his Melody asked from behind him. Mel walked to the window and took a look for herself. "Finally. I thought he would never figure it out."

"But we both knew he would."

"Did we? I think you're more of an optimist than I am."

Kevin smiled; Mel had *always* been his child with the best outlook on the world around them. Odd, considering the career she had chosen. He grabbed her shoulders and kissed her on the forehead. He had come so close to losing her over a year ago. Had come so close to losing Brynna, too. He *had* lost almost two decades with his Carrie. But he had them all now.

Carrie was happy in St. Louis; he couldn't have asked for more for her. Brynna was now happy with a man he liked and respected.

Jillian was finishing up her nursing degree and finally going to achieve a goal she'd wanted since she was fourteen. It hadn't been an easy road for his Jillian; of all of his children she had struggled the most in school, thanks to her reading difficulties. She had struggled, but she was also the one who had chosen years of higher education to fulfill her dream. He was so proud of her for what she had accomplished. Syd had finished all the requirements for her high school degree and had, like Mel had so many years before, chosen to graduate at midterm, even though this was technically only her junior year. She had worked hard.

All of his girls were hardworking, kindhearted, beautiful young women. But his Melody wasn't yet happy.

"She'll be happy, Mel."

"I know. It was in the way she looked at him, Daddy. She's never looked at a man quite like him before." Mel leaned her head on his shoulder as they continued to stare at the house across the street. "I can't believe he knew about that house."

"She must have told him. He bought it for her. He loves *her*." Kevin had deliberately not questioned Melody about Houghton Barratt. Not past that initial week when she'd returned from Mexico. Did she realize that *she* looked at Barratt in much the same way that Brynna looked at Chance?

Mel cared for the man; he knew that. Why else would Houghton Barratt be in Melody's bedroom sleeping off the drugs the hospital had given him instead of at the mansion in Barrattville where Mel had spent the last several weeks? He didn't quite buy the excuse that reporters were blocking the entrance to Barratt's house. The guy had armed guards—he could have gotten them inside his home somehow. Instead he'd let Melody bring him here. To where Jillian could help keep an eye on him.

"Melody, sweetheart, are *you* happy? Do you want to come home? If you do, Barratt won't be able to stop you. Not really."

His daughter was quiet for a long time. Then she shook her head "I...I need to be with him. But...oh, Daddy, why can't it be easier than this? I don't trust him. I don't know why he wants *me*."

"Honey, why wouldn't he?"

"Never mind, Dad. How do I know he's not just after what he can get from me and the TSP and Elliot and...how do I know if *any* of this is real?"

Oh, Melody. His little girl. "When it's real, it feels it, sweetie. How do you feel about him?"

"I don't have a clue."

Kevin would have questioned her more. Mel wasn't the type to share what she was upset about until she had already thought of solutions. She so rarely asked for help this way. He wanted to *help* her somehow. She was his girl—he wanted her happy. His phone shrilled, interrupting what he was about to say. "Hold that thought."

He looked at the screen. "Elliot."

He answered quickly, then cursed. Cursed loud enough to have everyone in the room looking at him. He questioned Elliot for a moment then disconnected.

He looked at his daughters and Lacy and Foster.

"Dad? What is it?" Mel asked.

"Charles Raymund." Kevin had tried to remember who the man was, and he may have arrested him before. He couldn't be sure. But that didn't matter now, did it? "A sniper just took him out as they were leading him into the Finley County jail."

Mel shivered and wrapped her free arm around her stomach. "It's not finished yet, Daddy, is it?"

Kevin thought of the literal hell his middle daughter had gone through lately because of Charles Raymund. Thought of Melody being shot at in a parking lot for the second time in her life, thought of Melody and Brynna almost being forced off the road in St. Louis.

He looked at his family surrounding him, thought of the two people probably loving each other across the street, thought of his daughter and son-in-law in St Louis with his beautiful granddaughter. Thought of the babies growing in Carrie and Brynna now. Thought of Syd just on the brink of adulthood—what had this done to her?

He even thought of that arrogant boy Houghton Barratt asleep on his daughter's purple sheets.

They were his family. He'd do anything to protect them.

Raymund was dead. Benny was dead. Handley Barratt was somewhere in Mexico—but Barratt was not one of the men in the video from the Marshall murders. That meant there were still three more out there.

Who were they going to come for next?

The
Finley Creek: Texas State Police *Series*
Continues!

If you missed Gabby and Elliot's story, check them out in book 1

Her Best Friend's Keeper

Mel finally gets her man—but he gets her first—in book 3

The Price of Silence

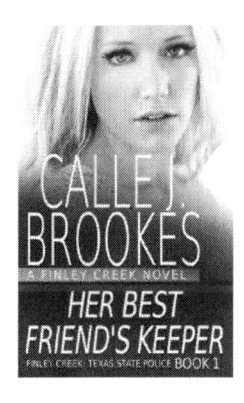

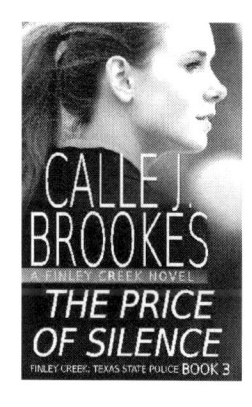

Available at Amazon, Kobo, Barnes & Noble, iBooks, Google Play and other participating retailers!